Murder of Crows

Shannon Riley

Table of Contents

About the Author

Shannon Riley is a writer, mental health professional, and community advocate whose work blends lived experience with sharp social insight. With more than 20 years in New York State's human services field, he has worked from the ground up, supporting individuals reentering the community after incarceration or psychiatric hospitalization, directing residential programs, supervising staff, and managing compliance.

A survivor of generational trauma, Shannon writes with an unflinching yet compassionate voice, weaving personal history, political awareness, and cultural critique. His fiction and nonfiction explore the intersections of faith, power, and community resilience, giving voice to those often silenced.

His novel Murder of Crows channels his lifelong commitment to truth-telling, exposing systemic corruption while honoring grassroots resistance. Currently pursuing his master's degree in Mental Health Counseling, Shannon also develops youth-focused trainings on domestic violence, sexual assault, and grooming prevention. Through his platform, Scott-Riley-INC, he champions the belief that "Kindness knows no enemy."

Prologue

The first time I noticed the crows, they were just shadows against the morning sky, quiet silhouettes lined up on the power lines outside my window. Back then, I told myself they were only birds. Ordinary. Uninterested.

But crows were never ordinary. My grandmother used to say they carried the language of the dead in their throats, passing it from branch to branch until the right ears were listening. Out on the corner, the old heads had rules: one crow meant trouble coming, two meant you were already in it, three meant somebody was going to the ground. Farther back, the Haudenosaunee told stories of Crow as a messenger, flying between worlds, making sure no secret stayed buried forever. And in African lore, the crow was a trickster and teacher, both reminding you that darkness can speak just as true as light.

Now they follow me. Not in the loud way you see in movies where flocks storm the sky. This is different. Quieter. A lone feather drifted onto my desk with no window open. A black shape gliding overhead when no one else bothers to look up. The soft brush of wings outside a closed curtain. Little signs that I am seen. That someone, somewhere, is keeping record.

People think death comes with sirens and shouting. Sometimes it does. But in Buffalo, death moves slow. It waits in policy meetings, in quiet approvals stamped behind glass doors, in the way a city block rots one brick at a time. The crows know this patience. They've been perched on wires through every winter storm, watching deals get cut and families pack up their last belongings. They see the things people step over and pretend not to notice.

And when the silence gets too heavy, when the truth sits too close to the surface, that's when I notice them most. The crows don't just watch, they measure. They seem to know where the story is headed before I do, like they're deciding whether I'm ready to follow.

If you're reading this, it means I've chosen to move forward. I can't promise I'll survive what's waiting. But I can promise this: when I go, I'll go knowing the truth is louder than the lies that tried to bury it.

The crows will make sure they reach you.

The crows don't mourn.

They watch.

And they wait.

Chapter 1
Rain on the roof

The sound of the rain reminded me of someone I hadn't thought about in years.

Mark. In high school, we were inseparable. We had this quiet ritual: I wore wine-colored penny loafers, he wore black, and we'd trade one shoe each so we both walked around with mismatched feet: one black, one wine. It was our way of saying we belonged to each other's world.

The rain tonight brought me back to the night he died. A rainy night atop a parking garage in Buffalo. Mark was scared, high, and trying to lean on an intellect that was trapped behind a mind hijacked by crack rock.

That night, he called me. I didn't pick up. I told myself I was done with him, that he wasn't the person I once knew and loved. Truth is, he was vulnerable, afraid, and reaching out to the only person he trusted.

Maybe I could have saved him. Instead, the Buffalo police chased him to his death because he tried to steal a steak from Wegmans, maybe to eat, maybe to feed the habit. The papers never said much; it was "an unfortunate incident." But I know what it was. The rain doesn't just hit the roof. It hits memory.

And this one? It hits like a crow tapping at the window steady, insistent, reminding me that beautiful minds can be broken and discarded, and that the city's gray sky has a long memory for the dead.

The morning, when she came to see me, the rain was doing that slow, sideways fall it does when the wind can't make up its mind. I was at my desk, pretending to work, staring at a coffee mug with a chip on the rim, wondering if it was worth walking down to the corner for something hot that didn't taste like boiled pennies. The blinds were half-open, letting in just enough light to make the dust on my filing cabinet look like it was trying to say something.

I heard the footsteps before I saw her. Not the quick, nervous steps of somebody coming in off the street, but measured, deliberate ones. Like she'd been rehearsing the sound. I'd been in this game long enough to know how a person walks into your office tells you more than their first sentence ever will.

When Yolanda Abrams stepped through my door, the room felt smaller. She didn't look like a woman who needed help. She looked like a woman who had already decided something and was now giving you the courtesy of catching up. Her coat was the color of wet stone, buttoned to the throat, but her hands were bare. The nails were short, clean, unpainted, practical hands. Her eyes… they were another matter. They carried a weight you didn't set down when you left the room.

"You're Harris Bushvill," she said. Not a question.

"That's what it says on the glass," I told her, nodding at the frosted door behind her.

She didn't smile. "I need to talk to you about my husband."

That word husband hung in the air like a bad smell. I'd read the papers, same as anyone. Pastor Ezra Abrams was found dead in his study, with no sign of forced entry. The official story said heart failure. The unofficial one was that a man doesn't just drop dead a week after calling out half the clergy in the city for being bought and paid for.

I gestured to the chair across from me. She sat, back straight, knees together, the way people sit when they're not planning to stay long.

"What is it you think I can do for you, Mrs. Abrams?"

Her eyes didn't flinch. "Find out who killed my husband."

There, it was no preamble, no soft landing. I leaned back, lacing my fingers behind my head, playing the part of the reluctant detective. Truth was, I'd been expecting someone like her. Deaths like Ezra's don't go unanswered forever; they just get buried until someone's stubborn enough to start digging.

"Police already have a file," I said. "And a conclusion. Heart stopped. End of story."

Her mouth tightened, just enough to tell me she'd already heard the same line a dozen times. "You think a man like Ezra just dies in his chair? After the week he'd had? After the things he was saying?"

I didn't answer right away. Outside the window, a crow landed on the ledge, slick feathers glistening in the rain. It looked at me the way only crows can, like it knew more than it should, and would enjoy watching me figure out the rest.

"What makes you think it wasn't just bad luck?" I asked finally.

She reached into her coat pocket and slid an envelope across my desk. No name, no return address. Inside, a single piece of paper, folded once. I opened it. On the page, printed in block letters: STOP DIGGING OR WE'LL BURY YOU NEXT.

I let the silence stretch. The rain tapped at the glass; the crow shifted its feet. "When did you get this?"

"Two days ago."

"You show it to the cops?"

Her laugh was dry, humorless. "And watch it end up in a drawer marked 'miscellaneous'? No, Mr. Bushvill. I brought it to someone who doesn't answer to City Hall."

That was the moment I realized she'd done her homework. She knew my reputation was too stubborn to play nice, too smart to scare easy, too broke to turn down work. She also knew the kind of enemies I'd made.

"I don't take cases like this," I lied.

"Yes, you do," she said, and for the first time, there was heat in her voice. "You took on the Gallaway job when everyone told you to leave it alone. You found the city contracts they were hiding."

"That was different."

"How?"

I didn't have a good answer, so I stood and walked to the window. The crow was gone. Down on the street, people moved through the rain, heads down, umbrellas up, the whole city pretending not to see each other.

When I turned back, Yolanda watched me like she was measuring how far she'd have to push.

"What else have you got?" I asked.

She slid a second envelope across. This one was heavier. I opened it to find a photocopy of what looked like church ledgers, tithes in, grants out, private donations from names I recognized from campaign posters. The numbers didn't add up. They weren't even trying to.

"This is the kind of thing that gets people killed," I said.

She nodded once. "Ezra called it the Sleeping Pill. Said the churches had been dosed years ago, and most of them didn't even know it. That's why he started the MANNA Covenant to wake them up."

I'd heard the phrase before. Street talk. A way of saying the church had been turned into a branch office of the government kept quiet, kept docile, kept dependent.

I sat back down, flipping the ledger pages slowly, like they might bite. "And you think the church is behind it?"

She didn't answer, but she didn't have to. Everyone in our part of town knew Ezra was going against the church, calling it a house without God.

I closed the folder and slid it back to her. "If I take this on, it won't end with a nice, clean answer. You understand that?"

She stood, pulling her coat tighter. "I'm not looking for clean. I'm looking for the truth."

And just like that, she was gone, leaving the smell of rain and the faint sound of her footsteps in the hall. I sat there for a long time, staring at the chipped mug, thinking about the crow on the ledge and the warning in that envelope.

I knew I should walk away. Cases like this didn't just get you killed; they made sure no one remembered your name afterward.

But the thing about a door like that? Once it opens, it doesn't close again.

Chapter 2
The First Crow

The next morning, the rain had given up but left behind a damp, gray hangover that settled over the city like a cheap wool blanket. I was at the office early, not because I'm the type to get a jump on the day, but because sleep had been restless. Yolanda's visit was still clinging to me: the smell of wet stone from her coat, the sound of her measured footsteps fading down the hall, the way she said "truth" like it was a debt she intended to collect.

I had the ledger she'd shown me sitting on my desk. It wasn't the kind of thing you left lying around unless you were looking to shorten your life expectancy. Numbers, names, grant codes. It was the kind of paper trail that could set a building on fire from the inside out.

The coffee was even worse than yesterday, but it gave me something to do with my hands while I stared at the columns. Churches are getting government grants for "community development," but when you followed the numbers, they looped back into the same three shell companies. One of those companies had a Tremaine, a Buffalo kid who made it big in real estate, on its board.

Ezra Abrams hadn't just been preaching against corruption. He'd been mapping it.

I thought about the way he must have worked on these late nights in his study, quiet except for the scratching of a pen and maybe the low hum of a lamp. That kind of work made enemies. And enemies like that don't forgive.

The door creaked open without a knock. Donell stepped in, carrying the kind of street energy you can't fake alert eyes, easy movements, like he was listening to the room breathe. He dropped into the chair Yolanda had used yesterday.

"You look like hell," he said.

"Thanks. Thought I'd dress for the part." I pushed the ledger toward him.

He flipped it open, scanning the pages without asking what it was. Donell's mind worked fast when there was danger in the mix. "These numbers don't match. And some of these names… yeah, I've seen a couple on campaign flyers."

"They're not just taking donations," I said. "They're cycling public money through the churches and into Tremaine's pockets. Ezra called it the Sleeping Pill."

Donell nodded slowly. "Fits. Keep the people comfortable, keep the preachers paid, and nobody rocks the boat."

"And Ezra was building something to wake them up. The Restoration Covenant. Yolanda didn't give me all the details, but I think this ledger was part of it.

Donell leaned back. "You think she's clean?"

I didn't answer right away. Outside, the street was starting to fill. People on their way to work, moving like they were on rails, eyes down. A bus hissed to a stop, coughing up a line of passengers into the damp morning.

"I think she's got skin in the game," I said finally. "Whether that makes her an ally or a liability, we'll see."

Donell tapped the ledger. "This isn't the kind of thing you investigate from behind a desk. You want answers? You've gotta talk to the people who handle this money. Pastors, board members, anyone who signed a grant form."

"I was hoping you'd say that," I said.

We started with the easy ones, names we knew wouldn't be dangerous to ask about. A pastor in a storefront church on the East Side, a deacon who doubled as a handyman for half the congregations in the district. Most of them got nervous as soon as we mentioned

Ezra. One even pretended not to know who he was, which was a lie so bad it almost made me laugh.

By noon, we'd got exactly nothing except a trail of eyes watching us from windows and doorways.

We stopped at a corner diner for lunch, sliding into a booth near the back. The place smelled like burnt toast and old grease. A waitress with a voice like gravel poured our coffee and didn't bother with a smile.

"You notice the way they shut down when we mention him?" Donell asked.

"Fear does that," I said. "Fear and loyalty. Sometimes it's hard to tell the difference."

The door jingled before he could answer, and a man in a tan overcoat walked in. He didn't look our way, but he didn't have to. I'd seen him before, hanging back near the recent funeral of a community activist, keeping his distance.

Donell caught my eye, his expression tightening just enough to confirm he recognized him, too.

"We finish this coffee," I said under my breath, "and then we find out if our friend's just here for the pancakes."

We didn't have to wait that long. The man ordered to-go, but he lit a cigarette outside instead of leaving. From the booth, we watched him position himself where he could see both the diner door and the street.

"Tail?" Donell asked.

"Maybe. Or maybe just making sure we know we've got one."

We paid, stepped out into the gray afternoon, and started walking without looking back. You don't want to give someone the satisfaction of knowing they've spooked you.

But I could feel that subtle hum under the skin when you're being watched. The city felt tighter, the air was heavier. And somewhere above, a crow called once, sharp and brief, like a warning.

By the time we looped back toward my office, the man was gone. But the feeling stayed.

Back at the desk, I opened the ledger again. The numbers hadn't changed, but they felt heavier now. Every line was a thread, and every thread led to someone who had a reason to keep their mouth shut.

"This is going to get loud," Donell said, reading my face.

"It already is," I told him.

And for the first time since Yolanda walked in, I realized that walking away wasn't an option.

The rain had been falling steady for hours, the kind of rain that didn't come down in sheets but in a constant hiss, like the city was leaking from every seam. My office smelled of paper, coffee grounds gone cold, and the faint mildew you get when a building is too old for anyone to care about fixing the pipes. The streetlight outside threw a pale orange wash across my desk, making the scattered case files look like autumn leaves no one had bothered to sweep.

Ezra's death was still fresh enough to keep the phone ringing and the whispers moving in circles. A good man gone, and not in any way that made sense. People wanted to say it was God's will, but I'd been around long enough to know that line was just a lazy cover for something dirtier. God didn't push people down stairs, or slip something in their drink, or make a man suddenly too dangerous to be left alive. People did that.

I'd been reading the transcript of his last sermon, my pen dragging across the margins as I underlined phrases. He'd been talking about liberation in a way you didn't hear from pulpits anymore, about how the church had traded its fire for the comfort of tax exemptions and government grants. That was the Sleeping Pill theory in its purest form: keep the people dosed, keep them docile. I knew the idea. I'd seen it play out in quiet ways for years. Ezra had been trying to shout it into the light.

And I remembered the first time I saw him work a room.

It was at the BFNC Summer Solstice, years back. I was seated at a table with Jan Peters, the sharpest mind I'd ever met, and the kind of woman who could make you stumble on your words just by raising an eyebrow. Jan was the Executive Director then, a walking library of wit, vocabulary, and unflinching logic. She wasn't much for church talk that afternoon, she said calmly but with surgical precision that the church was a waste of time and energy. Too much giving, too little change. She cited crime, sickness, and poverty as proof, concluding that no one was listening, so why bother?

Ezra didn't flinch. He quoted scripture with quiet authority: 'Faith without works is dead,' and reminded her that God was waiting on us, not the other way around. He made the case that the church was never meant to be a place of comfort but a launch pad for action. I watched Jan lean back, her lips pressed together, and though she didn't admit it then, I could see the wheels turning. By the time she passed years later, she knew God and had made her peace. That was Ezra's gift, making people who had sworn off the idea of faith stop and reconsider.

That memory lingered when I heard the tapping.

It wasn't loud, just a small rap against the window to my left. I turned, half expecting to see a branch swaying in the wind. But there it was, a crow, black as midnight, sitting on the narrow ledge, raindrops sliding off its feathers. It didn't move when I got up, nor did it flinch when I came close. Just stared at me through the glass, head tilting like it knew something I didn't. I told myself it was nothing, just a bird out of place. Still, it left a cold prickle at the back of my neck.

I was about to return to my desk when I noticed the envelope. It was on the floor, just inside the door, like someone had slid under it without making a sound. No name on it. I tore it open and pulled out a single folded funeral program. My face stared back at me in black-

and-white, the print still smelling faintly of ink. Tucked inside was a single black feather, slick from damp air.

I'd heard old street stories about feathers like that. The kind that meant you were marked not for death necessarily, but for attention. Somebody was watching you, and they wanted you to know it.

The door opened before I could think too long on it. Yolanda Abrams stepped in, umbrella in hand, coat still damp from the rain. She moved with controlled precision, like grief had taught her not to waste an ounce of energy on anything that didn't matter. Her eyes scanned the room, landing on the program in my hand.

"Someone dropped this," I said, holding it up.

She didn't look surprised. "Then you know what it means."

I didn't answer. I wanted to see if she'd say it first.

"It means," she continued, "you've been invited in. Whether you like it or not."

She set her umbrella against the wall and took the chair across from my desk. From her bag, she pulled a worn leather journal, the edges frayed from years of handling. "This was Ezra's," she said. "He kept it close. Notes for sermons, names of people he trusted, and ideas he was working on. Over the last few weeks, he started locking it up. The night before he died, he told me if anything happened to him, I should give it to you."

I flipped through the pages. His handwriting was tight and deliberate, each word chosen like it was meant to hold weight. About halfway through, I saw a page ripped out, the edges ragged. On the next page, faintly visible in the paper grain, was the outline of a crow in the watermark.

"I want you to find out what happened. And I want you to be ready for the answer."

Her voice was steady, but I could see the exhaustion around her eyes. She'd been living with the questions longer than I had.

I told her I'd look into it, knowing that "looking into it" meant putting myself square in the path of people who didn't mind silencing pastors or anyone else if the message got too loud. Tremaine's name was already a shadow in my mind, the kind of name that didn't need to be said out loud to change the temperature in the room.

When she left, the office felt heavier. I put the journal in my desk drawer and locked it. On my way out, I glanced toward the window. The crow was gone.

The rain had eased into a drizzle by the time I hit the street. I walked to my car, collar turned up against the damp, the funeral program was still in my pocket. That's when I saw it again, the same crow, or one just like it, perched on a lamppost across the street. Its feathers caught the light in an oily sheen, and its eyes never left me.

It cawed once, sharp and deliberate, before spreading its wings and lifting into the night. I stood there longer than I should have, watching it disappear over the rooftops. Somewhere in the distance, sirens wailed, and for the first time since Ezra's death, I felt the ground shift under me.

I didn't know yet that the crows weren't just birds. I didn't know they were part of a network with eyes in places I'd never see. All I knew was that something had been set in motion, and I was already in it.

Chapter 3
The Sleeping Pill

I didn't sleep much that night. Rain on the window has always been good for putting me under, but not when my head is filled with unanswered questions and shadows shaped like birds. Ezra's journal sat locked in my desk drawer like a live wire. Every time I closed my eyes, I saw that torn page and the faint crow watermark, like a ghost pressing against the paper.

The rain had stopped, but the air still felt wet. Buffalo has a way of carrying dampness in its bones. I made coffee black and strong enough to take the edge off the dull ache behind my eyes. A murder of crows. Not flying, not stirring, just perched like jurors waiting for me to open my mouth. Their black feathers rippled in the breeze, eyes glinting like they'd memorized my sins and were eager to recite them.

I stopped mid-block, tilting my head back. They stared down, unblinking.

And right there, I remembered Moses. Moses wasn't just a prophet to me. He was the man who told the truth nobody wanted to hear. He warned Israel plain and simple: forget who you are, forsake the covenant, and you'll lose everything. Not just land or livestock, your very freedom. He told them if they strayed too far, they'd end up as captives, shipped off to serve enemies in a land that wasn't theirs.

He didn't sweet-talk them. He didn't promise endless blessings without blood. He said, 'Choose life or choose death.' Blessing or curse. Freedom or slavery. That was the deal.

And under those wires, staring up at those crows, I felt his warning echoing across centuries, humming like the current running through the poles.

But then my mind shifted, as it always does, to the Slave Bible.

I'd studied it once, out of curiosity more than anything. Printed in London, shipped to the Caribbean in 1807. Almost ninety percent of the Old Testament cut out. Half of the New has been erased. Gone were Moses, Pharaoh, and the cry of the oppressed. Gone was the God who split seas and toppled empires. They left just enough to keep people docile: 'Servants, obey your masters.' They left Paul telling slaves to honor their earthly chains. But they stripped out the roar of Exodus, the judgment on Egypt, the promise that bondage is never the final word. It wasn't a Bible. It was a weapon. A muzzle dressed in leather binding.

And the longer I stood under those wires, the more I realized: Ezra kept preaching about was just the Slave Bible repackaged. Different century, same poison. Keep the flock obedient. Keep them quiet. Take away their history, their hope, their God of deliverance, and replace Him with a God who tells them to sit down and wait.

That's how they did it then. That's how they're doing it now.

The crows shifted, flapping just enough to let me know they were listening. Their wings looked like torn pages, black against the weak streetlight. I half-expected one to drop a verse at my feet, the parts they cut away.

I thought about Ezra then. My friend, a community compass, now a ghost. He dared to stand in a pulpit and speak like Moses, to tell the people the contract was broken, the covenant hijacked. He said if we kept pretending the church was free while it bowed to the state, we'd wake up one day to find ourselves slaves all over again, maybe not with whips and chains, but with grants, bylaws, and gag orders. Ezra saw it plain. He warned them, just like Moses warned Israel. And they killed him for it.

I started walking again, taking slow steps, as the crows hopped along the wires above, as if keeping pace. My reflection stared back at me from the puddles, broken by ripples with every drop that fell.

I asked myself the question I never say out loud: Am I supposed to be next? Am I the next voice in that long line of men who stood up, warned the people, to be cut down for it? Or am I just the fool who couldn't keep his mouth shut, doomed to end up like the rest, silenced, erased, footnoted in someone else's edited Bible?

The crows answered with a unified caw, loud enough to rattle the day. It sounded less like a warning and more like a verdict.

I pulled out the last cigarette I had, lit it, and let the smoke curl upward toward them. The flame trembled, then settled into a steady burn.

"You watching me?" I muttered, not caring if the neighbors thought I was drunk, talking to birds. "You keeping record? Or you just waiting for me to fail like the rest?"

Another wave of caws ripped through the air. They weren't mocking me. They were reminding me.

Moses warned. The Bible was twisted. Ezra preached. And now here I was, standing in the same current, feeling the wires hum overhead, the warnings vibrating through marrow and memory.

I finished the cigarette and crushed it under my heel. The rain started again, soft at first, then steadier. The crows didn't move.

That's when it hit me.

The warnings weren't for them. They weren't even for the church. They were for me. For anyone crazy enough to think they could play Moses in a world that crucifies prophets and buries truth. The crows weren't judges; they were witnesses. They were testifying that the story remained alive, no matter how many times it was censored, redacted, or rewritten. I took a breath that felt like it might crack my ribs. Looked up one last time and whispered, "I hear you."

And with that, the murder lifted, wings tearing through the mist, scattering like a black storm over the city.

The street was empty again, but I didn't feel alone. I felt marked. Called. Condemned. Maybe all three.

Either way, the warnings had reached me. And I knew better than to ignore them. Then headed down to The Lot, a cracked stretch of asphalt on the East Side, where Donell liked to post up in the mornings. Donell was a connector. If there was a whisper in the street, he could tell you who started it and who it was meant for. We'd worked together on a couple of cases, and he had a way of talking that made you forget half the things he said could get a man buried.

He was leaning against his car, a beat-up silver Maxima, when I got there. Hoodie up, cigarette between his fingers, scanning the street like he was waiting for someone who might not show.

"You look like hell," he said as I walked up.

"Appreciate the warmth," I told him.

He grinned. "What's on your mind?"

I told him about the feather, the program, the journal. I didn't tell him about the crow at the window yet. I wanted to keep that detail to myself until I knew what it meant.

Donell took a drag and nodded slowly. "Feather like that… you're in somebody's sights. Could be good, could be bad. Depends on somebody."

"You ever hear of a crow network?" I asked.

His grin faded. "Yeah. You don't want to be on their page. That's old-world stuff. Back when the Panthers were still moving in daylight, back when word had to travel without phones. The crows were signal men. They'd post up near certain spots, feed the birds, and send messages in plain sight. Now? Folks say it's more than that. Some say they watch, record, mark who needs marking."

"Connected to Tremaine?"

"Everything's connected to Tremaine if it's big enough."

The way he said it left no room for doubt. Tremaine wasn't a rumor in Donell's world; he was a constant.

We walked to the corner store for coffee. The owner, an older man with eyes that didn't miss much, slid our cups across the counter without small talk. As we stepped back outside, I caught sight of a crow perched on the roof of the church across the street. It was the same posture as the one from my office window, still watchful, like it had nowhere else to be. I told myself it was nothing, but my chest tightened anyway.

"You see it too," Donell said, nodding toward the bird.

"Yeah."

He sipped his coffee. "Don't look at it too long. That's how they know you're paying attention."

I let the words settle. We stood there in silence until the bird finally lifted off and disappeared behind the steeple.

I walked to my car, collar turned up against the damp. That's when I noticed it again not sure if it was the same crow or another cut from the same dark cloth perched on the lamppost across the street. The metal light caught its feathers and gave them that slick, oil-black shimmer, the kind you only see on things that live between worlds. It didn't move. Just stared at me like it knew my name long before I ever learned its purpose.

It let out a single caw, low and intentional, then opened its wings and rode the night wind toward the rooftops. I watched it longer than I care to admit, feeling the street tilt beneath my feet. Sirens broke somewhere in the distance, slicing the silence in thin blue lines.

Back then, I didn't understand what any of it meant. I didn't know crows carried messages or warnings or history. I didn't know they were part of something larger—an unseen signal traveling through the city, watching the watchers. All I knew was that the air changed after it left, and whatever had started with Ezra's death had already reached me.

And there was no stepping back from it.

I was halfway to my car when a voice came from the shadows near the alley.

"Bushvill."

I turned to see Clarence Dunne, a file clerk from City Hall who owed me a favor from years back when I kept his brother's DUI out of the papers. He wasn't the type to be out this late, or this wet, unless it mattered. His raincoat was buttoned high, hat pulled low, but his eyes darted like someone was keeping score.

"You didn't get this from me," he said, glancing toward the corner where the streetlight hummed. "But you're in the wrong garden."

"What's that supposed to mean?" I asked.

He shifted his weight. "You start pulling weeds where you're looking… the roots go deeper than the soil you think you're standing on."

I let that sit. Clarence had a way of talking like his words were already under review. "You talking about Ezra?"

"I'm talking about the people who paved the road he walked on. Some of 'em are still walking it. And some don't want any traffic." He glanced behind me, then back. "They already wrote your name on the ledger. Means they've noticed you."

I studied him. "Who's 'they'?"

He shook his head, almost smiling, but not with his eyes. "In this city? 'They' is whoever you don't want it to be."

Clarence stepped closer, lowering his voice until I could smell the cigarette smoke clinging to him. "If I were you, I'd stop asking where the water comes from. Just drink what's poured and walk away."

"That's not my style."

"I know," he said, almost sadly. "That's why I came out here tonight. You've got maybe a week before doors start closing on you. The kind you can't open again."

Before I could ask for more, he stepped back into the shadows. "You didn't see me," he said. And then he was gone, leaving nothing but the sound of his shoes slapping the wet pavement.

I stood there, a new truth settling in my gut: I was no longer chasing a case. I was trespassing on sacred ground, and the gardeners carried knives.

Back at my office, I unlocked Ezra's journal. The handwriting pulled me in again, neat lines of thought that built toward something. He'd been writing about the church's role in Black self-determination, how the 501(c)(3) status had become a leash. The Sleeping Pill, that's what he called it in his own words, wasn't just a metaphor. It was a doctrine of silence enforced with a velvet glove. No political speech from the pulpit. No mobilizing against the party in power. In exchange, the IRS left you alone, and the grants kept coming.

It was the kind of thing people suspected but didn't say out loud. Ezra had been saying it out loud. And now Ezra was dead.

I called Yolanda, told her I wanted to know more about the weeks before Ezra's death. She agreed to meet me that evening at her house. The rest of the day I spent making calls to old contacts reporters, retired detectives, pastors who owed me favors. Most of them didn't want to talk once Ezra's name came up. A couple hung up on me.

Around four, Donell called.

"You might want to take a walk," he said. "Basement of Greater Hope on Jefferson. Something's moving."

I grabbed my coat and headed over. Greater Hope looked like any other mid-sized church from the outside: brick walls, a faded signboard out front, a parking lot with more potholes than pavement. The front doors were locked, but I found the side entrance ajar. Inside, the basement lights glowed, voices murmuring in low tones.

I stayed in the hallway, close enough to hear but out of sight. A group of men was talking about "keeping the line" and "not drawing attention." One voice, deep and steady, mentioned Ezra by name. Said his death was "unfortunate but necessary." My stomach tightened.

A sudden flutter overhead made me look up. A crow was perched on the narrow basement window ledge, looking down through the glass. Its beak tapped once against the pane, a hollow sound that cut through the voices. No one else seemed to notice.

I backed away before anyone came out, slipping into the cold evening air. Donell was waiting in his car a block away.

"You hear them?" he asked.

"Yeah. And I saw another crow."

He didn't answer right away. "Then it's official. You're in it now."

I was in it, deep. It reminded me of something my uncle once told me.

I was eleven when I learned there were things you didn't talk about, even if they burned a hole in your chest.

It was summer in Buffalo, the kind of heat that makes the asphalt shimmer. I'd spent most of the day at the park shooting hoops with Marcus, our shirts damp and sticking to our backs. The sun was just starting to slide low, stretching shadows across the street.

I was walking home down Fillmore, dribbling the ball against the cracked sidewalk, when I heard voices in the alley behind the corner store. Not arguing hushed. The kind of talking grown men do when they don't want anybody to hear.

I should've kept walking. That's the truth. But curiosity's been my disease for as long as I can remember.

I leaned my shoulder against the brick and peered around the corner. Two men stood by a dented Oldsmobile, one of them holding a brown envelope thick enough to bulge. The other tall man, wearing a tan fedora even in the heat, was counting the cash. I recognized him. Everybody did. He ran numbers out of the barbershop and had a hand in damn near every hustle in our zip code.

The ball slipped from my hands and rolled into the alley. My stomach dropped.

The man in the fedora turned. His eyes met mine flat, cold, like he was measuring how much trouble I could be. I froze. My legs wanted to run, but I couldn't move.

The other man, a big one with shoulders like a linebacker, picked up the ball. He walked over slow, squatting so we were eye level. "You didn't see anything," he said. His voice was calm, almost friendly, but it slid over my skin like ice water.

I nodded, my throat dry.

He handed me the ball and glanced toward the street. "Go on home, kid."

I went. I didn't look back. I didn't dribble again until I was two blocks away.

When I got to the apartment, Uncle Raymond was on the stoop, rolling a cigarette. I must've still looked shook, because he squinted at me and said, "Who put the fear in you?"

I told him it was nothing, just the heat. But he wasn't buying it. He lit his smoke, took a drag, and leaned forward.

"Listen to me, Harris. There are two kinds of trouble in this world: the kind you make, and the kind that finds you. If the second one finds you, you keep your mouth shut unless you're ready to leave town. You hear me?"

I heard him. I heard every word. And from that day on, I learned to file things away instead of blurting them out. But I wasn't prepared to stay quiet and not leave town, Uncle Raymond would cuss me out.

By the time Donell came back, the sky had started to clear in patches, the kind of deceptive sunlight that makes you think the day will turn around. It wasn't, not for us.

He came in without knocking. Donell never did, carrying a brown paper bag that smelled like fried chicken and something sweet. He dropped it on my desk like an offering and took the same chair he always claimed, the one with the wobble in the front leg.

"Thought you could use lunch," he said. "And maybe a reminder that the world's still got a couple good things in it."

I tore open the bag, the smell filling the room, almost pushing out the ledger's stale-paper odor. Almost.

"You get anything?" I asked.

"Couple whispers," he said. "Nobody's talking loud, but there's movement. One of Tremaine's men was seen near the East River Baptist warehouse last night."

"That's where they keep the food donations?"

Donell gave a humorless grin. "That's what the sign says. However, the word is that Ezra had an interest in what came in and went out of there. He was asking questions."

The mention of that warehouse stirred something in me. I'd been there once, years back, on a different job, all polished on the outside but hollow and cold inside, like a stage set.

We ate in silence for a minute, the kind you only get with someone who's been around long enough to know you don't need to fill it. Donell had been with me through more than I could list, some clean, some dirty, some we never spoke of again.

"You think Yolanda's holding back?" he asked finally.

"I think she's giving us what she thinks we can handle," I said. "And I think she's testing to see if we'll break before she does."

He nodded, chewing slowly. "Then we'd better make sure we don't."

After lunch, we headed out toward the warehouse. I drove, Donell in the passenger seat, scanning the mirrors like he was reading another ledger only he could see. The streets were wet from the morning rain, reflecting the low sun in strips of gold that made the cracked asphalt look almost respectable.

We parked two blocks away and walked the rest of the way. The warehouse sat squat against the river, its brick darkened with age and neglect. The faded mural on the side still showed a family holding hands under the words "Faith Feeds All," but the paint had peeled away in places, revealing the brick-like bones beneath the skin.

A delivery truck idled out front, two men unloading boxes into the open bay. From where we stood, the labels read "Canned Goods" in bold black letters. Donell shifted his weight.

"You notice those boxes don't look heavy enough for food?"

I did. And I noticed how the men handled them carefully, not carelessly, like whatever was inside could hurt them if they weren't paying attention.

We didn't get closer. Not yet. Some places you don't walk into until you know precisely what you're walking into.

Instead, we circled back, heading for a coffee shop across the street where we could watch from the window. The place was nearly empty, and the barista was too busy scrolling her phone to care about us. We sat with our cups, watching the truck pull away, only to be replaced minutes later by a black SUV that rolled in slowly, as if it wanted to be noticed.

A man in a dark suit stepped out, talking into an earpiece. He disappeared inside, stayed about ten minutes, then came back carrying a small metal case.

"That's not soup kitchen business," Donell said.

"No," I agreed, "but it's definitely Sleeping Pill business."

We watched him drive off, the SUV disappearing into the thinning traffic. I didn't know where he was going, but I knew we'd cross paths again.

Back at the office, daylight was slipping, shadows creeping in before the streetlights had time to catch up. Donell leaned against the filing cabinet, arms crossed.

"You think we can pull this without Tremaine noticing?" he asked.

"He already noticed," I said. "The guy at the diner today wasn't there for the pie."

That got a nod out of him, slow and deliberate.

"Then we'd better make sure that when they look at us," he said, "they see something they don't want to touch."

The thing about Donell is that he never said "if." It was always "when." Like danger wasn't a possibility, but a certainty. And in our line of work, that was the closest thing you got to honesty.

I walked him out to the street. The air was colder now, and a damp wind rose off the river. Somewhere overhead, a crow cut across the fading light, its wings black against the gold sky.

Chapter 4
Feathers in the File

The morning of Ezra's funeral, the sky was too bright for the occasion. Sunlight spilled over the church steps, making the brick glow, as if the building wanted to be the centerpiece of a celebration instead of a burial.

The street was lined with cars, the kind you only see when a well-known pastor dies: luxury sedans, government plates, and tinted SUVs. Some of the people filing up the steps wore grief honestly; others wore it like a borrowed suit, something to be returned when the cameras left.

Donell and I parked a block away. He adjusted his tie in the rearview mirror like it was an enemy he couldn't quite get even with. "Place is crawling with city people," he said.

"That's the point," I told him. "They want everyone to see them here. Proof they cared."

We walked up the steps together, slipping into the current of mourners. The air inside was thick with perfume and cologne, a chemical sweetness that didn't cover the undertone of sweat and damp wool.

Ezra's casket sat at the front, closed. Dark wood, polished to a shine you could see your own doubts in. Two ushers in matching suits flanked it, their eyes scanning the crowd the way security scans a checkpoint.

I'd been in this church before, but never like this. Every pew was full. Along the walls, folding chairs had been brought in for the overflow. The choir loft was empty, the organ silent. At the pulpit stood Pastor Herb, all smiles and handshakes, moving through the front rows like a politician working the floor before a vote. He was a big man, his tailored robe doing its best to disguise the weight he carried. The gold trim caught the light with every movement. Beside him, his wife, round-faced, bright-eyed, handed out programs with the efficiency of someone used to keeping a show on schedule.

Herb spotted me and Donell from across the room, and for a moment, the smile faltered. Not enough for most people to notice, but I caught it. Then it was back, bigger than before, as he raised a hand in what could have been a blessing or a warning.

We took seats halfway back, close enough to see but far enough not to be seen too much. From here, I could watch the faces. Politicians in dark suits, leaning in to whisper to donors. Local clergy exchanged nods that looked more like negotiations than condolences.

The service began with scripture, read in a voice so measured that it sounded as if it had been rehearsed. Then came the eulogies, one from a city councilman, another from a pastor I didn't know. Words about community, about service, about how Ezra had "brought people together." Not one mention of the Restoration Covenant. Not one nod to the way he'd challenged the system that many in this room were part of.

When Herb finally took the pulpit, the room leaned forward. He had that kind of presence, loud and commanding, a performer who knew when to raise his voice and when to drop it low, so people had to lean in.

"Pastor Ezra," he began, "was a man of vision. A man who knew that unity was the only path forward. And in these troubled times, unity means working with those who hold power, not against them."

It was subtle, but the message landed. Ezra had stood against the powers; Herb was telling them the new direction was cooperation. Compliance. The Sleeping Pill, dressed up in Sunday clothes.

Donell shifted beside me. "He's already rewriting the story," he murmured.

I kept my eyes on Herb. He was good too good. He could wrap a sellout in scripture and make the crowd say, 'Amen.'

When the service ended, the mourners filed past the casket. Some touched the lid, some whispered prayers. When my turn came, I stopped long enough to place a hand on the wood. The polish was warm under my palm from all the hands before mine. I thought about the ledger on my desk, about the warning in Yolanda's envelope, about how easily Herb had turned this from a call to action into a lullaby.

Outside, the sunlight was even brighter, the air sharp with the smell of fresh flowers. Across the street, cameras caught the procession, city officials pausing just long enough for the evening news.

Yolanda stood near the steps, her coat open now, her face unreadable. She met my eyes for a second, then looked past me toward the line of cars.

Donell and I walked away without saying much. The whole thing felt staged, like the funeral was just another part of the city's choreography, one more way to put Ezra in the ground and make sure his voice didn't echo.

But I'd heard it. And so had Donell. And if Herb thought this was the last word, he was wrong.

I passed a corner bar on the walk back to my building. Murphy's. The same place I'd sat in a dozen times before I got sober. The smell of beer and fry grease drifted out every time the door opened, and for half a second, I thought about stepping inside. I could picture it too easily: the first shot burning on the way down, the beer after it hitting like an old friend's handshake.

But I also knew how that story ended. I'd wake up the next morning with my hands shaking, my mouth dry as dust, and the case files scattered like someone had come through and stolen my focus. Ezra's journal would end up under a pile of unopened mail. The crows would still be watching, but they'd see a man who'd chosen the wrong medicine.

I kept walking.

When I got home, I tossed my coat on the chair and sat at the kitchen table. I let the sound of the rain on the roof fill the silence, the way it used to when I was a kid. Back then, it was a comfort proof that the world was still moving even if I was stuck. Tonight, it was a warning. I thought of Mark again, my high school friend, the one who died at the hands of the police on a rainy night in Buffalo. I'd shunned him that night, told myself he wasn't the same person I'd grown up with, when in truth he was just scared and lost.

Maybe I'd been doing the same thing to myself lately, turning away when the fear crept in, convincing myself I was too strong to break. But the truth is, I'm still one bad choice away from falling back into that hole.

I poured myself a glass of water, sat with it like it was whiskey, and prayed a prayer I hadn't said in a long time:

God, don't let me throw this all away. Not for comfort. Not for fear. Not for anything.

When I opened Ezra's journal again, the ink on the page seemed heavier than before. Clarence's warning, the crow on the lamppost, and the smell of beer outside Murphy's it all felt connected, like the universe was making me choose which path I was going to take. And for tonight, at least, I chose to stay sober.

I awoke the following morning on a mission, excited because I had remained sober. Ezra's old office in the back of the church smelled like wood polish and dust. The kind of dust collects in places people avoid, either because they're too busy or don't want to disturb whatever's been left behind. I'd gotten permission from Yolanda to look through his files. She told me she hadn't been able to bring herself to go in here yet. I could understand that.

The desk was made of heavy oak, and the drawers stuck slightly when I pulled them open. Inside, neat stacks of sermon notes were bound with rubber bands, labeled by date in Ezra's tight, almost architectural handwriting. He was the kind of man who respected order, even in chaos.

I worked my way through the papers slowly, reading as I went. The sermons build on each other, calling for unity, strength, and independence. But woven into them, more in recent months, was language that was less Sunday morning and more manifesto. Phrases like "The sleeping don't march" and "Chains can be velvet, but they're still chains."

One stack in the bottom drawer felt different, heavier. Inside was a thin folder marked only with a small crow doodled in the top corner. I opened it carefully. Most of the pages looked blank at first. But the paper felt strange, smoother than the others. I held one sheet over the small desk lamp, letting the heat build. Slowly, faint lines of writing appeared.

"The sleeping don't march." Again. Below it, "When the pulpits go quiet, the streets grow silent." There was no signature or date. It wasn't a sermon draft; it was a warning, maybe to himself, maybe to someone else.

The missing journal page was still on my mind. The person who had taken it had done so cleanly, like a surgeon. Not torn in anger, but removed with precision. That kind of neat work meant intent.

I heard a sound, then a soft, quick one. I turned toward the window.

A crow was perched on the sill, feathers glossy in the pale light. It didn't startle when I moved. We stared at each other through the glass, and I felt that same prickle I'd had in my office. This was broad daylight. I told myself it was a coincidence, but the thought rang hollow.

I closed the file, locked it in my bag, and left the office. On the steps outside, I caught sight of Donell across the street, leaning against a hydrant like he'd been there a while.

"You've got company," he called, nodding toward the roof.

Another crow sat there, head tilted. Watching and always watching.

Chapter 5
The Watchers

It was a cold morning, the kind that made your breath hang in the air like you were carrying smoke in your lungs. I was downtown, not far from the federal building, following up on a lead about a grant Ezra's church had supposedly turned down. The sidewalk was busy with government workers, lawyers in dark coats, people who had the luxury of walking with purpose.

That's when I saw him.

An older man in a green parka stood at the corner, scattering something from a paper bag. At first, I thought it was bread for pigeons. But the only birds that came were crows, half a dozen of them, landing one after another, keeping perfect distance between themselves. The man's movements weren't random. He tossed, paused, tossed again, always in the same rhythm.

I watched for a while, trying to see the pattern. After a few minutes, he folded the bag neatly, slipped it into his pocket, and walked away without looking at the birds. The crows stayed a moment longer, then took off in pairs, heading in different directions.

I knew then I needed someone who could move in places I couldn't, ask questions I didn't even know how to form. Someone who could walk into a hornet's nest and not get stung.

That meant Donell.

Donell wasn't just family. He was the ghost of who I might have become if my mother hadn't forced books into my hands and fists into my pockets. My first cousin, but twice removed, is gentle. He came out of the womb with clenched hands and a jaw like stone.

Our bond had been sealed years ago in the kind of moment that gets burned into your blood. We were barely teenagers when it happened. My brother Devon and our cousin Mark, along with me, had jumped a kid named Toney in 8th grade. He was built like a grown man and carried a temper that could break glass. We caught him slipping after school, three on one. Left him bruised.

A week later, Toney came back with five cousins. We were outnumbered, scared, and stupid. We stood in the schoolyard waiting for fists we couldn't dodge. Mark made the call. He didn't say much. Just "Unc, it's bad," and the reply: "I'm sending Donell."

Just as Toney and his goons circled in fifteen minutes later, Donell stepped out from behind the bushes like a ghost with purpose. No words. No threats. Just presence.

Toney pulled a blade. Donell walked right to the point of it, slapped Toney so hard he staggered, took the knife from his hand, slapped him again, and handed the knife back. Toney, looking more embarrassed than injured, folded it and told his crew, "Let's go."

That was Donell. Fearless wasn't even the right word; he was unmoved. And he wasn't fearless because he thought he couldn't be hurt. He was fearless because he'd already decided pain didn't get to make his decisions for him.

I found him that night at Foster's, the same bar we used to duck into when we wanted the truth with our whiskey back before I quit drinking. He didn't look surprised to see me. We decided to take a walk.

The city always smells different at night. There is less exhaust, more damp brick, and trash left on the curb for too long. The kind of smell that reminds you of decay is patient. It'll wait.

Donell was returning from a meeting with one of Ezra's old allies, a storefront pastor who swore he knew nothing about the Covenant but couldn't quite look him in the eye when he said it. "You hear that?" he asked.

At first, it was just the hum of a transformer somewhere overhead and the faint slap of a loose sign in the wind. Then I caught its footsteps behind us, quickening when we turned a corner.

I didn't break stride. "Two?"

"Three," Donell said, voice flat. "And they're closing."

We cut left into an alley that smelled like wet cardboard and fried food, the kind of place you either avoided or used as a shortcut when you knew the ground rules. The footsteps followed.

"Stay cool," I said. "If they want to talk, they'll talk. If they want to do worse, they'll show their hand."

Halfway down the alley, the shadows separated themselves into men. Three of them, just like Donell said. Two in hooded sweatshirts, one in a leather jacket that caught the streetlight in flashes. The one in leather smiled, not the friendly kind.

"Bushvill," he said, like he was confirming a bet.

"That's me."

"You're making noise in places you don't belong."

I glanced at Donell, who was already angling his body between me and them. "Noise is a side effect of breathing," I said.

Leather Jacket's smile widened. "Tremaine doesn't like noise."

There it was. No dancing around the name now. The air felt tighter, like the buildings had inched closer.

"You boys always introduce yourselves this way?" Donell asked.

The one on the left stepped forward. "We're here to tell you this ends now. You back off, or you end up like your friend."

I didn't know which friend they meant, but I didn't ask. Sometimes the worst thing you can do is let someone see the question in your eyes.

Donell moved first, not with fists, but by closing the space between him and Leather Jacket until the man had to tilt his head back slightly to keep eye contact.

"Walk away," Donell said quietly.

For a moment, I thought they might. Then the one on the right reached under his jacket.

"Down!" Donell barked, and we dropped just as a flash lit the alley and the sound cracked against the brick.

We moved without thinking, me toward the dumpster for cover, Donell closing the distance on the shooter with a speed that didn't match his size. Two blows, and the man was down, weapon skidding across the wet pavement.

The others backed off, dragging their friend with them, but not before Leather Jacket leaned in just enough to let me see his eyes.

"This is your first and last warning," he said. "Next time, we don't miss."

Then they were gone, swallowed by the night.

I stayed crouched for a few seconds longer, listening for the echo of their footsteps, the thump of my own heartbeat in my ears. Donell picked up the dropped gun, checked it, then tossed it into the dumpster.

"You all right?" he asked.

"Yeah," I said, though I wasn't sure if it was true.

We walked the rest of the way to the car in silence. My mind kept circling back to how Leather Jacket had said Tremaine's name, not like it was a man, but like it was a weather system you couldn't stop from rolling in.

Back at the office, I poured two fingers of water into a glass and stared at it like I wished it were something more substantial. Donell leaned against the wall, arms crossed.

"They're not just warning us," he said. "They're marking us. Everyone in Tremaine's circle will know we've been touched."

I nodded. Somewhere outside, a crow called once, sharp and deliberate.

Blood in the water. And the sharks had our scent now.

"His wife hired me. She thinks it wasn't a heart attack."

Donell leaned back, jaw flexing. "You want me to keep digging?"

"I want to know what the streets know."

He tapped the table once. "Then you came to the right place."

"Tell me about crow feeders," I said.

There was a pause. "You've been watching one?"

"I think so. Downtown, near the federal building."

Donell sighed. "That's old code, back before cellphones, before beepers. You feed the birds in certain ways, at specific spots, and at specific times. Anybody who knows the pattern gets the message. Could be a meeting spot. Could be a signal to move. Could be a mark on somebody."

"Mark?"

"Means they're being watched. Or worse."

"Don't get cute with this," Donell warned. "If you see feeders, you're closer to the center than you think. And the center doesn't like the company."

His words stuck. The network wasn't just superstition. It was organized, alive, and old enough to blend in seamlessly.

Chapter 6
The MANNA Covenant

The night after the alley, I couldn't sleep. Every time I closed my eyes, I saw the flash of the gun, the tilt of Leather Jacket's smile, and the way Donell moved like he'd been here before because he had.

I sat at my desk long past midnight, the city's noises fading to the occasional car horn or the rattle of a truck hitting a pothole. The ledger Yolanda had given me was still open, its pages full of careful handwriting and numbers that told a story no one wanted read aloud.

Ezra's Restoration Covenant.

Before he died, Ezra had been more than a preacher with a flair for scripture. He was an organizer, a strategist. The Covenant wasn't just about faith; it was about structure, self-determination, and economic autonomy for Black communities in a city that had been engineered to keep them dependent.

The plan had layers. At first glance, it appeared to be a straightforward church-union model: congregations pooling resources to fund housing, education, and small business grants for their members. But beneath that was the political layer, a base that could, in time, function like a voting bloc, independent from party politics, beholden to no one except the people funding it.

That's what made it dangerous.

It was one thing for a pastor to talk about helping the poor. It was another for him to create a system that could rival the city's political machines. And Ezra wasn't shy about saying the quiet part out loud, that the churches had been fed what he called "The Sleeping Pill" for decades. Government grants, nonprofit partnerships, strings attached so tight they cut off circulation. Keep the sermons tame, keep the people quiet, keep the checks coming.

I turned the ledger to a page marked with a paperclip. Here was the Black Treasury idea: a separate, independent bank for pooled church funds. It had never been announced, nor had it been mentioned in a sermon. Maybe only a handful of people even knew it existed. But on paper, it was viable.

Donell came in around two, carrying a bag that smelled like late-night diner food. He dropped it on my desk without a word, then leaned over to look at the ledger.

"You're still on this," he said.

"I can't stop thinking about it. If Ezra had pulled this off, it wouldn't just have shaken the city. It would've changed the game."

Donell nodded. "And Tremaine doesn't like the game changing."

We ate in silence for a while. The food was greasy and good, the kind of meal that soaks up adrenaline and regrets in equal measure.

"You ever meet Ezra?" I asked finally.

"A couple times," Donell said. "Didn't like wasting words. He looked you in the eye like he was trying to figure out if you were going to help or get in the way."

I could see that. And I could see why he'd be a threat to men like Tremaine and to men in City Hall who pretended not to know Tremaine at all.

Donell leaned back in his chair. "So what's our move?"

"First, we figure out who else knew about the Covenant," I said. "Not the people who just heard him preach about unity. The ones who saw these numbers."

"That's going to be a short list."

"Short lists are easier to follow," I said.

The next morning, I called Yolanda. She answered on the second ring, her voice clipped, like she'd been waiting for the call.

"You've been reading," she said.

"I have. And I've got questions. Who else knew about the Treasury?"

There was a pause on the line. I could hear the faint hum of traffic behind her. "Three people," she said finally. "Ezra, me, and a lawyer named Reuben Ellis. He helped draw up the bylaws."

"Where is he now?"

"Hiding. Last I heard, he was downstate. Said he had a 'close call' with his motorcycle and decided the city wasn't safe."

I wrote the name down. Reuben Ellis. A thread I'd follow later.

When I hung up, Donell was leaning in the doorway. "You look like you just got handed a map."

"Not a map," I said. "A key."

The sun was coming up, cutting through the blinds in sharp lines across the ledger. Outside, the city was going to sleep, but it felt like we were moving in a different time altogether, slower, heavier, every step pulling us further into Ezra's unfinished business.

And somewhere, I knew, Tremaine was already figuring out how to make sure we never finished it.

The rain had stopped, but the streets still held its memory. Puddles reflected the streetlamps like tiny mirrors, each one cracked by the oil-slick shimmer of a city that had been playing dirty for too long. I parked across from Kingdom Restoration Tabernacle, a grand name for a building that looked like it had been a bingo hall in a past life. The lot was half full, too full for a Thursday night.

I sat low in the driver's seat, a Styrofoam cup of black coffee in hand, the kind that burns your tongue but keeps your mind sharp. The main doors opened every few minutes. Some people came in dressed like it was Sunday service suits pressed, dresses crisp, the kind of outfits you wear when you want to be seen. Others slipped in wearing hoodies and jeans, heads down. No Bibles in their hands, no kids in tow.

On the far side of the lot, a black Escalade pulled up. Windows tinted darker than legal. Two men stepped out, both wearing overcoats, both too clean-cut to be from the neighborhood. They didn't go inside. Instead, they carried a black duffel bag between them and disappeared through a side door.

I watched the pattern repeat itself three times in an hour. Different men, same door, same bag shape. These were not church ushers or deacons; this was business, the kind you don't list in your mission statement.

I could see shadows moving through the stained-glass windows, but no sound carried across the street. Then, at 9:15 sharp, the side door swung open again and Herb stepped out. Even from here, I could see his grin wide and empty, like he was born knowing how to sell something he didn't believe in. He shook hands with one of the overcoat men, clapped him on the shoulder, and glanced around the lot like he was expecting someone. His gaze lingered in my direction just long enough to make me shift in my seat.

A group of women exited the main doors next, all in heels, laughing too loudly, each one carrying a gift bag with gold tissue paper peeking out from the top. Whatever was going on inside, it wasn't choir practice.

A city truck rolled past, headlights sweeping over my car. In that brief wash of light, I saw movement in my side mirror: a crow, perched on the lamp post across the street, watching me the way I was watching Herb. I didn't know if it was the same one from before, but it didn't matter. Either way, it meant I wasn't the only one keeping score tonight.

By the time Herb went back inside, my coffee was cold and my pen had filled with two pages of notes. I didn't have proof not yet, but I had enough to know that walking through those doors tomorrow wouldn't just be a conversation. It would be a test.

And I wasn't sure yet if I was ready to pass it.

Chapter 7
In Their Book

I lit a cigarette I didn't need and started walking toward the diner two blocks over. Donell had texted me an hour before the service even ended: We need to talk. No punctuation, no pleasantries. That was his way of saying it wasn't optional.

The bell over the diner door gave a tired jingle when I stepped inside. The place smelled of burnt coffee and fried onions, a scent that clung to your clothes. Donell was in a booth by the window, hoodie up, hands wrapped around a mug. He didn't wave me over. Didn't need to.

I slid into the seat across from him.

"You look like a man who just saw the inside of the machine," he said.

"I saw enough," I told him. "And I got this." I slid the folded note across the table. That read your in the book.

He read it once, twice, then set it down as if it were nothing more than a receipt. "You know what that means, right?"

"I have a guess."

He leaned forward, eyes narrowing. "It means they've decided you're worth the time. The crows don't watch anybody, Harris. They watch people who can hurt them. And once your name's in the book, it stays there until one of two things happens: you stop moving, or you stop breathing."

The waitress came by with a pot of coffee. Donell didn't break eye contact with me as he nodded for a refill. "That feather you got? That wasn't a warning. That was your welcome mat."

I sipped the coffee. It was bitter enough to make my teeth ache. "So who exactly is 'they'?"

"Tremaine's network," he said flatly. "Politicians, preachers, street bosses, contractors, the kind of people who smile in your face while they move pieces you'll never see. The crows are their eyes. They don't all work for him directly, but they all feed the same nest."

"And Ezra?"

Donell's jaw tightened. "Ezra started talking about the nest. They started discussing the idea of cutting the strings on the churches and waking people up. That doesn't fly. The Sleeping Pill works because the pulpit's quiet. You get a pastor saying 'stop swallowing it,' and suddenly folks start asking why their preacher's got a new Cadillac but won't speak on a police shooting."

A gust of wind rattled the diner window. I glanced outside and froze. A crow sat on the hood of my car, feathers ruffling in the breeze. It wasn't pecking or moving, just facing the diner, head tilted.

Donell followed my gaze and muttered, "Persistent little bastards."

"You think that's a coincidence?" I asked.

"You still asking that?" He shook his head. "Look, man, they're not subtle because they don't have to be. They want you to know they're there. Makes you paranoid, makes you slip. And when you slip, they're there to clean it up."

I let the words sink in. The crow hopped down from the hood, landed on the curb, and then lifted into the air, disappearing over the rooftops.

"So what's my next move?" I asked.

"That's the thing," Donell said. "You can't just go chasing feathers. You gotta figure out which part of the nest Ezra was poking at before they clipped him. Yolanda trusts you, that's your in. But she's being watched too, make no mistake. You want answers, you move carefully. You start with who benefited from Ezra being quiet."

I thought about the handshake I'd seen between the elder and the man in the gray suit at the funeral. Not grief, not comfort agreement. A deal in plain sight.

"You know who was at the service that didn't belong," I said.

Donell nodded slowly. "I know some. But the ones you gotta worry about? You won't find their pictures online. They're the kind that make sure cameras turn the other way."

We finished the coffee in silence. When I left, the sidewalk felt emptier than it should have. No birds in sight, no feathers underfoot. But I could feel them, somewhere just out of view.

I drove with the windows down despite the cold, letting the air clear my head. The note was back in my pocket, the paper warm from my hand. You're in their book now.

I didn't know how many pages the book had or how long my name would stay in it. But I knew this Ezra had died for trying to close it, and I wasn't ready to let them write the ending.

I didn't sleep that night.

Not because I was scared, at least not the kind of fear you admit to, but because my mind was tracing lines between Herb's church, those black duffel bags, and the names I'd been hearing whispered since Ezra's death. Lines that didn't stay on one map.

By sunrise, I was at my desk, coffee on one side, Ezra's journal on the other, and a stack of county records spread like a gambler's hand in front of me. Carr's name didn't show up anywhere directly; men like him never put their own fingerprints on anything. But the church's 501(c)(3) filings told a different story.

A side entity. Kingdom Youth Empowerment Initiative. Cute name. Listed as a mentorship program for "at-risk male youth." Received over $200,000 in city grants last year alone. According to the paperwork, they had three full-time staff, a summer basketball league, and a life-skills training program.

Except the address wasn't a rec center.

It was a second-floor suite above a check-cashing place on Bailey.

I drove there mid-morning. The hallway smelled like old carpet, and someone was frying fish behind a closed door. The "office" door had a vinyl decal peeling at the edges, and the logo was a pair of hands cupping a cartoon basketball.

Inside, the place looked like it had been furnished from a church basement giveaway. Two folding chairs in the waiting area, a dented file cabinet, and a potted plant on life support. A desk sat behind a cloudy plastic window divider, and behind the desk was a young woman, perhaps in her mid-twenties, with a thin frame and a hoodie featuring the nonprofit's logo.

She smiled when I walked in, but it was the kind of smile people wear when they're trained to. "Can I help you?"

I kept it casual. "Looking for someone who runs this place. Pastor Carr."

Her eyes flickered, not fear exactly, but the kind of tight blink that says you just asked the wrong question. "Uh… Pastor Carr's not in. He's… usually not here during the week."

"Right. But this is his program?"

Her smile faltered. "It's… community-led."

I nodded, pretending to buy it. "Mind if I ask how the mentorship program works? Got a nephew who might need something like this."

That seemed to relax her a bit. "We… mostly do workshops. And events. The basketball league is in the summer. Right now we're… uh… between cycles."

I glanced at the bare bulletin board behind her. No flyers. No schedules. No photos of kids at last summer's league. Just a single city grant award letter tacked to the cork, like they wanted anyone walking in to know they were legit.

"You keep records here?" I asked.

Her hands dropped into her lap. "Everything's… at our other office."

I smiled back, slow. "Right. The other office."

The phone on her desk rang. She answered, listened, then gave me a quick nod. "We're closing early today."

I left without pushing it further. Pushing would only scare her into silence, and I had what I needed: the smell of something rotten wrapped in the language of "community uplift."

Back in the car, I wrote one line in my notebook: Follow the money.

Because no matter how clean the sermons or how loud the hallelujahs, the books never lie.

Chapter 8
The First Thread

The street was mostly quiet except for the hum of a bus a block away and the distant bark of a dog. No crows this time, not in sight, but I kept scanning rooftops and streetlamps out of habit. Donell's voice was still in my ear: They don't all work for him directly, but they all feed the same nest.

I drove without a destination for a while, letting the city pass by, with liquor stores featuring neon signs buzzing in daylight, laundromats where tired women carried baskets, and corner boys leaning against brick walls with eyes sharp enough to cut glass. This was the Buffalo I'd always known, the Buffalo Ezra had tried to wake up. I found him sitting where he always did on Fridays, back booth at Dee Dee's Soul Kitchen, sipping black coffee and eating eggs slow like he had nowhere to be. Folks called him Bramble now, but back in the day, his name made city hall sweat. He'd been a field organizer, strategist, and one of the last men in Buffalo to wear a leather jacket like it was a second skin. His hair was gray now, but his eyes still had that sharpened edge like he could cut through your story before you'd even finished telling it.

"Bushvill," he said without looking up. "If you're here, that means you're either looking for trouble or trying to remember what the truth smells like."

I slid into the booth. "Maybe both."

He smirked. "And you think I'm the one to give it to you?"

I didn't answer right away. I just pulled the manila folder from my coat and slid it across the table. Inside were copies of Carr's nonprofit filings, a grant ledger, and a photo I'd snapped of the duffel bags being loaded into the church's side entrance.

Bramble flipped through it without surprise. "Tremaine," he muttered.

"You know him?" I asked.

"I know his type. Always been here. Always will be. Only the names change." He tapped the folder. "See, the government doesn't just react to movements; they manage them. Keep the lid on the pot. That's COINTELPRO 101. Back in my day, they used snitches, fake leaflets, and wiretaps. Now? They use grants, 501(c)(3) rules, and pastors with a taste for the finer things."

I leaned back. "You saying Tremaine's working with the feds?"

Bramble chuckled, but there wasn't anything funny in it. "Working for, working with the same thing if the checks clear. They learned from the '60s. You don't have to kill the movement outright. You just starve it, dilute it, or buy out the people leading it. That's what this is. Ezra was the wrong kind of preacher, not for sale, too loud, and trying to teach people they didn't need permission to fight for themselves."

I thought about Ezra at the BFNC Summer Solstice, going toe-to-toe with Jan Peters about the role of the church. His verses had pulled her closer to God that day, but it was more than scripture; it was the kind of defiance you couldn't fake.

Bramble went on. "Tremaine's a broker. He navigates between the church world and the political world, ensuring that both sides receive what they need or what they believe they need. He's not interested in the truth, Bushvill. He's interested in balance. And if one man tips that balance…"

"They take him out," I finished.

Bramble nodded. "They call it 'stability.' I call it murder with paperwork."

We sat in silence for a beat. Dee Dee's clatter filled the air plates, laughter, and a gospel track low in the background.

Bramble leaned in. "You want to keep digging? Fine. But don't think you're just up against Carr or Tremaine. You're up against a system that's older than both of us. And if you start making noise like Ezra, they'll find your pressure point and they'll push until something breaks."

He finished his coffee, slid out of the booth, and clapped a hand on my shoulder. "Question is, Harris, what's your pressure point?"

By the time I parked in front of my office, the note in my pocket felt heavier. I unlocked the door, flicked on the light, and sat at my desk without taking my coat off. I laid the note flat, stared at the words until they blurred. Then I pulled out Ezra's journal again.

I wasn't looking for sermons this time. I was looking for patterns, names, initials, and dates. Ezra's handwriting was tight, deliberate, but here and there he'd circle a date or underline a phrase twice. "Jefferson 8," "T.R. meet," "Fifteenth St. lunch." The one that stopped me cold was "Grantman silent."

Grantman was a councilman I'd seen at the funeral, sitting near the back. A small man with a sharp suit and a way of staying just outside the spotlight. If Ezra had written "silent" next to his name, it meant one of two things: he'd kept his mouth shut when Ezra needed him to speak, or he'd been paid to keep it shut.

The phone rang. I let it go twice before I picked it up.

"Harris?"

It was Yolanda. Her voice was low, the way people talk when they're not sure if someone's listening.

"I can't talk long," she said. "But there's something you need to see. Not over the phone."

"Where?"

"I'll text you. Don't come right away. Give it an hour."

The line went dead.

I leaned back, staring at the ceiling. The room was quiet except for the hum of the radiator. Then I heard a faint tap at the window. Not the steady rain from before, but a single, deliberate tap.

I crossed the room. There, it was a crow on the ledge, head cocked. It didn't move when I approached. Its beak tapped the glass once more before it lifted off, wings flashing in the streetlight as it vanished into the night.

An hour later, I was parked two blocks from the address Yolanda had sent, a small community center on the edge of the East Side. Most of the windows were dark except for one on the second floor. I watched for a while before getting out, the cold biting through my coat.

Inside, the place smelled of old books and floor wax. Yolanda was in a small office at the back, a file folder on the desk in front of her.

"These are copies of some of Ezra's grant applications," she said, pushing the folder toward me. "He started making notes on them a few months before he died. Look at the last one."

It was an application for a city improvement grant for sidewalk, lighting, and community repairs. The signature at the bottom wasn't Ezra's. It was Grantman's.

"He submitted it after Ezra died," she said. "Same proposal, same numbers. Just changed the name."

I flipped through the rest. The paper smelled faintly of tobacco. "You think this is why Ezra was killed?"

"I think it's one piece," she said. "And I think Grantman's not working alone."

The sound of footsteps in the hall made us both freeze. Yolanda slid the folder into my coat pocket and motioned toward the back exit.

Outside, the night was sharp and empty. We didn't see anyone, but as I walked to my car, I caught sight of something on the hood: a single black feather, slick with dew.

Chapter 9
New Blood

She couldn't have been more than twenty-one, maybe twenty-two, but she carried herself like she was already outgrowing the room. Shoulder-length twists, gold-rimmed glasses, a denim jacket plastered with protest buttons the kind of look that said she didn't just read history, she wanted to set it on fire and watch what grew from the ashes.

I'd met Kristen twice before, both times in passing, both times in places where people spoke in lowered voices and didn't linger at the door. She had a way of being present without inviting questions, the kind of person you only noticed because she didn't seem to want to be noticed.

When Donell told me she wanted to meet, I asked where she wanted to meet. He said she'd pick the spot. That told me two things: she was careful, and she was testing me.

The place she chose was an all-night laundromat on the West Side. Old machines lined up like sentries, their chrome dulled by years of soap residue. The hum of dryers filled the air, mingling with the scent of detergent and the burnt coffee from a vending machine in the corner.

Kristen was sitting near the back, a half-full basket of clothes at her feet, folding a shirt like she meant it. She didn't look up when I slid into the chair across from her.

"You're early," she said.

"You're cautious," I countered.

That got me the faintest flicker of a smile. She reached into her bag and pulled out a paperback book, the kind you find in grocery store racks. Inside, where the middle pages should have been, was a folded sheet of paper. She slid it across the table without breaking her rhythm with the shirt.

I unfolded it. At first glance, it appeared to be a grocery list. Milk, bread, coffee, and paper towels. But next to each item was a string of numbers. I recognized the pattern addresses.

"These are churches," I said.

"Not just churches," she replied quietly. "These are the ones still in the Covenant, or at least sympathetic to it. The ones that haven't taken Tremaine's money yet."

I looked at her for a long moment. "Where'd you get this?"

"Does it matter?"

"It does if I'm going to use it."

She met my eyes then, and I saw the calculation there. "Let's just say I have a friend who works in grant processing. She sees where the money goes. And where it doesn't."

The addresses were spread across the city, the East Side, the West Side, and even a couple in the suburbs. A map was already forming in my head.

Kristen leaned forward. "You've got maybe two weeks before half these names disappear. Tremaine's people are moving fast. They're offering 'community improvement stipends.' Sounds harmless, right? But once they take it, they're bound. They can't back the Covenant without losing the money."

Her voice had a tension to it, not fear exactly, but urgency. She was giving me something valuable, and she was aware of the risk.

"Why bring this to me?" I asked.

"Because you're not on anyone's payroll. And because Ezra trusted you."

That last part landed harder than I expected.

Before I could answer, a man stepped inside, scanned the laundromat with a quick, empty sweep of the eyes, and slipped back out without a sound. Kristen watched him the whole way to the door, her jaw tightening the way it does when she senses trouble before I do.

"We're done," she said, standing with a calm I didn't trust. She pressed the folded white button-down into my hands and walked out with her basket balanced against her hip, like she had already decided where we were going. I followed her, partly curious, partly uneasy, because she carried herself like someone older than she was like someone who had seen too much and refused to flinch at any of it.

The street felt colder once we stepped outside. Kristen didn't say a word; she just moved with purpose, cutting through the late-morning quiet as if she'd been walking beside me her whole life. I trailed a half-step behind, thinking about that man in the doorway, the look in Kristen's eyes, and the strange pull in my chest that wasn't quite fear but wasn't comfort either.

By the time the tension had settled enough for me to speak, we were already standing in front of my office door.

She pushed it open like she belonged there, and the story shifted.

 I opened the shirt. Inside, tucked into the fold, was a small flash drive.

"I'm working on my senior project," she said, "A profile on Pastor Ezra Abrams. His work, his message, and… his death."

The way she said it, "death" carried a certainty that didn't match the official story. She wasn't here for the heart attack narrative. She wanted the raw edges.

She had that look in her eyes, the same look I'd seen in Ezra's the first time we met at the BFNC Summer Solstice. A mix of faith, doubt, and a refusal to sit still while the world burned.

Part of me wanted to push her out the door. Not because she wasn't sharp, she was. But sharp gets you cut if you don't know how deep the blade goes.

"You know what you're stepping into?" I asked.

Her jaw tightened. "I've done my research."

"Research doesn't prepare you for the phone calls at three in the morning. Or the black car parked outside your apartment for two nights straight. Or the fact that the people you think you can trust might be the ones who hand you over."

She didn't flinch.

I sighed, glancing at the framed photo of my friend Mark on the bookshelf, the one killed by Buffalo PD on that rainy garage roof. I thought about the nights I'd almost poured whiskey down my throat just to quiet the ghosts.

Mentoring her could mean turning her into one more ghost.

But something about her reminded me of me before the cracks set in. And maybe, if I played it right, I could help her navigate the storm instead of being swallowed by it.

"Alright," I said finally. "I'll feed you information. But you follow my lead, you don't chase shadows on your own, and if I tell you to walk away, you walk."

Her smile was small but sure. "Deal."

When she left, I found myself staring at her name scrawled in my notepad. I underlined it twice.

Because if things went bad, and they usually did, I'd need to remember exactly who I'd let into this.

The black feather sat on my desk where I'd left it, but I ignored it. Tonight wasn't about birds or symbols. Tonight was about a list and the trail that leads to a dead pastor.

I kept my lights low, only the desk lamp on, and spread Yolanda's file across the surface. The pages were clean copies, the kind you'd pull from a city records room if you had the right clearance. Signatures were neat, practiced the kind of signature that had been written on numerous public checks. But the proposal? Word for word, it was Ezra's. Same block improvements, same budget lines, even the same typo in "recreation."

I started making calls. First to the City Clerk's office, posing as a reporter. No one there remembered any issues with the grant. "It was approved without comment," the woman said. "Standard process." I could hear her typing while she spoke, probably looking up my number to see if I was legit.

Next, I contacted an old acquaintance in the Department of Public Works, a man named Mills who'd once owed me for helping his nephew avoid a vandalism charge. "That sidewalk money?" he said when I asked. "Went through a contractor in Cheektowaga. B&B Infrastructure. Quiet job, no bids posted."

"No bids?"

"Not on paper," Mills said. "But if you want my guess, it was greased before it left the council floor."

B&B Infrastructure. I wrote it down, then dug through an old drawer for my laptop. A quick search yielded a bare-bones website, stock photos of construction workers, a generic email address, and a mailing address located in a strip mall. I recognized the location; half the units were empty, while the other half housed cash-based businesses that nobody really looked too closely at.

I closed up and decided to drive over. It was late, but sometimes that's when you see the real face of a place. The lot was mostly dark when I got there. A single light glowed above B&B's door, illuminating a metal security gate. No vehicles with company logos, no signs of actual construction work.

As I walked back to my car, I noticed the first movement in the reflection on the glass of the barber shop window. A figure, leaning against the corner across the street. Not moving toward me, not away, just... there.

I got in the car, started it, and pulled out slowly, keeping a close eye on the mirrors. Two blocks later, the figure was still behind me, a dark sedan three cars back.

I took a left turn when I didn't need to. The sedan followed.

I didn't floor it. That's a rookie move. Instead, I kept my pace steady, weaving through side streets until I found one with a narrow alley and cut hard into it. From there, I killed the lights and waited.

The sedan cruised past the alley without slowing. No plates I could read from here, no window roll-down to check a face. Just a shape in the dark.

When I finally pulled out, I didn't go home. I went to Donell's. He answered the door in sweats, eyes narrowing when he saw my face.

"You're being followed," he said.

"Yeah," I told him. "By who?"

"Could be anyone tied to the grant. Could be someone wanting to scare you off before you get to the why." He stepped back to let me in. "And you are gonna get to the why, right?"

I dropped onto his couch, the file folder heavy in my hands. "B&B Infrastructure," I said. "Ever heard of it?"

He smirked. "Yeah. And I also know they don't lay damn brick unless it's for show. Money runs through them, that's it. They build fake jobs, pad invoices, and kick back to whoever made the call.

"On paper," Donell said. "But it's just a face.

I leaned forward. "You know who?"

He shook his head. "Not yet. But I know who might."

He gave me a name I hadn't heard in years, Curtis Vale. An accountant who used to work for a nonprofit until they caught him moving money into "special projects." He'd done time, got out, and now freelanced for anyone who didn't want their numbers public.

"Curtis owes me," Donell said. "We can talk to him, but it's not gonna be friendly. He doesn't like being reminded of his time inside."

I nodded, the map already forming in my head. B&B to Curtis. Curtis to whoever was really pulling the strings.

When I left Donell's, the street was quiet. No sedan, no figure in the shadows. But I knew better than to think they'd just lost interest.

The game had shifted, and I'd just taken my first step onto their side of the board.

Chapter 10

Donell's methods were less cautious.

Where I leaned on conversation, subtlety, and the slow gathering of facts, he preferred something quicker, pressure applied directly where it hurt.

We tracked a lead to Reggie, a low-level hustler who moved between dice games and corner stores like he was allergic to staying in one place too long. Word was, he'd been making small deliveries for Curtis Vale, nothing flashy, just envelopes and unmarked packages.

We found him behind a bodega on Jefferson, the alley choked with the smell of frying grease and rotting fruit. He was counting cash, the kind of roll that said the streets liked him just enough to keep him breathing.

Donell didn't waste time. He stepped into Reggie's shadow, grabbed him by the jacket collar, and shoved him hard against the dented dumpster. The metal boomed, startling a stray cat that darted past my feet.

"Vale," Donell said flatly. "How do you know him?"

Reggie tried to play it cool, but his eyes kept darting to me, like I might be the one to save him.

"I don't know," he started, but Donell cut him off with a sharp forearm across his chest.

"Wrong answer," Donell growled. "Don't waste my time."

Reggie's voice cracked. "Man, I just run errands. I don't ask questions."

"That's the thing about errands," Donell said, leaning in so close I could see Reggie's breath fog against his cheek. "They start and end somewhere. You're gonna tell me both."

Donell pressed harder, enough to make Reggie's shoes squeak against the wet pavement. Finally, the name dropped Tremaine. He's an accountant; he moves money. Along with a description of a warehouse, Vale visited twice a month, always at night, always after church meetings.

Donell let him go; the man was slumping against the dumpster like air leaking from a tire. He adjusted his jacket, smoothed it like he hadn't just wrung information out of someone.

"That's how you handle liars," Donell said, wiping his hands on a rag he pulled from his back pocket. "You don't wait for them to feel comfortable. You make the truth the easiest thing they can say."

Donell, through his connections, discovered where Curtis Vale lives.

The drive to Vale's place took us out past the city's glare, into streets where the porch lights looked like small moons keeping watch over the dark. Donell kept his eyes on the road, hands loose on the wheel, but I could feel the unspoken between us. We didn't know if we were heading toward an ally or a memory.

Vale lived in a two-story brick house that had seen better decades. The shutters leaned, and the yard was trimmed but tired. A single lamp glowed in the front window. He answered our knock without asking who it was, as if he'd already read the ledger of our intentions.

"Harris. Donell," he said quietly. "Come in."

Inside, the place had a faint smell of paper and old coffee. Bookshelves lined the walls, heavy with binders, ledgers, and boxes labeled in blocky handwriting. The living room was neat but lived-in, as if someone had kept it ready for guests they hoped would never come.

We sat. Vale took the armchair opposite, a leather-bound journal balanced on his knees. His eyes were steady, the kind of calm that doesn't come from safety but from deciding fear has no more leverage.

"I knew this day would come," he said. "Ezra called it the 'Manna Covenant.' Not many knew that name. Fewer still knew what it meant."

Donell leaned forward. "We've heard pieces. Church unions, pooled funds, and political leverage for FBA causes. But not the full picture."

Vale opened the journal. The pages were dense with diagrams, arrows connecting names, amounts, and dates. "Ezra wanted a resource stream for our people. Something not tied to the government's purse strings. Manna from heaven, but in this world, manna had to be accounted for, every penny. That was my role. I made sure the Covenant's ledgers were clean, unassailable. No matter how hard they dug, they couldn't say it was criminal."

I watched Vale's finger trace the ink like it was a scar. "Tremaine's network… It's built like a spider web. LLCs, shell companies, and grant laundering. He uses prosperity preachers and community 'nonprofits' as funnels. The money moves in circles until you can't tell where it started. But I followed it. Every rotation. Every shadow account."

"You gave this to Ezra?" I asked.

Vale nodded. "Piece by piece. I didn't dare put it all in one place until now. Ezra was the only one I trusted with the whole picture. I knew what it would cost him. I knew it might cost me." He closed the journal, hands still resting on it. "After he died, I thought about burning this. But then I thought about what he'd say."

Donell's voice was low. "He'd say keep going."

Vale gave a tight smile. "He'd say, 'The manna wasn't for me. It was for the ones coming after.'"

Silence settled over the room, heavy but not hopeless. I felt the weight of what Vale was offering, not just numbers, but a map of the rot. A weapon disguised as a book.

"You ready for this, Harris?" Vale asked. "Because once you have it, Tremaine will know the Covenant didn't die with Ezra. He'll come for you like he came for him."

I thought about Ezra's last sermon, about the leash he told us to burn. "Then he'll have to come," I said. "Because we're not burying this manna in the desert."

Vale slid the journal across the coffee table. Its weight hit my palms like a verdict.

"Vail tapped the arm of his chair, thinking. "He wanted to flip the script. Use the same tax code that muzzled the church to free it. He was attempting to pool tithes from multiple congregations, mostly pastors who were tired of dancing for crumbs. He had this idea that if you combined that money, you could build a fund big enough to do three things: buy property, bankroll candidates, and pay out direct reparations to FBAs in the congregation."

Donell whistled low. "That's not just church reform. That's a war chest."

Vail nodded. "Yeah. And it scared the hell out of people. Because if you get enough churches moving in the same direction, you don't just have a religious network. You've got a political machine. Ezra was building a voting block of Foundational Black Americans only. No outsiders coming to water it down. That block could've swung local and state elections overnight in a few years."

"And reparations through tithing?" I asked.

Vail grinned faintly. "He called it 'restoration giving.' Ten percent in the plate, ten percent out to the people. Direct payments. No politicians touching it, no nonprofits skimming. Straight from the church to the folks who built the country. That's dangerous thinking in this city. Dangerous thinking anywhere."

I could feel the weight of Yolanda's note again in my pocket. *You're in their book now.*

"Where was the money?" I asked.

"In a trust," Vail said. "Names of the contributing churches kept off the books. Only Ezra and two others knew the full list. One's dead. The other…" He trailed off.

"Who?"

Vail shook his head. "If I say it, I'm next. And I'm not in the mood to be next."

Donell leaned forward. "You're already in the book, Vail. Only question is which page."

For a moment, the only sound was the hum of his monitors. Then Curtis swiveled, opened a drawer, and pulled out a manila envelope. He slid it across the desk.

"Copies of the first disbursement plans," he said. "Ezra never got to send them. Names are coded, amounts rounded, but you'll see the scale. This wasn't pennies in a jar, this was enough to start flipping neighborhoods."

I opened the envelope. Inside were spreadsheets and maps marked with colored dots. Churches clustered across the East Side, each with a figure next to it. The totals added up to a number that made my chest tighten.

"This is why he's dead," Vail said. "It wasn't the sermons. It was the math."

Vail leaned back, stirring his coffee so slow it looked like he was winding time backward, but his words were meant for me.

"You know why Ezra wouldn't let this go?" he asked. "It wasn't just about the church. It was about the gap, what he called the value gap."

I raised an eyebrow.

"See, Ezra knew white life in America is treated like a blue-chip stock," Vail continued. "Protected, insured, grown at all costs. Black life? They treat it like a risky penny stock worth something only if it can be flipped for profit or controlled so it doesn't disrupt the market. That's math. And Ezra? He couldn't stomach that math."

He took a slow sip, his voice softening but sharpening at the same time. "He'd see a white neighborhood get a new arts center 'cause they asked for it, while a Black neighborhood had to beg just to keep the library open. He'd see banks hand a loan to some twenty-year-old white kid with nothing but a smile, and turn down a Black man with a perfect payment history. And he'd tell me, 'Vail, this ain't about talent or hustle, it's about what they decided we're worth before we even step in the room.'"

Vail set his cup down, the sound heavier than it should've been. "That's why he went after the power structure. Not 'cause he thought he could win quick. But 'cause he knew if you don't call out the gap, they'll convince you it's your fault it exists. And once they do that, they own you."

He finally looked at me. "That's why Ezra had to go. Not because he was wrong but because he was telling the truth loud enough that even the quiet folks started listening."

Before we left, I asked one more question. "Why give this to us?"

Vail looked at me like it should've been obvious. "Because if someone's gonna burn for this, it's not gonna be me alone. And maybe... maybe you're stupid enough to finish what he started."

Outside, the air felt heavier. Donell lit a cigarette and stared at the envelope in my hands.

"That right there?" he said. "That's the kind of thing people kill movements over."

I didn't answer. I was too busy thinking about the map, the dots, and the idea that maybe Ezra hadn't been preaching to save souls. Maybe he'd been preaching to save the people who'd been carrying everybody else's weight for four hundred years.

And maybe that was exactly why they'd put him in the book.

Chapter 11
Paper Saints

The envelope from Curtis sat on my desk like a loaded gun.

The black duffel bags, the church fronts, all pointed to something bigger. But bigger how? That night, Donell found the trail leading not just into sanctuaries and nonprofits, but into political coffers.

We trailed a stack of grant checks stamped with the name Sable Equity Holdings, but then crossed paths with "Allied Futures PAC", a recently registered political action committee. A PAC reaches higher, gives more it was meant to channel funds into campaigns or legislation. But something about Allied Futures reeked of setup.

It was the kind of PAC that was registered with the FEC, had a treasurer whose name led only to a P.O. box, and filed filings so sparse they could've been drawn in crayon. It was a typical decoy, transparent enough to appear legitimate, yet obscure enough to conceal its true purpose. Late that night, Donell flipped through the county's campaign disclosure database. Allied Futures had quietly donated six-figure sums to a State Representative running for public safety reform. The figure didn't fit in the official ideological box; it was too strategic, placed right when reform was likely to hit a nerve. A smokescreen, maybe. But the trail didn't end there.

A second entity a 501(c)(4) "Social Welfare Organization" turned out to be funneling "soft money" into Allied Futures. Unlike 501(c)(3)s, these can actively influence elections and keep their donors obscured.

In one county filing, a donation from Sable Equity appeared as a lump sum to Allied Futures. The PAC spent it on a statewide mailer supporting criminal justice "balance." The cleverly vague mailer praised the same reforms Ezra publicly pushed, nowhere mentioning Tremaine, but the optics made the candidate look progressive, all while serving as a diversion from what Tremaine's network was actually doing.

"Look at this," Donell said, voice low. "It's a loop. The church receives repurposed funding, which is then funneled to a shadow PAC. PAC sends it to the legislature. And the public sees reform, while the reorder of power happens behind screens." He tapped the screen. "That's how you own more than churches, you buy the platform they speak from."

The numbers didn't lie. Less than a year old, Allied Futures had already spent over $500,000, enough to sway local endorsements, media mentions, and compliance committees. Every dollar was obscured in paperwork, and every donor was hidden behind shell entities.

Tremaine didn't just whisper in pulpits; he funded them, controlled the message, and shaped the city in the legislature's image.

I'd read through the spreadsheets three times since we left his place, tracing the dots on the map in my head. Churches I knew. Churches I'd passed a hundred times without looking twice. Storefront sanctuaries with peeling paint. Stately brick buildings with stained glass that caught the afternoon sun like it was still holy.

I pulled one sheet from the pile, a small Baptist church on Jefferson. I knew the place. Ten pews across, a choir that could raise goosebumps, a pastor with a wardrobe that looked like a men's haberdashery downtown sponsored it. I opened my laptop and typed the church name into the IRS's online database.

The record popped up. 501(c)(3) determination granted: 1989. I stared at that date. Back then, crack had been flooding the East Side, the jobs were drying up, and the same federal government choking our neighborhoods was granting churches tax exemptions in exchange for political silence. Ezra had called it The Sleeping Pill for a reason.

I leaned back in my chair, staring at the ceiling, letting the thought unspool.

The modern Black church had become a strange kind of theater. The flash, the lights, the praise of dancers in sequined gloves, celebrity preachers with radio spots and livestream services, hashtags, and merch lines. All the while, the blocks around them crumbled. Potholes big enough to swallow hubcaps, boarded-up houses next to buildings with LED screens flashing "God Loves You" in colors bright enough to burn retinas.

It was a show, a Sunday dopamine rush. You walked in carrying the weight of the week and left floating on music, charisma, and the practiced cadence of a man or woman who could make a scripture sound as if it were written just for you. But by Monday? Monday, it faded, and you were back where you started. Bills, layoffs, the hum of police cars outside your window at night. You chased the feeling like a junkie, because the high didn't solve anything.

Ezra's plan was dangerous because it wasn't about making people feel good for a few hours; it was about changing their lives. It was about giving them power real, usable, and dangerous power. Money is pooled and directed at tangible goals. A voting block built on shared history, not imported talking points. Reparations paid from the collection plate before it ever had a chance to be siphoned away into building funds that never seemed to finish building anything.

I closed my eyes and found myself back in another church, another time. Easter Sunday. I was maybe ten. My aunt had pressed a too-tight tie around my neck, the kind that made swallowing feel like a chore. The sanctuary smelled of lilies and hairspray. The choir was loud enough to make the walls hum.

I remember looking up at the front of the church and seeing him in the picture. Jesus, pale-skinned, straight-haired, eyes the color of the sky I never saw in my neighborhood, looked nothing like me or anyone in the pews.

Something in me broke open in that moment. It wasn't anger, not yet. It was with certainty that I didn't belong here. This wasn't built for me, even if they said it was. I'd slipped out during the altar call and never gone back. At least not to stay.

Ezra must've known that feeling. That's why his sermons cut past the pageantry and went straight for the roots. He didn't want the Black church to be a stage; he wanted it to be a base. And the people who run this city, who profit from us staying docile, couldn't afford that.

I turned back to the spreadsheet and ran the church's 501(c)(3) date against the voting patterns in the neighborhood. The correlation was ugly every election year after '89 showed a drop in turnout, sharper among the congregations with those tax-exempt plaques hanging in their foyers. It wasn't proof, but it was a scent.

I kept digging. Three more churches were removed from the list, all with status granted between '85 and '95, all in districts that had once been politically restless and now barely stirred at the polls. The pattern was too neat to be random.

These neighborhoods had been engines, once marching in the streets, voter drives on the corners, meetings that went past midnight. Now the engines were cold. The fire went out right around when the pulpits started preaching patience instead of pressure.

And every single one of those districts? Blue. Deep blue. Generation after generation, voting Democrat was like paying a Sunday tithe. Not because the policies were delivered but because tradition said you were supposed to. The same candidates came through every election cycle, shaking hands in church basements, promising the world and leaving the same potholes, boarded-up houses, and underfunded schools.

You could stand on the corner of Genesee and Fillmore and see it, liquor stores where the libraries used to be, shelters where the rec centers used to be, a line at the methadone clinic stretching farther than the one at the voting booth. This wasn't representation. This was management. The kind that kept a lid on the pot while the water boiled down to nothing.

The Democrats held the keys to these cities, and somehow the locks only seemed to tighten. The streets were no safer, the jobs were no better, and the schools were no fuller. However, the sermons continued to instruct people to "pray and participate," which essentially meant "vote and wait." And we waited so long, we forgot what moving forward looked like.

It was hard not to wonder if the 501(c)(3) wasn't just a tax code; it was a muzzle to keep pastors from talking about real political power. The moment people woke up and started questioning the deal they'd been getting, someone's gravy train was over.

Somewhere in this list was the key to unlocking Ezra's map. One church name would lead to another, and eventually to the core part of the plan, no one wanted to see daylight. But first, I needed to understand the network from the inside.

I shut the laptop and sat in the half-dark, the envelope still on my desk. Outside, the city was quiet. Somewhere, pastors were writing next Sunday's sermons, polishing their stories, timing their pauses. And somewhere else, people like Tremaine were counting on those words to keep the flock exactly where they were warm, fed, and asleep.

I wasn't a preacher. But I was awake. And that was going to have to be enough.

Chapter 12
Both Sides of the Pulpit

I left my office with my coat collar pulled up against the wind, the file from our meeting tucked under my arm. I was headed to John's. It was one of those spots where the espresso was bitter enough to make you feel like you were still alive, and the regulars knew how to keep their eyes to themselves. It was the kind of place you could talk in half-sentences and still be understood.

Halfway down the block, I felt it, not saw, felt that faint itch between the shoulder blades, the one that tells you the air behind you is carrying more weight than it should. I kept walking, slowing my pace just enough to catch a reflection in the pawnshop window.

A dark sedan, two cars back, rolling slower than traffic demanded. There were no plates I recognized or faces clear enough to pin, but the rhythm was wrong. A city has its own heartbeat, and this was off-tempo.

I took the next corner without looking over my shoulder, ducking into a side street lined with shuttered storefronts. A delivery truck sat at the curb, engine idling. I slipped between it and the wall, watching the sedan ease past at the end of the block. No brake lights. No pause. Just a glide, like they didn't want to break character.

Cat-and-mouse. The only question was, which one was I?

When I finally circled back to my car, the street was clear. No sedan. No eyes in the rearview. But the tension stuck with me, so I went home. Whoever they were, they wanted me to know they were there, close enough to touch, far enough to stay a rumor.

Donell used to say the real danger wasn't the bullet you saw coming. It was the one you didn't notice until the light left your eyes. The next day

I started with the churches that had the largest dots on Ezra's spreadsheet, pulling in the tithes that could fund something significant. One name stood out: Mount Hope Baptist. It has a mid-size brick façade and has been sitting on the corner of Filmore and Carlton since the late sixties. I'd driven past it a hundred times, but I'd never been inside.

According to Curtis's coded list, Mount Hope was among the first wave of churches Ezra had locked in for the pooled-tithing plan. The disbursement amount next to its name wasn't pocket change; it was enough to buy two houses in that neighborhood or pay for a serious campaign ad in a city council race.

Wednesday afternoon, the parking lot was nearly empty. Midweek meant no service, no choir practice, just the church's "business day," the side most of the congregation never sees. I pushed through the glass doors into a lobby lined with fading photographs of past pastors, each looking more removed from the street than the last.

The secretary at the front desk looked up from her paperwork. "Can I help you?"

"I'm here to see Pastor Williams," I said. I used my real name sometimes; the truth throws people off more than a lie.

She hesitated, then picked up the phone. A short exchange, a nod, and she motioned me down the hall. "End of the corridor, second door on your right."

The hallway was quiet except for the hum of fluorescent lights. Halfway down, I noticed something on the baseboard, a single black feather, small, perfectly placed if it had been set there on purpose. I kept walking, but the back of my neck tightened.

Pastor Williams' office was warm, thanks to a space heater, not central heat. He was in his late fifties, heavyset, with a suit that looked too small and eyes that studied you like they were counting your sins.

"Harris," he said, motioning to a chair. "Donell told me you might stop by."

So, he already knew my name.

I sat. "I'm looking into Ezra Abrams' work. I think you were part of it."

His mouth twitched, not quite a smile. "Ezra had ideas. Dangerous ones."

"Dangerous for who?"

"For everyone," Williams said. "You start pooling money like he planned; you threaten the balance. People often become accustomed to church as a place for comfort, rather than confrontation. You change that, and you'll have the IRS breathing down your neck, the city pulling grants, the banks calling in loans."

"That's The Sleeping Pill talking," I said.

His eyes narrowed.

"Tax code's a leash," I continued. "501(c)(3) status buys silence. The city pays for peace. Ezra wanted to break that."

Williams sighed. "You think I don't know? I sat in on those meetings. He had math. He committed half a dozen pastors, maybe more. But he underestimated the reach of the people he was going up against."

"Tremaine."

Williams didn't flinch at the name. "Him, and others. You think this is just local? The networks reach further than you want to know. And they've got... messengers."

"Messengers?"

He leaned back. "Have you ever seen the same bird twice in different places?"

I didn't answer.

"They know how to make you feel watched," he said. "They don't have to break your windows. They remind you they can."

I thought about the feather in the hallway. "So, you stayed quiet."

"I stayed alive," Williams said. "You think I like preaching about blessings and breakthroughs while my congregation lives on food stamps? You think I don't see the hypocrisy in new choir robes when the streetlights outside are busted? But the minute you speak about policy, money, and self-determination, they find a way to shut you down. And if they can't shut you down, they shut you up for good."

"Ezra didn't shut up."

"No," Williams said quietly. "And now he's gone."

We sat in silence for a moment. The hum of the heater filled the space.

"I can't do what he did," Williams said finally. "Not openly. But I can point you in the right direction." He opened a desk drawer and slid a folded paper across the table. "That's another church from the list. They've still got leaders who believe. But they're being squeezed."

I picked it up. No name, just an address.

As I stood to leave, Williams said, "Harris… you're in their book now. Don't think for a second that the crows won't follow you to the altar."

I didn't turn around. "Let them watch. I'm not here for the show."

The feather was still in the hallway when I left.

Chapter 13
The Bottle and the Bloodline

Home was quiet, but not the kind that rests you. It was the kind that makes the walls seem closer and the air heavier. My coat hits the chair by the door, and I go straight to the kitchen, not because I am hungry, but because that's where I keep it.

On top of the fridge, pushed back behind an old coffee can, was the bottle. Jack Daniel's. Empty, but I couldn't throw it away. It was the last thing my uncle and I shared before he died, sitting right here at this table, talking about nothing that mattered because we were both too drunk to handle the things that did.

I set the bottle on the table and sat across from it like it could talk back. My hands itched, like they wanted to go through the motions pour, raise, swallow, repeat. I'd been dry for a while now, but sobriety isn't a trophy you win. It's a fight you wake up to every day, and some days the bell rings before you're ready.

The situation worsened when I thought about my father.

He died of a drug overdose when I was in my forties. Crack and heroin were a cocktail that was killing men in my neighborhood like clockwork. When my father caught the disease, it was criminal, not an epidemic; it wasn't some accident of fate. It was a flood, and it came from upstream. And the people upstream never drowned.

I didn't go to his funeral. I didn't want to stand over his body and remember him as the man I'd spent years resenting. I thought he was weak. I thought he'd chosen the pipe over his family. I thought if he'd just been stronger, he could've quit. Back then, I didn't understand the gravity that addiction puts on a person's soul.

Now I do.

Now I know how a man can promise to stop and still find his feet, carrying him toward the corner store. How can the mind draw a line in the sand, and the body step over it without asking permission? Now I know my father wasn't weak; he was drowning in a current that was designed to pull him under.

What I didn't know until much later was how much hope he'd had in the church. Not in God in the institution. He believed the church could redeem and support him when he couldn't stand alone. I remember him coming home from revival nights, still smelling of cigarette smoke but with a Bible tucked under his arm, talking about turning over a new leaf.

But the church wasn't built for men like my father anymore. His demons were too powerful. It wasn't built to carry the weight of the broken. It was built to stage a show on Sunday, collect an offering, and let Monday swallow you whole. They didn't follow up when he stopped coming. They didn't knock on the door when he missed service. They didn't pull him back when he slipped.

When he died, I told myself I was better than him. Stronger. I said I'd never let a substance take my dignity. But here I am, staring at an empty bottle like it's an old lover, knowing damn well I've lost that fight before.

The only difference between him and I is that I still have a choice.

I reached for the bottle. Not to mimic pouring a drink, but to put it away. Back on top of the fridge, out of sight but never out of mind. I wasn't doing it for me. I was doing it because this fight I'd stumbled into, Ezras' fight, needed me sober. You can't go against the machine half-drunk and think you'll live long enough to win.

I went to the desk in the corner of the living room and pulled out the folded piece of paper Pastor Williams had given me. It did not have a name, just an address. I ran my finger over it, thinking it might tell me more if I touched it long enough.

Whoever was at that address was part of Ezra's network or had been before the squeeze started. If Williams trusted them enough to point me there, they had something worth protecting. It also meant Tremaine's people were aware of them.

The clock on the wall ticked louder than it should've. I grabbed my coat.

Before I stepped out, I looked back at the bottle on the fridge. It would be there when I got home, whispering the same promises as it always did. But for now, I had somewhere else to be.

The rain had stopped when I returned to my office, but the place still smelled like damp paper and yesterday's coffee. I dropped my coat over the chair and was about to pull the spreadsheet back out when I noticed something odd: my desk lamp was tilted just a hair to the left. I never leave it like that.

I froze.

It wouldn't be paranoia if you'd been tailed an hour ago. I scanned the room; my eyes settled on the framed photo of my brother on the bookcase. It was shifted forward, just enough that the dust ring underneath didn't line up.

I picked it up, and that's when I saw it was a pinhole mic, no bigger than a shirt button, stuck to the back of the frame. Black wire, flat battery pack, the kind you could buy online if you knew where to look.

Somebody had been in here. Somebody had been listening.

I sat down, the bug in my palm. My first thought was to smash it, flush it, erase the signal. My second thought was meaner. If they wanted to hear something, maybe I'd give them something worth choking on.

I pictured feeding them a steady diet of fake leads, names that didn't exist, meetings in neighborhoods where I'd never set foot. Let them chase ghosts while I kept digging. But the risk was real. The more I let them listen, the more chance I gave them to catch something real by accident.

I weighed it for a long minute, listening to the hum of the radiator and the faint traffic outside. Finally, I set the bug back behind the frame, right where I found it. I'd play along, for now. Whoever was on the other end thought they had the upper hand.

They didn't know I'd just invited myself into their game.

Chapter 14
The Address

When I stepped out, the city was quieter than usual, too quiet. Even the usual bass thump from the bar two blocks down had faded, like someone had turned the volume down on the street.

The air was heavy with the damp that clings to you, a leftover from the afternoon rain. My shoes scuffed against the slick pavement, every step echoing louder than it should have. That's when I felt that weight between my shoulder blades, the itch in the back of my neck, the feeling you don't get from nerves but from experience.

I slowed, letting my eyes adjust to the dark. Across the street, a streetlamp flickered, and in that strobe light pulse, I caught movement, a shadow slipping just beyond the halo of light, keeping pace.

Then came the sound. Not footsteps. Wings.

Above me, a burst of crows exploded from the power lines, scattering into the night with a chorus of rough caws. Feathers floated down like slow black snow, spinning in the glow of the streetlamps. I stopped walking. So did the shadow.

The crows circled once before disappearing over the rooftops, their noise still ringing in my ears. I turned my head just enough to catch the faint outline of someone leaning against the corner of a building, smoking. No face, just the ember of the cigarette flaring as they took a drag.

I kept moving, faster now, telling myself I wouldn't run. Running would confirm what I'd noticed. Running would make it a chase.

Half a block later, I glanced back. The corner was empty; whoever it was had melted into the city like smoke in the wind.

The crows didn't scatter without reason. And neither did I. Rev Feagan's place. The building was a converted corner store with a brick façade, a faded green awning, and a hand-painted sign that read "New

Hope Deliverance Tabernacle." It was the place you'd miss if you weren't looking for it. No stained glass, no digital marquee, just a single bulb over the door and a cross painted in peeling white.

Through the glass, I could see a man stacking chairs in the front of the room. Midweek service must've just ended. A few women lingered, gathering hymnals and folding tablecloths. I pushed the door open, and the sound of their conversation dropped half an octave.

The man straightened, wiping his hands on his slacks. "Can I help you?"

"I'm looking for someone who knew Ezra Abrams," I said.

His eyes shifted, just enough to notice. "A lot of people knew Ezra."

I stepped forward, lowering my voice. "Williams sent me."

That changed the air. He looked past me toward the door, then nodded toward a side room. "Let's talk in here."

The office was cramped, paper stacked high on every surface. He sat behind a desk and gestured for me to take the other chair.

"Name's Deacon Miller," he said. "What's this about?"

I pulled the folded spreadsheet Curtis had given me from my pocket. "You're on this list. Ezra had you down for pooled tithes restoration giving."

His eyes stayed on the paper, but he didn't read it. "You shouldn't have that."

"I do."

He exhaled slowly. "We believed in what Ezra was building. Still do. But beliefs don't stop bills from coming due. You know what it's like to have the city threaten to pull your permits? Or have your insurance company decide your coverage doesn't meet standards?"

"That Tremaine's doing?"

"Some of it. The rest is the system knowing how to squeeze without leaving fingerprints." He leaned forward. "We were ready to move. Ezra had the plan, and the other pastors were in. Then the pressure started. Fire inspections every other week. Noise complaints that came from nowhere. Even the bank started talking about 'reassessing' our mortgage."

I thought about the quiet street outside. Too quiet. "And you backed out."

"We paused," Miller corrected. "Ezra told me once, 'A dead man can't vote, and a bankrupt church can't lead.' I figured he was talking about someone else. Now I think he was talking about himself."

There was a knock on the office door. A young woman poked her head in. "Deacon, someone is asking for you."

He stiffened. "Tell them I'll be a minute." She closed the door.

"You need to go out the back," Miller said.

"Why?"

"Because I've been getting visits. Not the kind where they talk first."

I stood. "Who's here?"

He shook his head. "Don't know. But I see the same car parked across the street every week. Different driver, same eyes."

I slipped out the back door into an alley that smelled faintly of damp concrete and fryer oil. The cold cut sharply against my face. I made it halfway down the block before I glanced back.

At the mouth of the alley, a man stood watching. He wasn't moving toward me, but he didn't have to. He just needed me to know he was there.

Chapter 15
The Visit

The church looked smaller than I remembered from the last time I'd driven past. Midday light didn't do it any favors, peeling white paint, gutters sagging like tired shoulders, and a patch of weeds choking the front steps. Still, the sign out front flashed "Sunday Service 10 a.m." on a small electric marquee, as if nothing was wrong inside.

Reverend Carter answered the door himself. Mid-sixties, wiry, with a smile that could warm a room. I'd met him once at a community event with Ezra, and I remembered how they'd stood together, two men talking about possibilities like it was already in their hands.

"Brother Harris," he said, shaking my hand. "Come on in, come on in. I just put on some coffee."

His office smelled faintly of paper and lemon polish. The desk was clean except for a well-worn Bible and a framed photo of his congregation in matching choir robes.

We traded a few minutes of small talk before I brought it up. "I've been looking into Ezra's pooled tithes plan. Restoration giving. Your church was on the first-round list."

The warmth in his face cooled slightly. "That was a long time ago."

"Not so long. The plan could still work. You know what it meant: direct reparations to our own, a real political block for FBAs. You believed in it once."

Carter leaned back, folding his hands. "I still believe in the people, Harris. But the church... we must follow the law. The IRS doesn't grant you 501(c)(3) status so you can operate as a political action committee. We start endorsing candidates or organizing voting blocks, and they can yank our status. That's not just taxes, that's losing the building. Losing everything."

"That's The Sleeping Pill talking," I said quietly.

His eyes flickered, but he didn't deny it. "I have a responsibility to my flock. I can't lead them into a fight that'll leave them standing in the street come Monday morning."

Before I could respond, his phone buzzed on the desk. He glanced at the screen, and something in his face shifted, a tightening around the eyes, a quick swallow. He answered, said nothing for a few seconds, then murmured, "Yes. I understand." He hung up without looking at me.

I followed his gaze to the window.

Outside, a man in a dark coat was scattering something along the curb. Black shapes swooped down, landing in precise spaces. Five crows, evenly spaced, jerked their heads as they ate. The man never looked at them, nor did he look at the church. He just fed, paused, and fed again.

Carter stood abruptly. "I think our meeting is done for today, Brother Harris. I've got to prepare for this Sunday's message."

The shift was too sudden, too deliberate. "You know him?" I asked, nodding toward the window.

"Best if you go out the side door," he said, ignoring the question. "Less eyes."

When I looked back toward the street, the crow feeder and the birds were gone.

I didn't need anyone to explain what I'd just seen. This was the machine at work: the spiritual muzzle of the 501(c)(3) paired with the psychological chokehold of the crows. One kept you compliant, and the other kept you afraid. Together, they kept you quiet.

I'd just left a meeting at the church on Jefferson. My contact had been nervous, glancing at the window like the rain outside might be carrying messages. The air was heavy when I entered the street, and the light slid toward dusk. I didn't hear the footsteps until they were too close two of them, maybe three. The rhythm was wrong, not the casual stroll of neighbors, but the tight, deliberate pace of people who'd already decided where the night would end.

I kept walking, my hands in my coat pockets, one brushing the handle of the small blade I carried out of habit more than faith. The echo of their steps picked up, and when I glanced at a darkened store window, I caught them hoods up, shoulders squared, moving in the way wolves move when they've sighted something they think will be easy.

The first one closed the distance fast. I turned, just enough to make out his face under the hood. That's when another shadow peeled itself from the mouth of the alley; it was Donell.

He didn't speak. Didn't need to.

In three long strides, he was between me and them, his coat swinging open just enough for the metal at his hip to gleam in the dying light. His voice was low, but it carried a weight I'd heard before, the kind that makes grown men remember they have somewhere else to be.

"You boys looking to die on a Wednesday?" he said.

The tallest one tried to hold his ground, but Donell stepped in, close enough that their noses almost touched. "Nah. You ain't built for this," he murmured. "And you sure as hell ain't built for me."

The three exchanged glances, and I saw the moment when bravado turned back into common sense. They backed away, slow at first, then quicker, until they melted into the side streets.

Donell turned to me, his face unreadable. "You really ought to start checking your six, Harris."

I managed a half-smile. "Guess you've done it for me twice now."

He shrugged. "That's what families are for. But keep walking blind, and even I won't be fast enough."

I didn't tell him, but I knew the truth that night would've ended differently without Donell. And the fact that he'd been there, without me even calling, told me something else: Donell had his way of watching over me. Quiet. Relentless.

Chapter 16
Pressure Points

We sat in the dim light of my office, the rain tapping against the window like an impatient visitor. Yolanda had been silent for a long time; her hands wrapped around a mug of coffee she hadn't touched.

Finally, she spoke. "The last month before he died… Ezra wasn't himself."

I leaned back, watching her. "How so?"

"He'd always been bold," she said. "Too bold for his good sometimes. But lately… it was like he knew something was closing in on him. He'd check the locks twice, sometimes three times, before bed. He started leaving his phone in the kitchen drawer and told me not to answer it after a certain hour.

Her fingers were resting on the edge of my desk like she was holding onto something she didn't want to drop. Her eyes had that glassy stillness you see in people right before they confess something they can't take back.

"There's something I didn't tell you," she said.

I leaned back, watching her. "I figured as much."

She looked down at her hands. "I told him to stop. Ezra. I told him to… to follow the script."

The words came out small at first, but their weight was heavy enough to bend the air between us.

"What script?" I asked.

"The one they hand you when you take the grants. Keep the sermons safe. Keep the politicians close. Smile at the cameras. Never talk about the wrong kind of justice. Never make the wrong enemies." She looked up at me then, and her voice had that brittle edge of someone rehearsing this guilt for a while. "I told him the Covenant could wait. I told him we had time."

"And now he's dead."

Her silence was answer enough.

I didn't let her off the hook. "Why tell me this?"

"Because you need to know what you're walking into. These people… they don't just kill a man's body. They erase his voice, his vision. They rewrite him until even the people who loved him thought he was something smaller than he was. I helped them in my way. I thought I was protecting him, and I was helping bury him before they ever touched him."

She reached into her coat pocket again and pulled out a small, worn leather notebook. The kind you keep in your purse for grocery lists and phone numbers. She slid it toward me like it was burning her fingers.

"His notes," she said. "The parts he never preached. The ideas he kept off the pulpit because I told him it wasn't the right time."

I flipped it open. Short phrases. Scripture references. Meeting dates. Between them, scattered like seeds, were lines as sharp as any headline: The church is the last untapped voting bloc. Economic power without political independence is a leash. The Sleeping Pill is not just money it's permission to speak.

I closed the notebook gently, the way you might close a coffin.

Yolanda stood, pulling her coat tight. "If you take this on, Harris, understand something: you're already in the script. And the only way out is to rewrite it."

I didn't interrupt.

She stared into the steam of the coffee. "He said the sermons weren't enough anymore. The truth was bigger than the pulpit, but the pulpit had chains. He told me…" Her voice faltered, then hardened. "He told me he felt like the walls were listening. That even our prayers weren't private anymore."

I thought about the bug I'd found in my office, now sitting in the drawer like a venomous insect. Rendered useless.

She shook her head. "He wouldn't tell me everything. Said it was safer if I didn't know. But he kept talking about a network, explaining how the money moved and who was pulling the strings. He'd sit up late with that old ledger, scribbling notes, and then the next day he'd burn them in the fire pit out back. Not throw them away, burn them."

The way she said it sent a shiver down my spine. "Did he say who was after him?"

She met my eyes then, and it was like she was searching for the right words. "Not who. What. He called it 'the machine.' Said once you saw it, you couldn't unsee it. And once it saw you, you were already in the gears."

I let the silence sit between us, heavy and sharp. Outside, a crow called once, its voice cutting through the air.

She sat at the table with a stack of papers spread in front of her: city inspection reports, code violation notices, letters from grant offices.

"Every one of these churches was on Ezra's list," she said, tapping the papers. "And every one of them got hit right after a planning meeting. Fire inspections, building code citations, and even zoning disputes. Some of these pastors hadn't had an inspection in years, but suddenly, they're getting visits every other week."

Donell was leaning against the counter, arms crossed. "That's not random. That's someone upstairs making phone calls."

"It's worse than that," Yolanda said. She reached into a folder and pulled out a manila envelope. Inside were grainy photographs taken from across streets or through car windows. In almost everyone, a man stood near the church in question, tossing something to the ground.

"Crow feeders," I said.

Yolanda nodded. "Different men, same pattern. They're there before, during, or right after the inspections. Always in plain sight."

I flipped through the stack. "You're saying the feeders are working with the city?"

"I'm saying it's coordinated," Yolanda said. "They hit the church from both ends. The government arm waves the rule book; the street arm waves the fear. Together, they don't need to threaten you directly; you already know you can't fight both at once."

Donell joined us at the table. "I tracked one of these guys after he left Mount Hope last week. He walked three blocks and met with a man in a suit outside a coffee shop. They didn't shake hands or talk long, but money changed hands."

"Who was the man in the suit?" I asked.

Donell smirked. "City Development Office. Name's Price. Runs point on business permits. If he tells the Fire Marshal to look at a building, they look."

The papers in front of me stopped feeling like documents and began to feel like a map. Not Ezra's map, theirs. A system was established to keep every pulpit free from politics and every congregation silent in the voting booth. The Sleeping Pill wasn't just theology; it was backed up by bureaucracy and enforced by the crows.

"Ezra saw this?

Yolanda didn't answer right away. "He called it the 'two-handed choke.' One hand holds the law, the other points the barrel. You never see them together, but you feel both at once."

I leaned back, running my hand over my face. "We need to know where these feeders report. Who gives them their orders?"

Donell grinned. "I was hoping you'd say that." He pulled a folded paper from his jacket pocket and slid it across the table. It was a list of locations, dates, times, and the initials of the feeders.

"This is the next week's schedule," he said. "Some of them I pulled from watching, some I got from a friend who's not supposed to be talking to me. If you follow one, you'll see where he lands."

"Why not just go after Price?" I asked.

"Too high up," Donell said. "You spook him, he disappears and takes the network deeper underground. We follow the feeders; we find the middle ground. That's where the connections are loose enough to break."

I looked at the list. One name, J.T., was scheduled to visit a small AME church near Broadway tomorrow afternoon.

"I'll take him," I said.

Yolanda frowned. "Alone?"

I nodded. "Too many eyes otherwise. If I can see where he goes after, we'll have our first link in the chain."

Donell slid the list back toward himself, leaving J.T.'s line visible. "You be careful. These guys aren't just tossing bread to birds. They're marking territory."

I stood, folding the paper and putting it in my coat pocket. "Then it's time we see who they're working for."

Chapter 17
Following Feathers

The AME church on Broadway was a squat brick building tucked between a pawn shop and a boarded-up grocery store. Its white cross was faded to gray, and the marquee out front leaned at an angle, advertising Women's Day All Are Welcome from three months ago.

I parked a block away, far enough not to be obvious but close enough to keep the front doors in view.

J.T. showed up right on time, mid-forties, his ball cap pulled low, and a bomber jacket zipped to his chin. He didn't go inside. Just stood on the sidewalk, scanning the street like he was waiting for something.

Then he started the routine. Hand in the jacket pocket, pulling out bits of bread or seed, tossing it to the curb slowly and deliberately. Within a minute, the first crow landed. Then another. They spaced themselves perfectly, like they'd rehearsed it.

I stayed in the car, looking through the side mirror. Every so often, J.T. glanced toward the church doors. The whole thing lasted maybe ten minutes before he brushed his hands together, turned, and started walking.

I let him get half a block ahead before I pulled out, keeping two cars between us. He wasn't in a hurry, but he wasn't wasting time either. He cut down a side street, past a row of houses with sagging porches, and into a part of the city where the streetlights hadn't worked in months.

Eventually, he stopped in front of a corner coffee shop, one of those faux-rustic places with Edison bulbs and reclaimed wood counters. Inside, the warmth and chatter didn't match the cold outside. J.T. ordered something at the counter, then sat near the back.

Five minutes later, a man in a gray suit came in. Tall, clean-shaven, with the polished ease of someone who'd been shaking hands for a living a long time. I recognized him from Donell's file, Price, the City Development Office official.

Price didn't order. He just slid into the seat across from J.T. They didn't shake hands, and there were no smiles. Price leaned in and said something short. J.T. nodded. Then Price slid a small envelope across the table, resting his hand on it until J.T. picked it up.

The conversation lasted less than a minute. Price stood, buttoned his jacket, and walked out without looking back.

I snapped a photo through the gap between two coffee drinkers. It wasn't perfect, but it caught both faces and the envelope between them proof that the feeder network wasn't just street-level intimidation; it was directly tied to the city's political machine.

J.T. finished his drink, tucked the envelope into his jacket, and left through the side door.

JT posted up outside a corner store on Jefferson. He was leaning against the brick like he had all the time in the world. He was eating sunflower seeds, spitting the shells into a paper cup, his eyes scanning the street in slow, deliberate sweeps.

Feeders aren't in a hurry. That's their advantage. They let the street breathe around them until you forget they're there, and then they pass whatever they've got: a phone, a package, a word to the next link in the chain. By the time you notice, it's already moved twice over.

I'd heard his name for weeks in the same breath as Tremaine's mid-level operators. JT had a way of moving between church events, block parties, and city hall corridors without ever looking like he belonged anywhere, which, in this line of work, meant he belonged everywhere.

Half a block back, I stayed as he left the store and headed south. He didn't walk like a man in a rush; he walked like the route was his and everyone else was trespassing.

We passed storefront churches with sun-bleached banners and corner lots where the grass had given up the ghost. A low and slow crow cut across the sky ahead of us, its shadow sliding over JT before it reached me.

A kid no older than fifteen was waiting at the bus stop, earbuds in. JT didn't sit, didn't say a word. He just brushed past, slipping something into the kid's hoodie pocket. The kid never looked up. That's how feeders work smoothly, unnoticed, and forgettable.

JT kept walking, and so did I. We ended up on a back street near the old rail yards, where a man could vanish without the courtesy of a goodbye. That's when I closed the gap.

"Busy day?" I asked.

He didn't flinch. Just turned his head slightly, like he'd been expecting me. "Bushvill. Thought I felt eyes on me."

I stepped in front of him. "You're moving messages for Tremaine. I want to know who's giving you the routes."

JT chuckled, low and dry. "Routes? Ain't no routes, man. Just instructions. You get told, you move, you forget. That's the whole point."

"And the crows?" I asked.

That made him stop. Not freeze stop. Like he was taking the weight of the question in his hands.

"They ain't just birds," he said finally. "They're markers. You see a crow where it ain't supposed to be? Means eyes are on you. One crow is a warning. Two means you're in play. Three…" He shook his head. "Three means you're done."

"Who tells them where to be?"

He smiled at that, but it didn't touch his eyes. "Same people who trained me. The same people who trained the ones before me. They watch the watchers, Bushvill. Old heads, some still in the game, some so far out you can't trace 'em. You don't meet 'em, you know you're working for 'em."

"Names," I said.

He spread his hands. "Even if I had 'em, you think I'd hand 'em to you? I like breathing."

We stood there for a long moment. JT wasn't rattled, and I wasn't sure if that was because he was fearless or because he'd already decided this conversation wasn't worth remembering.

"You're playing in a deep game, Bushvill," he said. "Deep enough, you start asking the wrong questions, and the crows ain't warn you. They'll just be there when it happens."

He brushed past me and kept walking, his pace never changing.

I let him go. Some answers you take by force. Others you let sit, knowing they'll come back around when the circle closes.

Above me, a single crow landed on a telephone wire, tilted its head, and stared. One. Just one.

For now, back in the car, I texted Donell a single line: Confirmed. The city's feeding the feeders.

Before I could start the engine, a tap on the passenger window made me jump. I turned, ready for anything.

It was a boy, maybe twelve, holding something in his hand. He pressed it to the glass, and I saw that it was a black feather.

When I unlocked the door, he was halfway down the block, disappearing into the shadows. The feather profoundly affected me, maybe because it was handed to me by a little black boy. It took me back to the only time I was afraid like this.

I was seven when I learned God could be terrifying.

Mama pressed my hair down with spit before we left the house that morning. The suit was stiff and smelled like the cedar chest in the back room, which she only opened for funerals and Easter. The shoes were too tight, biting into the sides of my feet with each step.

The church on Jefferson was already full by the time we got there. Heat pressed down like we'd stepped into a furnace, and every breath smelled of lilacs and sweat. The women wore hats with flowers the size of plates, their perfume thick enough to taste. The men had polished shoes that caught the light, their hands folded as if waiting for an important announcement.

And then the wailing began.

It started with one voice, an old woman rocking in the second pew, hands gripping her knees. A low moan at first, then higher, sharper, like someone was twisting her soul. Another woman joined in, then a man, and before I could understand what was happening, half the room was crying at a picture of a white Jesus nailed to a cross. His eyes were pale blue, fixed somewhere above us, and for a second, I thought he was looking past me toward something I couldn't see. I didn't understand the words in their prayers. I just knew they were begging. Begging like they were at the end of something and didn't want to fall off.

A drumbeat started. The organ swelled. Voices rose, tangled in each other, singing and sobbing, and I felt my heart race. My chest tightened. The air got thick. I didn't want to be there anymore.

Mama was swaying, her eyes closed, her lips moving fast. I tugged on her sleeve, but she shook me off like a fly.

The preacher's voice cut through the noise deep, rolling, sure. "He died for you," he said, pointing at the picture. "And what have you done for Him?"

My throat burned. My legs moved before my mind caught up. I slipped between knees, skirts brushing my face, and pushed through the heavy door to the outside.

The street air was cold, sharp. I sucked it in like I'd been underwater for too long. The sounds from inside were muffled now, just a hum behind me. I stared at the cracked pavement, trying to steady my breathing.

I didn't know it then, but that was the first time I made a deal with myself: trust the feeling in your gut more than the words in your ear.

Years later, I'd remember that day when I watched men with Bibles in one hand and cash in the other tell people how to live. I remember the way fear crawled up my spine. The same way it is today.

Chapter 18
Yolanda's Warning

Yolanda opened the door before I knocked twice. She must've seen me pull up from the window. Her eyes went to my face first, then down to my hand clutching the manila envelope of photos.

"You got something?" she said, stepping aside to let me in.

Her living room was warm but not cozy. Papers were on the coffee table, and a corkboard with names, dates, and pushpins was on the far wall. It was the closest thing I'd seen to a war room.

I set the envelope down and slid out the photo of J.T. with Price. Her breath caught.

"City Development," she whispered. "He's not just a bureaucrat; he's Tremaine's pipeline to everything in the books. Building permits, zoning, and business grants. If he's meeting with the feeders, it's bigger than I thought."

I nodded. "And coordinated. The feeders mark the territory, the city applies pressure, the pastors choke themselves to keep the heat off."

"That's The Sleeping Pill at work," she said. "It's not just a doctrine, it's a machine. You strip the political voice out of the pulpit, then you keep the body on life support so it can still collect tithes and preach obedience."

I could hear the edge in her voice. She'd seen this up close, probably more than she'd ever told me.

"This is exactly what Ezra wanted to stop," I said.

Her eyes softened for a moment. "Ezra thought pastors would rebel if he could prove the connection between the pulpit's silence and how power moves in this city. Some did. Most knew and didn't. They've got mortgages and families too."

I leaned forward. "You're saying they're scared."

"They're terrified. And they should be." She pointed at the feather I'd brought, the one the boy had pressed to my window. "Those birds aren't just for show, Harris. Every pastor on that list has seen them. Ezra used to say the crows were the only machine part that didn't need an office. They can be anywhere and don't mind letting you know they're watching."

Her voice dropped. "If you push this, you'll be on every page of their book. And once you're in that deep…"

She didn't finish the sentence.

I thought about my father. About my uncle. About all the men I'd known who'd fought smaller fights and still lost. "I'm already in it, Yolanda. I'm just trying to write my ending."

She gave a small, sad smile. "Ezra said something like that once. It was right before he… well." She looked away. "Just remember, he wasn't afraid to die for this. But that's exactly what they were counting on."

I rose from my seat, but her hand on my arm held me there. "If you're serious about moving forward, photos will not be enough. You will need names, dates, money trails, the kind of proof they cannot twist into lies. And there is only one person I know who keeps it all in one place."

"Who?"

Her fingers tightened around me. "They call him The Bookman. He is the one who holds Tremaine's ledger." Then she looked me in the eye and said quietly, "You are going to need prayer." The last time I had prayed was when I was begging for my brother's life.

It was winter, the kind of night when the cold sits heavy in your bones. I was in bed, tucked under two blankets, listening to the radiator hiss. That was when I heard the shouting. Not the usual street noise, this was frantic, like the sound you make when you're not sure you'll get another breath.

I sat up. The air smelled wrong, sharp, bitter, and burning, making my throat tighten. Then the sirens came.

I ran to the window. Down the block, an orange light flickered against the brick buildings. Smoke curled into the night sky, black and heavy. My brother was supposed to be at Calvin's house, three doors from the glow.

I didn't think about shoes. I didn't think about the cold. I bolted. Mama's voice chased me down the hallway, telling me to stop, but my legs didn't hear her.

By the time I reached the corner, the whole block was out. People stood in their nightclothes, arms folded tight against the wind. The fire roared, swallowing wood and glass like it was starving. I pushed through the crowd until I was close enough to feel the heat on my face.

And then I saw my brother at the upstairs window. Smoke rolled out around his head. His hands slapped at the glass, and his eyes were wild and searching.

I froze. I could hear people yelling, "Get back! Get back!" but I couldn't move. The ladder wasn't up yet. The firemen were yelling to each other, trying to find a way in.

Somewhere in all that chaos, I dropped to my knees. I didn't think about what I was doing; I just knew I couldn't stand there and watch him burn. I looked into that black sky and started talking to whoever would listen.

I prayed to God first, because that's what I'd been taught. I promised him I'd be better, do better, keep my head straight if He just got my brother out alive. But somewhere in the middle of that prayer, another thought slid in.

If God were too busy or didn't care, maybe the other would.

So, I switched. My voice dropped low, so no one could hear. I offered the devil the same deal. Said I'd pay whatever he wanted if he got my brother out. My stomach turned even as I said it, but the words came fast, like they'd been waiting inside me.

The next thing I knew, the ladder was up. A fireman smashed the window, and smoke poured out like it was alive. My brother climbed through, coughing, his hair singed at the edges, and third-degree burns over 80% of his body. When they rushed him to the hospital, I felt something inside me unclench.

Mama was crying, trying to hold him like she could pull the heat out of his skin. I just stood there, my knees shaking, wondering which one of them had heard me, God or the devil.

That night stays with me. Not just the fire, but the bargain I made in the dark. I didn't know if I'd signed something invisible, or if I'd been stupid enough to think I could make deals with the sky. But from then on, I understood two things: one, you can't ever be sure who's listening, and two, you'd better be ready to pay for what you ask.

Chapter 19
The Ledger rewrite

Donell didn't like the name "The Bookman."

"Sounds like some comic book villain," he said, pacing in my office. "Except this guy's got something scarier than a superpower, he's got receipts."

I sat at my desk, the photo of Price and J.T. still on top of the pile. "Yolanda says it's all in there. Payoffs, contracts, which pastors got squeezed and which ones got the payday. A whole map of the machine."

Donell stopped pacing. "And you think we can just walk in and take it?"

"No. I think we have to find him first."

The Bookman wasn't a street guy. He didn't need to be. He was a record keeper, the kind you only trust if you believe he's more afraid of you than he is of dying. The man held Tremaine's operation in his hands, both the spiritual chokehold of the Sleeping Pill and the muscle and fear tactics of the crows. In typical Donell fashion, he said, "Let me check it out."

Doubt started to cling to me as I reflected on the task ahead and the threat that came with the pursuit.

The work wasn't just dangerous, it was the kind of danger that liked to get personal, the kind that didn't just come for you but for the people around you.

Then I thought of Rick.

And just like that, the doubt was left. Determination to finish Ezra's work hung over me like a direct message from God.

There's a memory I don't talk about much, not because it's painful, but because it's the kind of thing you keep close, like a talisman you don't want to wear down from handling too much.

It was after my brother came home from the hospital. He'd survived something most people wouldn't have burns so severe that they said he'd probably never feel right in his skin again.

He'd died twice from his injuries before they brought him back. But each time, he came back anyway.

When he finally got home, the doctors gave us the warning in a low, careful voice: He may be suicidal. Said it like they were preparing us for an inevitability, like you prepare for bad weather you can't stop.

They didn't just mean the physical pain; they also meant the emotional distress. They meant the weight of living inside that pain, every single day.

I took it on myself to watch him. Day and night. Sleeping light so I could hear if he moved. I made it my job to stand between him and whatever edge the doctors thought he might be heading toward.

For a while, he stayed in bed. The burns made moving an act of will. He'd stare out the window for hours, and I'd wonder if he was seeing the same street I saw, or something far away from here.

Then, one night, I couldn't tell you what time it was - maybe two, maybe three in the morning - I heard the floorboards creak.

I got up quick, ready to stop him if he was heading for the door. But he didn't go outside. He went down to the old basement, the one we never used except to store boxes and the rusted weight bench that had been there since we were kids.

I stood at the top of the stairs and watched.

He sat down on the bench, gripped the barbell with hands still marked from the burns, and started lifting. No warm-up, no stretching, just raw determination pushing that weight up like it was the only thing keeping him alive.

I don't know how long I stood there. It could've been five minutes, could've been an hour. All I know is, at that moment, something shifted in me.

I realized he wasn't just fighting the pain; he was choosing life, over and over, with every rep.

And I thought, if I've got the same blood in my veins that he's got in his, then I've got no excuse.

Up until then, belief in myself had been a fragile thing. It cracked easily, crumbled under the weight of doubt, mistakes, and what the world said I wasn't.

But watching him in that basement, I understood something I hadn't before; maybe it was God's gift to me to witness that night.

Because God doesn't always speak in sermons or dreams, sometimes He speaks in the sound of an iron bar clinking back into its rack, in the quiet grit of someone deciding not to die.

From that night forward, I couldn't look at myself the same way.

And every time I felt like giving up, I remembered my brother in that basement, lifting his way back into the world.

Donell pulled a folded paper from his jacket. "I asked around. He's been spotted twice in the last month. Both times at the same place, an old Masonic Hall on the East Side. Nobody uses it for meetings anymore, but the building's still in good shape. Private. Quiet."

I knew the hall. Stately brick, big wooden doors, the place that looked like it remembered better days.

"What's the catch?" I asked.

"Catch is, you don't just knock. You get invited." Donell smirked. "And I just happen to know a guy who knows a guy who can get us in. But it's not free."

I waited.

"He wants two grand and a favor."

The favor would come back to bite me later, I knew. But the ledger was the kind of thing you didn't pass up. "When?"

"Three nights from now. Late. The place is lit just enough to see who's coming, but not enough for you to see where the cameras are. We get in, keep our heads down, and if we're lucky, we walk out with a picture of that book."

"And if we're not lucky?"

Donell shrugged. "Then the ledger gets a new chapter with our names in it."

That night, I went home and sat at my kitchen table, staring at the empty Jack Daniel's bottle on top of the fridge. The old itch was there, stronger than usual. I wanted something to take the edge off the idea of walking into Tremaine's den.

Instead, I grabbed a glass of water and the envelope of Curtis's spreadsheets. I kept thinking about what Yolanda had said about how the Sleeping Pill worked because it was quiet, polite, and respectable, while the crows worked because they weren't. One hand soothed you to sleep, the other ensured you didn't wake up.

The Bookman had both hands on the same body. If we got to him, we might finally see the whole thing for what it was.

Three nights later, Donell didn't show up at my door. He didn't need to. We'd agreed he'd go in alone, with less noise and less chance of being made. I'd be the clean one who could still move without Tremaine's eyes on me.

But when the clock hit 2 a.m. and I heard the low rumble of his car outside, I knew something had happened. The way he stepped out told me. Slow, deliberate, a stiffness in his right arm like he was holding himself together.

He walked in and dropped a small flash drive onto my desk. I noticed the dried blood on his knuckles before I noticed the faint smell of cologne mixed with sweat and concrete dust.

"What happened?" I asked.

Donell didn't sit. "The Bookman won't be showing up at the Hall for a while. Caught him just as he was leaving. He had the ledger in a briefcase and wouldn't let it go."

I stared at his hands. "So, you persuaded him?"

Donell smirked, but it didn't reach his eyes. "Let's say we had a conversation he won't forget. Pain can be a motivator when words don't work."

"Is he?"

"He's breathing. And he'll stay that way, as long as he keeps his mouth shut. I made sure he never saw my face. Didn't know what hit him."

I picked up the flash drive. "Ledger's on here?"

"Back-up copy. He was smart enough to keep one off-site. Stupid enough to tell me where it was after I convinced him the alternative was worse."

I turned the drive over in my hand. It was small, light, and carried the weight of a city's hidden machinery.

"Where's the original?" I asked.

"Somewhere safe for now. But this" Donell tapped the drive, "this is enough to burn half the Sleeping Pill network if you can get it in the right hands."

I plugged it into my laptop, and there it was. The ledger. Names, payment trials, meeting dates. Pastors, politicians, developers, all connected by invisible wires running straight to Tremaine's pocket.

Blood money.

I scrolled through entry after entry, my stomach turning at the sheer volume. There were notes on blackmail, on "moral adjustments" for pastors unwilling to embrace the new, inclusive theology, and on grants timed to kill grassroots movements before they could gain momentum.

And there it was, Herb Lane, multiple entries. Payouts were tied to city contracts, televised endorsements, and his sudden rise from a storefront preacher to the man with the most prominent pulpit in town.

I looked back at Donell. "You realize what we're holding?"

He nodded. "Yeah. A death sentence, if we're not careful."

I leaned back in my chair, the screen's glow throwing deep shadows across the room. "We need to copy this. Hide it in three different places. And then we need to decide who will see it first."

Donell flexed his hand, wincing slightly. "Whatever you decide, we move fast. The Bookman's absence won't go unnoticed. And if Tremaine gets wind of his missing records, he'll turn this city inside out and look for them."

I pulled a blank envelope from my desk, slid the flash drive inside, and sealed it. My pulse was pounding, but my mind was clear.

The war Ezra started was about to change fronts.

And now, we have the receipts.

Chapter 20
Crow at the Door

The city pulsed under a dull gray sky, the kind that smothered sunlight and hope in equal measure. Harris walked with his collar turned up, his trench coat flapping against his legs like a warning. The world felt different now, not just dangerous, but watchful. The weight of secrets shadowed every step he took, and the more he uncovered, the more he understood how far Tremaine's network extended. It wasn't just about money laundering or blackmail anymore. It was a quiet war for control over information, over communities, over futures.

He reached the converted warehouse off Seneca Street, Jordan House Ministries' old printing facility, which had once been used for church bulletins and food pantry flyers. Now, it stood abandoned, another husk in the wake of Ezra's assassination. Harris keyed in the code Ezra had once scribbled into a copy of The Fire Next Time, a precaution, maybe, or a breadcrumb. The keypad blinked green. He stepped inside.

Dust coated the floor, but the place wasn't untouched. Someone had been here recently. Footprints in the grime. A Styrofoam cup, still damp inside. Harris moved cautiously toward the back, where an old office stood barricaded with filing cabinets and a makeshift steel door. He knocked.

A slit opened in the door. "Bushvill?"

The voice was female, sharp, familiar.

"Yolanda?" Harris asked.

The door creaked open. Yolanda Abrams stood there, her hair wrapped in a scarf, eyes red but alert. She didn't hug him. She just stepped aside.

"You shouldn't be here," she said flatly.

"Neither should you," Harris replied, stepping in.

The office had been converted into something between a safe house and a resistance cell. Walls were covered in maps, red yarn connecting pins like an urban spider web. Old newspapers, photos of Harris, Xeroxed documents detailing nonprofit funding cycles, church land sales, and IRS audits.

"You've been following Tremaine's trail," Yolanda said. "So had Ezra. That's why they killed him."

She pulled down a dusty file and handed it to Harris. "He was building something, Harris. A media hub. Black-owned. Underground but public enough to pressure policy, policing, zoning laws, and school boards. Real change. But first, he needed to dismantle the false authority propped up by the 501(c)(3)."

Harris flipped through the pages of legal filings, shell company registrations, and IRS exemption statuses. Ezra had traced church leaders being coached, even bribed, by think tanks with political motives. Ezra got hold of the ledger and began digging, and someone informed the authorities. That's why Ezra became so vocal; why did his sermons change? Why did he shift from personal salvation to structural confrontation?

"He called it The WatchTower," Yolanda said, voice cracking. "Ezra was going to set up a decentralized media platform, newsrooms in barbershops, sanctuaries, and rec centers. To spread truth like gossip. But vetted. Documented. Irrefutable."

A chill ran up Harris's spine. Yolanda nodded. "Bought, trained, and bound. Ezra called it the new plantation. The pulpit was the porch."

They sat in silence for a moment. The weight of what was uncovered wasn't just damning, it was revolutionary. He hadn't been naïve. He knew the cost. But he'd moved forward anyway.

Yolanda stood and pulled out a USB drive. "Here. This is part of the archive. The sermons he never got to preach. Names. Financial records. Video testimonies from whistleblowers. But we're missing one piece, Tremaine's link to the city. The broker. The one who connects the church grants, real estate shell companies, and the laundering. Harris felt a sense of achievement in telling Yolanda that he and Donell had secured the ledger that connected all the dots. Harris stood. "I need to move. This can't stay in one place."

Yolanda handed him a backup drive and looked him dead in the eye. "They won't just come for you. They'll smear you first. Then erase you like they did Ezra. You ready for that?"

He didn't answer. But the look in his eyes said yes.

Outside, the cold air hit him like a slap. He walked briskly back to his car, parked two blocks away. As he started the engine, he noticed a small drone hovering two stories above, like a buzzard circling roadkill. He floored the gas, zigzagging down alleys, finally pulling into a packed parking lot behind a Chinese takeout. He disabled his phone, pulling out a burner.

Back at his apartment, he closed all the curtains and dimmed the lights. He pored over the files from Yolanda. Ezra's plan was even more elaborate than Harris imagined: community journalists trained in ethical reporting, anonymous tip lines to expose corruption, and a digital map of land grabs and church property transactions. Ezra hadn't just been trying to wake people up. He was building a new way of seeing the world.

Then came the real revelation.

Harris stumbled upon a coded document labeled "MANNA." It outlined a proposal for re-educating church leaders, deprogramming them from the "gospel of delay," as Ezra called it. It quoted the Slave Bible, highlighting verses removed to pacify enslaved Africans. It showed how modern sermons paralleled those omissions quietism, submission, and forgiveness without justice.

Ezra wanted to break that cycle.

He wasn't just a preacher. He was an insurgent.

And now, so was Harris.

He leaned back, exhaling sharply. They'd crossed the Rubicon. There was no going back.

Tomorrow, he'll make contact with Donell. They had to finish what Ezra started.

Because silence wasn't survival anymore.

It was a surrender.

And Harris Bushvill wasn't ready to surrender.

Chapter 21
Inside the Nest

The following day arrived under a sky smeared with gray, the kind of dull overcast that felt like an omen. Harris stood in his kitchen, staring into a mug of cold coffee that had gone untouched for over an hour. Sleep had eluded him again. Ezra's Watchtower plan and the revelation of MANNA hadn't just haunted his thoughts; they'd possessed them.

It wasn't just a story anymore. This was the kind of movement that got people killed.

Donell arrived just after noon, shoulders hunched, his face etched with a worry he tried to cover with his usual bravado. "You look like hell," he said, half-smiling.

"Mirror says the same," Harris replied.

Donell pulled out a folder from under his jacket, thick with documents and manila envelopes. "You're gonna want to see this," he said, sliding it across the table.

Inside were blueprints, photos, and a thick outline of Ezra's media infrastructure plans. The project was broader than Harris had realized. What began as a simple newsletter had evolved into an entire communications network, including encrypted podcasts, peer-to-peer streaming, anonymous tip lines, and a physical printing press hidden beneath the church kitchen.

"Underground media, literal and digital," Harris muttered, flipping through the schematics.

Donell nodded. "Ezra was building his own news pipeline, one that wouldn't be controlled by white editors or foundation funding. The idea was to train community members to report what they saw. Shootings. Displacement. Police corruption. Political sabotage."

"Decentralized truth," Harris whispered.

Donell leaned in. "Ezra had lined up tech people, teachers, even old radio heads who knew how to build transmitters from scratch. He called it a return to the Black press. You remember that old quote? 'Until the lion learns to write, every story will glorify the hunter.' Ezra was teaching the lion."

Harris exhaled slowly. "That's why they killed him."

"That's one reason," Donell said grimly. "There's more."

Harris pulled a thumb drive from his coat pocket and slid it toward Donell. "Encrypted files. I only cracked two folders. One's a roster of Black pastors from across the country, Ezra rated them. 'Compromised,' 'Silent,' or 'Unbought.' He knew who was on the payroll, who was lost to prosperity theology, and who might still fight."

Harris's pulse quickened. "He was organizing them?"

"Recruiting, in secret. Part of MANNA."

Donell's voice lowered. "This wasn't just local. Ezra was quietly and deliberately building a national resistance. He had plans to fly under the IRS's radar, creating parallel institutions. If his plans had leaked before he could secure his infrastructure... the blowback would've been fatal."

Harris suddenly felt cold. "It was."

Donell nodded, face grim. "Someone leaked it. Tremaine or one of his proxies. I don't have proof, but I got a name."

He opened his phone and showed Harris a grainy surveillance still. The image showed a white man in a red ballcap shaking hands with a Black pastor. Harris recognized Bishop Alton Clay from Charlotte, North Carolina. Clay had publicly supported the Reparations Act but quietly retracted his statement days before Ezra's murder.

"That's Walter Briggs," Donell said. "He's ex-military intelligence. Works in 'faith-based engagement' for a federal contract outfit now. I tracked his car at the church the day before Ezra's last sermon."

"White man in faith-based operations?" Harris's eyebrows raised.

Donell's face darkened. "Briggs specializes in surveillance. His outfit does quite work with Black Muslim and Christian organizations.

Technically legal, but morally disgusting. They frame it as 'preventing extremism.' Really, they're keeping tabs on who's organizing outside the government's playbook."

Harris stood, pacing slowly. "So Tremaine had access to people like Briggs. That's how Ezra was compromised."

Donell nodded. "They knew about the press. About MANNA. And once Ezra started speaking too openly, calling out the 501(c)(3) compromise, calling for reparations, they decided to move."

Harris turned, eyes blazing. "This isn't just a murder. It's a damn counterinsurgency."

Donell raised a brow. "Say it louder."

A moment of silence fell between them. The weight of what they were uncovering stretched beyond Ezra, beyond Buffalo. This was a national effort to suppress Black prophetic voices. Harris was staring down the very apparatus that had once tried to neuter King, that had driven Malcolm to the edge.

And now, it had killed Ezra Abrams.

But Ezra hadn't just left a body; he had left multiple blueprints, but fragments remained.

Donell nodded. That evening, Harris met Yolanda in a candle-lit back room at a jazz café off Michigan Avenue. She was wearing black, her eyes tired but resolute. The room smelled of sage and something older, sacred.

"You've read his journals," she said. It wasn't a question.

"Yes."

"Then you know the risk."

"I do. And I'm still in."

She studied him for a long moment, then opened a black leather binder. Inside was a single sheet with six names.

"These are the unbought pastors. Ezra vetted them himself. They don't take federal money. They don't push prosperity. They don't hide behind 'pray and wait.' They speak. March. Feed. Protect."

Harris ran his eyes down the list. "You want me to contact them?"

"No," Yolanda said. "They're already watching. What I want is for you to do what you do best: uncover, investigate, and continue to connect the dots. And tell the story."

Harris looked up. "The watchtower lives?"

Yolanda smiled. "Only if someone dares to publish."

Outside, the night had deepened. Harris stepped into the darkness not as a detective chasing ghosts, but as a man standing between two worlds: one dying in silence, and the other rising in truth. The storm wasn't over.

It had only just begun.

Chapter 22
The Army I'd Need

I sat at my desk long after the night punched in, the hum of the city outside dull and steady, like the sound of boots shuffling on concrete. The kind of night where you can hear yourself think is both a blessing and a curse.

An underground network was no longer just a dream. It was moving, breathing, but it was fragile, the kind of thing that could be shattered by one wrong word in the wrong ear. To keep it alive, I'd need more than passion. I'd need an army.

Not the kind you see in uniforms marching in straight lines. No flags, no salutes. My army would be quiet, trained to disappear into crowds, to pass information in handshakes and grocery store conversations. People who could live in plain sight but see everything. A chessboard of lookouts, messengers, digital ghosts, and street philosophers.

I'd need fighters who could withstand the heat, hold their ground, and not flinch when the system bared its teeth. I'd need the thinkers, the architects who could blueprint the next move before the enemy even knew they'd made one. And I'd need the believers whose faith in the mission would carry them through the sleepless nights and close calls.

The thing about armies is you can't just recruit bodies. You have to recruit blood. People whose lives, like mine, have already been split open and rearranged by the very forces we're fighting. You can train a skill, but you can't train a scar.

That's why I'm glad Donell is on my side.

Donell isn't loud, but he's dangerous in the ways that matter: patient, methodical, eyes like he's mapping escape routes in every room. We've both been burned enough times to know the value of moving slowly. Where I see angles, he sees patterns. Where I'd rush, he'd wait. And when it's time to strike, he hits with precision.

I don't trust it easily. But with Donell, it's different. He's the kind of man you'd want in the shadows watching your back. The kind who understands the cost of this fight because he's already paid in full.

The network will need soldiers like him who aren't afraid of the dark, who can keep their hands steady while the world shakes, people willing to fight a war without medals, to disappear if it means the cause survives.

I leaned back in my chair, staring at the city lights. Somewhere out there, the opposition was sharpening their knives. Somewhere, Tremaine was moving pieces on his board. But I wasn't playing alone anymore.

And with Donell in the ranks, I had the first piece of the army I'd need.

There aren't many people in this city I feel safe standing next to. Donell is one of them. Not because he's the loudest man in the room or the one flexing for attention, it's because he's the opposite. Donell has that stillness you can't fake, the kind that makes men with bad intentions stop and think about their next move.

I've seen it work in real time.

A few years back, before Ezra's death pulled us into this war, I was in a parking lot argument with a man who decided words weren't enough. He pulled a folding knife, flicked it open, and closed the space between us. I was weighing my options, and none of them were good, when Donell appeared from behind him. He didn't reach for a weapon, didn't shift his weight, didn't even blink. He just stood there, tall and still, shoulders squared, the faint outline of muscle filling his coat. The alley seemed to shrink around him.

The man's gaze climbed Donell like a wall he wasn't sure he wanted to scale. His fingers tightened on the knife for a heartbeat, then loosened. Slowly, deliberately, he folded the blade. The click of the metal locking shut was the loudest thing in the alley.

He slipped it into his pocket, eyes dropping to the cracked pavement, and stepped aside without a word.

We walked on. I never asked Donell what he said to him, because I don't think he said anything at all.

That's why I trust him. In a fight, Donell's not the man swinging first; he's the man making sure there doesn't have to be a second swing. And if there is, you won't see it coming.

Sitting across from him in the diner tonight, I realized that's exactly the energy I need on this road Ezra laid out. The ledger is essential, yes, it's proof of the Sleeping Pill in action, proof of the crows as enforcers. But proof alone won't change anything. We must carry the message that Ezra died for.

"The only way we win," I told him, "is if we make it impossible for them to choke this off at the source. We build something quiet, something they can't see until it's already moving."

"Underground," Donell said, stirring his coffee.

"Underground," I repeated. "Trusted pastors, neighborhood leaders, people who know what's at stake. We keep the circles small; the conversations are even smaller. We don't let them know where the road leads until it's too late to block it."

Donell nodded. "And if they find out?"

"Then we've already built enough momentum; they can't stop it."

He leaned back, that half-smile of his breaking through. "You draw the map; I'll keep the road clear."

Walking out into the cold night, I thought about Ezra's words: If the pulpit can't speak truth to power, then the street must. And if the street can't, then we'll build our own road.

Donell was that road's first brick. And if he could make a man walk away with his own knife, maybe we had a chance at making a whole system back down, too.

Chapter 23
The Remnant Plan

The thing about ghosts is they don't always haunt places. Sometimes, they haunt legacies.

That truth hit me hard as I stood outside the Monroe Street Community Center the next morning. The building looked tired, like it carried the weight of too many dreams deferred. Chipped brick, rusted gutters, a mural half-covered in graffiti. A crow perched on the sagging gutter, watching me like it was checking attendance.

Inside, the echo of children's laughter was long gone, replaced by the hum of flickering lights and the sterile buzz of bureaucracy. I nodded at the janitor, a man who'd once seen me here during a volunteer campaign years ago. He gave a nod back, the kind you give someone who's still alive but might not be for long if they keep walking the road they're on.

Ezra's old office was still here, though it now belonged to a part-time grant writer. She shrugged when I asked to see it and stepped out to give me a few minutes alone.

The room was nothing special battered desk, a crooked filing cabinet, and a faded corkboard still holding the thumbtacks of ideas never pinned. But I knew better. This had been ground zero for something Ezra called The MANNA.

I pulled out my phone and opened the folder from the flash drive Yolanda had given me. One file stood out: Covenants and Contradictions. Ezra had drawn a map of relationships between major Black churches, local political campaigns, and national philanthropic foundations. At the center was a name that stuck in my teeth: The Harmony Fund.

Founded by the widow of a tech billionaire, Harmony was celebrated as a progressive champion of racial equity. But Ezra saw it for what it was: control disguised as charity. Almost every church it funded had taken IRS 501(c)(3) status under its "guidance," along with a quiet list of rules: no political advocacy, no involvement in grassroots protests, and an "apolitical posture" in all public ministries. Perfectly legal. Perfectly pacifying.

Then I opened the next file: MANNA.

Ezra's blueprint wasn't just criticism but an insurgency in ink. Page after page outlined how to reclaim institutional power in Black communities without asking permission. He laid it out like scripture for revolution:

• Mass Incarceration: End cash bail, overturn mandatory minimums, and free non-violent offenders. Churches to directly fund legal defense teams.

• Miseducation: Build independent supplemental schools to teach real Black history, financial literacy, and job skills free from state censorship.

• Homelessness: Convert church-owned property into permanent housing linked to work programs.

• Institutional Control: Create a community-controlled banking cooperative to manage tithes and pool funds, keeping wealth in the community.

• Police Reform: Establish independent civilian review boards with the power to terminate officers and reallocate funding.

• Political Power: Finance unapologetically Black candidates directly, bypassing white political gatekeepers.

• Legal Infrastructure: Fund law school scholarships with a binding agreement to serve FBA communities, "an army of our own lawyers."

• Single-parent Household: Provide direct financial support for housing, childcare, and education, allowing single parents to raise strong families without state control.

Ezra's plan dripped with urgency. He wasn't asking to share power; he was preparing to take it. And it became clear why so many of his peers met his death with silence. They weren't shocked. They were relieved.

I called Donell.

"Found something," I said. "Check your email."

A minute later, his voice came back, low and edged. "This ain't just dirty, man. This is fossil-fuel filthy."

"Yeah."

"Let me tell you what I dug up. Rubber-stamped by a federal office called the CSEC Community Stabilization and Equity Commission. Sounds friendly, right?"

"Sounds like a cover."

"Exactly. Guess who lobbied to create it?"

"Who?"

"The Harmony Fund."

The words chilled me. This wasn't just Buffalo politics. This was national infrastructure. A system so elegant in its execution that most people would never even realize they'd been bought.

That night, I sat with Yolanda. We spread Ezra's files across her coffee table.

"They had him boxed in," I said.

Her eyes stayed on the pages. "He knew."

"He must've realized how deep it went. Harmony, CSEC, pastors, and politicians all in the same nest."

Yolanda's voice softened, almost like a prayer. "Ezra wasn't paranoid. He was prepared. But knowing the truth doesn't mean you survive it."

"Surviving's never been my strong suit," I said.

She looked at me hard. "Be careful, Harris. Not of dying but of living too long in a world that punishes the awake."

Back at my apartment, I dug out an old box from the back of my closet: case files, newspaper clippings, and letters from whistleblowers, most of whom were dead or had vanished. I found the one I was looking for: a photo of Julian Thorne shaking hands with then-Senator Linda Conway, the same senator who'd pushed the federal faith-based partnership act that expanded church access to public funds and muzzled their politics in return.

I pinned it to my corkboard alongside fresh printouts from Ezra's files. At the top: Ezra Abrams. Below him: MANNA. To the left: The Harmony Fund. To the right: Julian Thorne. At the bottom, a single red string is connected: Rodney Bell Ezra's marked leak.

Ezra had died with his eyes open.

Rodney Bell wasn't always the man in the glass pulpit. Before the billboards, before the Highmark Stadium revivals, he was a storefront preacher barely keeping the lights on. Eleven people in the pews on a good Sunday, and two of those were his wife and her cousin. The plate went around twice, sometimes three times, because the rent didn't take rain checks.

That's when Ezra found him.

Ezra saw potential in people the way a master carpenter sees furniture in raw wood. He'd stop by Bell's services sometimes, slip an envelope into the plate without saying a word. He liked Bell's grit, the way he preached with his whole chest, even if the only "amen" came from a half-asleep deacon in the back row.

"He's got the heart," Ezra told me once. "Just needs to see the bigger picture."

The bigger picture, for Ezra, was the MANNA Covenant uniting independent pastors, pooling resources, breaking free from the strings that came with 501(c)(3) money. He thought Bell could be a soldier in that army. Maybe even a general. For a while, it looked like he was right. Bell sat in our meetings, nodded in the right places, and asked sharp questions. He preached sermons that slipped through the Sunday comfort crowd, about economic self-determination and resisting the quiet chokehold of political silence. Ezra trusted him enough to put him on the short list of pastors who'd get the Covenant charter first.

Then Tremaine got to him.

It didn't happen all at once. First came the invitation expenses for the "Christian leadership conference," which included hotel accommodations. Then came the consultants offering to help "expand his ministry footprint." Before we knew it, Bell had traded the flickering fluorescent lights of his storefront for the high-gloss stage of a newly purchased mega-campus, paid for in cash through a Delaware-incorporated "faith foundation" that traced back to Tremaine's network.

The change in him was fast and brutal. The man who once preached about freeing the flock from government entanglements now spoke about "working within established partnerships." He swapped sermons on accountability for slogans about "seizing your season" and "walking in overflow."

Ezra didn't give up on him right away. He went to see Bell in his new office, three times the size of the old sanctuary. He told him the money came with a price, that Tremaine's hand on the scale meant the message would never be his again.

Bell's answer was smooth and cold. "Ezra, blessings come in many forms. Sometimes God sends a raven to feed you. You don't ask the raven where it's been."

I didn't see it as just a sellout. It was a betrayal. Bell hadn't just walked away from Ezra's plan; he'd started holding "pastor leadership forums" funded by Tremaine's people, and guess whose name never got invited into the room. He used the same networks Ezra helped him build to recruit other pastors into Tremaine's orbit, pulling them away from the Covenant before it even launched.

Ezra built that man up and fed his flock when he couldn't. Put him in rooms he didn't even know existed. And he sold him out to the same people who'd burn this whole thing down if they could.

Bell's betrayal confirmed something he'd been trying not to believe: that the fight wasn't just against the wolves outside the flock, but the ones dressed like shepherds inside it.

Now, whenever I see Bell on those giant screens at Highmark Stadium, striding across the stage while the crowd shouts and the lights flare, I can't help but see Ezra, faced, grieved.

Bell's revivals include free parking, free shuttle buses, and free tote bags. The only price is silence. The only requirement is never to ask why a man who once preached about resisting control now speaks the language of those who hold the leash.

And the crowd loves him for it.

Donell says Tremaine's strategy is simple: find those on the edge of collapse, the ones just humble enough to think a miracle has dropped in their lap, and make them feel chosen. Then put them on stages so big, their voice will drown out the truth-tellers.

Rodney Bell was perfect for that role. And maybe he knows it. Maybe he doesn't care.

I know this: when Tremaine's network is finally exposed, Bell's face will be one of the first people to recognize. Some will still defend him because the betrayal wrapped in scripture always goes down easier.

The Judas in Ezra's life didn't kiss him in the garden. He shook his hand at a pastor's breakfast, smiled for the cameras, and told everyone in earshot that Ezra was "passionate but misguided." Then he went back to the table with the city councilman and the developer, who were buying up Black neighborhoods.

That's the image I can't shake, not the betrayals done in anger, but the ones done in comfort.

Now I had to decide how to carry what he left. Not just expose it. Live it. Spread it.

Because the truth doesn't just set you free, it makes you a target. And in Buffalo, where justice moved slower than winter and died faster than trust, I was about to become a very loud problem. That's when the thought hit me how resistance had its own flag, even if it didn't fly from any pole. I'd known since I was a boy that the pledge of allegiance was an abstraction. The colors didn't mean the same thing to me as they did in school.

The red wasn't courage or sacrifice, it was sweet, cheap wine, the kind I used to drown myself in before I got sober. The white wasn't purity; it was the mental haze that came every time some smiling white stranger got too curious about who I was and what I thought. And the blue wasn't freedom, it was the persistent sadness I carried with me, the one that settled in my bones no matter how far I ran.

Maybe that was the real cost of resistance, not just the risk of a bullet, but carrying those colors in your heart every day, knowing the fabric they made would never wrap around you for warmth.

Chapter 24
The Black Treasury

The room smelled like ink, old carpet, and the kind of stale policy air you only get in City Hall.

Councilwoman Reva Stokes closed her office door and turned the blinds one slat at a time, shutting out the afternoon light. She was one of the few elected officials in this city who still walked neighborhoods without a press photographer two steps behind her. She'd made her name pushing the boldest Black equity and reparations proposal Buffalo had ever seen. And then, just days after it was introduced, it vanished like it had never existed.

"You're digging in places that were meant to stay buried," she said, still looking at the blinds.

"Ezra was working with you, wasn't he?"

She hesitated not out of fear, but calculation. "He believed in it," she said finally. "Not the watered-down version that made the papers. The real plan. The one that actually meant repair."

"Then why pull it?"

Her eyes were bloodshot from exhaustion, but the anger behind them was awake. "Because someone made it clear there would be consequences. Financial. Political. Even… personal."

From her desk drawer, she pulled a single-page document and slid it across to me.

A grant evaluation from the Harmony Fund. At the top, in red letters: DEVIATES FROM ACCEPTABLE COMMUNITY STABILITY NARRATIVE.

"I was told that if I didn't walk it back, every nonprofit in my district would lose funding. Food banks. Youth centers. Housing programs. All of it. And then came the threats, calls at night, emails, and my tires slashed twice. Ezra told me to hang on. Said he'd deliver the plan himself."

"But he never did."

She shook her head. "No. He didn't."

Reva's voice dropped lower. "Ezra believed the Black church had a role to play in reparations, not just spiritually, but structurally. He called it The Black Treasury. He wanted every church to contribute a percentage of its holdings, real estate, tithes, and investments into a collective reparations trust. Not waiting on Washington to send us crumbs but building our own table."

"And?"

"The minute the idea leaked, they came for him, not with bullets, not at first, but with letters, audits, zoning raids, and threats to revoke tax status. One church got its nonprofit charter suspended. Another had its accounts frozen. It was surgical."

She reached into the drawer again and handed me a second document, a draft of the original proposal, with Ezra's handwriting in the margins.

Build the treasury. Don't wait for permission. God doesn't ask Caesar.

Back outside, the wind had that metallic taste Buffalo gets before snow. A crow flapped overhead, cutting across the gray sky, and for a moment I imagined it circling City Hall, watching every meeting from the ledges.

I drove straight to Ezra's church, or what was left of it. The sign out front now reads:

Community Wellness Center Coming Soon Powered by Harmony Fund.

Inside, the sanctuary was gutted. The pulpit gone. The stained glass was covered in plastic sheeting. Workers in hard hats are measuring spaces for yoga mats and nutrition stations.

A young man with a Harmony badge told me, "We're transitioning the space to better serve emotional and nutritional needs."

I chuckled. "Still getting the same grant, though, huh?"

He didn't answer.

In Ezra's old study, his war room, I found a worn notebook tucked behind a row of untouched books.

Inside were his last notes:

The Sleeping Pill works because it feels like rest.

They don't destroy prophets. They repurpose them.

If the church can't speak, it will sing. If it can't organize, it will host potlucks. If it can't march, it will dance. And in the end, it will forget it ever had fire.

On the last page, underlined twice:

FBI using pastors as informants. Paid to report on "radicals" inside the movement.

The handwriting was jagged, rushed like he'd written it knowing someone could walk in any second. It wasn't paranoia. It was a warning.

Back in my office, I laid it all out:

• Reparations plan too radical to survive daylight.

• A Black Treasury that could have shifted economic power overnight.

• A pastor willing to risk everything to make it real.

• A grant system designed to muzzle the church.

And now, proof that some of those muzzles were wired directly to federal law enforcement.

The FBI wasn't just watching. They were recruiting shepherds to point out which sheep were "straying" too far from the fold.

Ezra hadn't been killed for dreaming too big. He'd been killed because he refused to become one of their eyes and ears, too.

I leaned back in my chair and stared at the notebook. In my line of work, truth was never just about right and wrong; it was about survival.

And the truth here was simple:

MANNA had a price.

And silence was the down payment.

Chapter 25
The Message

Kristen Brooks was the kind of young reporter who made you remember why journalism mattered. Fresh out of Howard, sharp with her questions, stubborn with her principles. She had that mix of curiosity and fire that made her a problem for people who liked their secrets kept.

She'd been helping me chase down the MANNA Covenant money trail, city contracts, shell nonprofits, quiet transfers into church accounts. Nothing in print yet, but she was piecing the bones together faster than I could.

The night it happened, I was in my apartment going over a list of 501(c)(3) grants when my phone buzzed. Unknown number.

"Bushvill?"

"Yeah."

"This is Marcus from County. You know Kristen Brooks?"

Something in his voice made my gut tighten. "Yeah. Why?"

"You'd better get down to Mercy General. Now."

The ER smelled like antiseptic and old coffee. Fluorescent lights hummed overhead, turning every face pale. I spotted Marcus by the security desk, a big man with a county badge clipped to his belt. He didn't have to say a word; his eyes told me enough.

"She's in Trauma Two," he said. "Stable, but," He shook his head. "They worked her over, Harris. Whoever did it knew what they were doing."

I pushed through the curtain.

Kristen lay on the bed, her face swollen, a strip of gauze above her right eye. Her left arm was in a sling. The machines beeped steady, but her breathing was shallow. When she saw me, her eyes welled.

"I told you they were watching," she whispered. Her voice was hoarse, like her throat had been squeezed.

I pulled a chair close. "Tell me."

"I was leaving the office… I parked in the lot behind the paper. It was late, maybe 9:30. I heard footsteps. Before I could turn," She stopped, blinking hard. "One of them grabbed me from behind. Another hit me in the ribs. They didn't take my purse. Didn't even check my pockets. Just… kept saying, 'Stay away from Bushvill.'"

My stomach turned cold. "They said my name?"

She nodded. "Twice. And when I hit the ground, one of them knelt and said, 'He's not worth dying for.'"

I felt the room shrink. This wasn't just a warning. It was a claim they were letting me know exactly how close I'd gotten, and how far they were willing to go to keep the trail cold.

A nurse came in, checked her vitals, and gave me the look that says "wrap it up." I leaned closer.

"Kristen, you don't have to keep going with this."

Her eyes hardened. "That's exactly why I have to."

That fire was why I'd trusted her with the threads I couldn't pull alone. But looking at her now, pale and bruised, I knew they were going to try again. And next time, they wouldn't stop at broken bones.

I left the ER with my fists clenched in my pockets. Outside, the air was heavy with the smell of rain. A single black feather lay on the hood of my car. I didn't touch it. Didn't need to.

They'd made their point. I turned and walked back inside, determined to stay.

The night nurse let me slide into the chair by Kristen's bed, as long as I promised not to make trouble. The lights were dim, the kind of half-dark where machines cast shadows on the walls, and the only steady sound was the monitor beeping in time with her heartbeat.

She was asleep, sedated, they said, but her face twitched now and then, like her mind was still dodging blows. Her lip was split, her left eye swollen shut. Somebody had made sure she'd see herself in the mirror and remember.

I sat back, the plastic chair creaking under me, and thought about all the times I'd told myself I could keep people safe by being careful. Truth is, careful only works when the other side plays by the same rules.

They weren't just sending me a message tonight; they were testing me. They wanted to know how much it would take before I folded, before I told myself the story wasn't worth another name on the list of collateral damage.

I looked at her and thought about my brother in the fire all those years ago. About the deal I'd made in the dark, promising whoever was listening that I'd do anything if they spared him. That night, the price was faith and a piece of my innocence. Tonight, I didn't know what the cost would be, but I could feel the meter running.

A janitor pushed his cart past the door, the wheels squeaking in a rhythm that reminded me of an old bicycle I had as a kid. I remembered riding that bike to the corner store for my grandmother, bringing back bread and milk, knowing if I took too long, she'd be at the window watching. She said the streets had eyes and ears, and if you learned to listen right, you could hear them talking.

That's what this felt like now, being in a room where the walls whispered. I kept thinking about the feather on my car hood, how deliberate it looked. No rush, no fear of being seen. They could've taken the car, slashed the tires, smashed the windows. Instead, they chose something quiet. Elegant. Creepy as hell.

Kristen stirred, a low groan escaping her throat. Her good eye cracked open, unfocused.

"You're still here," she murmured.

"Yeah," I said. "Where else would I be?"

Her gaze drifted toward the ceiling. "They think they scared me."

"They didn't?"

She gave the smallest shake of her head. "Hurts like hell. But it's not fear. It's… knowing I'm right."

I wanted to tell her I admired that. I wanted to tell her she reminded me of myself, back before I knew how long the fight could drag on. But I didn't. Some truths are better left unsaid until the moment they're needed.

Sometime after midnight, I walked down to the vending machines. The hallway was empty, but my skin prickled like it wasn't. I bought two cups of bad coffee and sat back down in the chair, one cup cooling untouched on the table beside her.

I thought about Ezra, how close he'd been to breaking the story before they silenced him. Maybe I'd been lying to myself, saying I was just finishing his work. Maybe what I was really doing was testing the same noose, seeing how much rope they'd give me before they pulled it tight.

Kristen shifted again. "You know they won't stop, right?" she said without opening her eyes.

"I know."

"Then why keep going?"

The question hung there. I could've told her the truth that sometimes you keep going because stopping feels worse than bleeding. I could've said that I was tired of the game and wanted to flip the board. But instead, I just said, "Because they told you I'm not worth dying for."

Her eye opened a little wider. She understood.

At 3 a.m., the nurse came back, took her vitals, and gave me another hour before I had to leave. I watched the slow rise and fall of her chest, the way her hand twitched like she was still holding a pen, still writing.

I thought about the quiet after the fire when my brother was safe, how it wasn't relief so much as a reprieve. That's what this night felt like: a pause between blows.

When I finally stood to leave, I leaned close to her ear. "Get some rest, Brooks. We're not done."

On the way out, I passed the nurses' station. The TV in the corner was tuned to a local news feed. The ticker scrolled a headline about a councilman's charity gala. I wondered if he was one of the hands in the envelope, one of the shadows behind the feather.

Outside, the rain started. My car was parked under a streetlight, glistening wet. The feather was gone.

Chapter 26
The Compass

The church was small, with barely fifty seats, tucked between a laundromat and a tax preparation place, its façade marked by a flickering neon sign. No steeple, no stained glass, just a white wooden door with peeling paint. I'd been told this pastor wanted to talk, but the note that reached me said we needed to meet after hours, "when the flock is gone."

Inside, the air smelled faintly of lemon oil and dust. The sanctuary lights were dim, casting long shadows across the pews. Pastor Micah Lane emerged from the side door wearing a worn cardigan and carrying a Bible that looked older than he was. His handshake was firm, but I felt the tremor in it.

"I've been following your work," he said, glancing toward the door like someone might be listening from outside. "And Ezra's. I knew him when he was just starting. Before the… before the storm."

We sat in the front row, the pulpit looming above us like it might be listening in.

"I want in," he said quietly. "The Restoration Covenant… It's what the church should've been all along. We've been feeding souls while letting bodies starve. Ezra was right Faith without works is dead."

"Then what's stopping you?" I asked.

His eyes dropped to the worn carpet between his feet. "You think Tremaine doesn't have eyes in these pews? Half my board is tied to grant money that runs through his network. The city audits us every year, looking for any reason to find fault. If I make one wrong move, I lose this place. I lose my livelihood. My wife…" He stopped himself, his throat working. "She's already telling me to leave it alone. Says she doesn't want to bury me like Yolanda buried Ezra.

The words hung heavily between us.

"You know," I said, "Ezra knew the risk. He also knew what would happen if nobody took it."

Micah leaned closer, his voice almost a whisper. "If I join, I need to know I'm not signing my death warrant. That there's more than just talk. That the Covenant can protect its own."

I met his gaze. "No one can promise you safety. But I can promise you that staying silent won't keep you safe either. It just makes the people killing us more comfortable."

He sat back, chewing on the thought. Then he nodded, but the fear was still there, sharp and alive in his eyes.

As I left, I noticed the blinds in the sanctuary window shifted ever so slightly. Whether it was wind or a watcher, I couldn't say. But I knew Micah wasn't imagining the eyes on him. Tremaine's reach ran deep, and even those ready to fight were fighting the kind of fear that could choke a man before the bullet ever came. I needed to learn more about Ezra. I needed to find the man who mentored him.

I found Robison Erns on his porch, sitting in a weathered cane chair that looked older than I was. The wood had gone gray and smooth, worn down by decades of Buffalo winters and quiet conversations that stayed on these steps.

Robison didn't just carry years, he carried rooms. The kind of man who could sit silent long enough to make you speak the truth without asking a question.

To most people, he was just a retired janitor from the Monroe Street Community Center, the man who fixed the boiler, polished the floors, and nodded when you passed him in the hall. To Ezra, he'd been something more. A compass.

And now, with Ezra gone, I needed to know which way the needle had been pointing.

"Bushvill," he said, spotting me before I reached the porch. "Figured you'd come by sooner or later."

He waved me into the empty chair beside him. The air smelled faintly of Pine-Sol, old wood, and the bitter curl of smoke from the cigarillo in his hand. His presence had that quiet gravity you don't rush.

"I wanted to talk about Ezra," I said.

"You and half the city," he muttered, flicking ash into a chipped mug. "The difference is, most folks want to talk about the saint or the scandal. You're here for the man."

"I'm here for the truth."

He studied me for a long moment, like he was weighing the price of what he was about to say. "Truth's a funny thing, son. It'll bless you one day and have you digging your own grave the next."

I didn't flinch.

Robison leaned back, eyes half-closed as if searching through the years. "Ezra used to come here when the noise got too loud. Politicians breathing down his neck, elders in the church whispering about him. He'd sit where you're sitting and listen while I told him how not to lose himself."

"What'd you tell him?"

"That there's always a bill for telling the truth. You just gotta decide if you can pay it."

Silence settled in. With Robison, silence wasn't empty; it was a tool.

Finally, he said, "He told me they were gonna kill him."

I let it hang in the air. "Why?"

"Because he knew enough to burn the whole house down. Not just the politics inside the Black church, but how the whole thing had been roped into the bigger game: The Harmony Fund, CSEC, politicians writing gag orders into grant agreements. And yeah... even the FBI."

Robison nodded. "They've been using certain pastors as informants for years. Smile in the pulpit on Sunday, file a report on Monday about who's getting too loud in the movement. Ezra found proof. Said he was going to call it out. I told him, once you start naming names like that, you'd better be ready to disappear.

"Did he listen?"

A sad laugh escaped him. "Ezra was his father's son. Too stubborn for his own good. Too committed to the idea that God gave him a mouth for a reason."

I'd heard pieces about Ezra's father, but never the whole story. Robison filled it in.

"They came up from Mississippi. My dad and I both knew the soil and the price of working it. Ezra Sr. tried to reform the local church back home. Wanted it to stop being the sharecroppers' chaplain. Got himself blackballed and broke before forty. Heart gave out from too much fight and not enough rest."

Yolanda had told me Ezra carried a weight he didn't choose. Robison confirmed it.

"Some men inherit money. Others inherit a fight," he said. "Ezra carried his father's unfinished business like it was sewn into his jacket."

"What was he planning near the end?" I asked.

Robison leaned forward. "He wanted to build The Black Treasury. A coalition of churches pooling their resources, including tithes, land, and investments, into a reparations trust that we controlled. No government permission. No corporate strings. Just us. And he wanted to cut loose from the 501(c)(3) leash so the pulpit could actually speak."

"That would have shifted power."

"That's why it scared them. It wasn't just the money; it was the voice. You take the leash off a Black pulpit; you've got the makings of a third political party. One rooted in the people, not in the mayor's crumbs."

We sat in the kind of quiet that makes you hear the street breathe. The hiss of his cigarillo. A lone crow settled on a power line across the way, watching like it had an appointment.

"Two weeks before he died," Robison said, "Ezra told me he was being audited again. Pastors he trusted wouldn't take his calls. That's when he told me about the informants, the preachers who could shout 'freedom' on Sunday and hand over names to the feds on Monday."

"And they knew he knew."

"Oh, they knew. And when a man like Ezra refuses to be quiet, they stop negotiating."

I asked what I already knew the answer to. "Was it worth it?"

Robison looked past me, into the rows of houses. "Worth it's a luxury question. He did it because he couldn't not do it. That's what made him dangerous and holy."

He stubbed out his cigarillo, stood slow, joints popping. "If you're chasing his trail, understand this truth doesn't set you free. It tells you exactly who's willing to lock the gate. And in this city, those gates are everywhere."

I rose with him. "I'm not walking away."

His eyes locked on mine. "Then make it loud, Bushvill. Loud enough to wake the ones who got used to sleeping through the sermon."

When I left, the sun was dropping behind the houses, the air faint with smoke. Two blocks away, a dark sedan idled at the curb. The driver's face was just a shadow.

They didn't move when I passed. They didn't have to.

They already knew I'd been to see Robison Erns.

And now they knew I wasn't done.

Chapter 27
First Stones

By the time I got back to my apartment, the sedan from Robison's block had disappeared. That didn't mean they weren't still watching, just that they'd changed vantage points. The crows always did.

I pulled the blinds and spread my notes across the kitchen table. Robison's words were still ringing in my ears: Truth doesn't set you free. It tells you exactly who's willing to lock the gate.

If I was going to keep Ezra's fight alive, I needed to know which gates could be rattled and which ones had padlocks forged by Harmony money and federal contracts.

The underground couldn't start with noise. It had to start with whispers.

I made my calls on my burner.

Not the kind you keep in your phone's contacts. These were numbers passed on scraps of paper, memorized for a week, then burned. Numbers that rang twice before clicking into silence, waiting for you to speak first.

"Looking to buy airtime," I'd say, knowing that was the wrong phrase to anyone but the right people. "For something that matters."

The Watchtower Network wasn't going to run on sermons or slogans. It was going to run on signal, the kind you couldn't shut down with a city permit or an FCC fine. Pirate radio. Hidden streams. Basement podcasts no one admitted to hosting. The kind of places where a preacher's voice could still shake a man without a commercial break.

The first voice I reached belonged to Moth, an ex-college DJ who'd been banned from public radio for airing a speech from Assata Shakur. "You want clean sound, or you want reach?" she asked.

"Both," I said.

"Then you're talking money. And not the kind that shows up on a bank statement."

I told her I'd find it.

The second was Keyman, a tech ghost who could bounce a livestream signal off a satellite twice before it touched a laptop. "If you're trying to be invisible," he said, "you already waited too long. Someone's watching your hands right now."

I didn't bother denying it. "Then make my hands look like they're doing something else."

Keyman laughed. "I like you. You sound like a man who knows his obituary could already be written."

By midnight, I had five names: broadcasters, hackers, and street-level archivists all willing to push Restoration Covenant messages into the cracks of the digital world. But every deal came with a warning: Say the wrong thing, and it won't be the government that silences you. It'll be the people they convinced you were your audience.

When I finally hung up, I sat in the dark of my office, listening to the rain on the roof. Somewhere outside, a crow called twice and fell silent.

The Watchtower Network was breathing now, but like anything living, it could die just as quick.

I drew three columns on a legal pad: Possible, Uncertain, No Go.

- Possible was for the people Ezra trusted to the end, the ones who'd already paid a price for speaking up.

- Uncertain were the ones I'd have to test folks who talked a good game on Sunday but kept their Monday schedule a mystery.

- No Go was for the names tied directly to Harmony grants, CSEC, or the pastors Robison suspected of being informants.

I called Donell

"You free?" I asked.

"I can be," he said.

Donell was already waiting at the diner when I got there. He sat in the corner booth, coffee steaming in front of him, the kind of spot where you could see the door and the street at the same time. He didn't wave me over, just gave a slow nod.

"You look like hell," he said as I slid into the seat.

"Feel worse."

He leaned forward. "How's Kristen?"

I took a breath. "She'll live. They broke her arm, cut her face. Told her to stay away from me."

Donell's jaw tightened. "Said your name?"

"Twice. Like they wanted her to remember every syllable."

He looked out the window, eyes scanning the street. "That wasn't random, Harris. That's not even about her. That's about showing you they can get to anybody in your orbit."

I stirred my coffee without taking a sip. "I know

For a moment, neither of us spoke. The clink of dishes and the hiss of the grill filled the silence.

"You remember what I told you when this started?" Donell said, finally. "About the cost?"

"Yeah. I thought I understood it back then."

"And now?"

I looked down at the table. "Now I know you can't count it until it's paid."

He nodded, slow. "See, people think the fight's just between the ones holding the gun and the ones in the crosshairs. But it's the families that get carved up the worst. They carry the weight without the bruises to prove it."

I thought about Mama, the way she'd sit up waiting for me to come home when I was a kid. About the nights she'd call out the window for my brother, about Kristen's mother, who was probably sitting in her own kitchen right now, staring at the phone, wondering why her daughter got hurt for a story she hadn't even seen in print.

"Your mama ever tell you not to bring trouble to the door?" Donell asked.

"All the time."

"That's what these people count on. They don't have to break your jaw if they can make your mother cry. They don't have to kill you if they can make your girl stop sleeping next to you. They go after your faith, your name, your place in the world until you start asking if the truth is worth losing everything that makes you who you are."

I leaned back, the booth's vinyl sticking to my shirt. "They've been doing that to us for generations. Same playbook, different century."

"Exactly," Donell said. "Back then, they'd burn your church. Now, they buy it. They put a clause in your 501(c)(3) paperwork that tells you what you can't preach about. And you watch men who once thundered from the pulpit about freedom start preaching patience instead. That's how they work on faith, slow poison, one Sunday at a time.

"And identity?" I asked.

Donell smirked without humor. "You already know. First, they call you too Black, then not Black enough. They split you from your own people. They tell the diaspora you're spoiled and tell you your FBA roots make you selfish. They'll fund ten immigrant organizations before they give one dime to a group talking about reparations. Before you know it, you're fighting folks who look like you while the real enemy walks right past with the bag."

I felt the heat rise in my chest. "And race?"

"Race is the easiest one," he said. "They turn it into theater. You get a diversity panel, a photo op, maybe a scholarship fund with somebody's name on it. Meanwhile, the neighborhoods stay gutted, and the same hands keep writing the rules."

I stared into my coffee, watching the surface ripple as the ceiling fan above us stirred the liquid. "Kristen didn't sign up for this. She thought she was chasing a story. She didn't know she was stepping into a war."

Donell's eyes met mine. "None of us ever really knows. Not until it's too late to walk away."

We sat there in the low hum of the diner. Outside, a bus rolled past, its windows full of faces looking anywhere but at each other. I wondered how many of them were carrying invisible bruise marks left by fights they never chose but still had to live through.

"You gonna keep her in it?" Donell asked.

"She wants to stay. Says it proves she's right."

He sighed. "That's the thing about people like her. Like us. We don't scare easy, but that's not always a blessing."

When we left, the air outside was cool and damp. A few crows perched on the power line above the street; their heads tilted like they were listening.

"You ever notice," Donell said, glancing up, "how crows show up after something bad?"

"Yeah."

"They're not just scavengers. They're messengers. They remember faces. Somebody crosses them, they'll follow for miles, wait years if they have to. That's how we gotta be."

I watched the birds shift on the wire, their feathers ruffling in the wind. "Long memory," I said.

"Long fight," Donell answered.

We shook hands, but neither of us smiled.

"I'm starting Ezra's network. Quiet. Need your eyes on my list before I make any contact."

"You thinking safe house or safe circuit?"

"Both. We need a place to meet that doesn't show up on paper, and a way to pass information that doesn't touch a cell tower."

He let out a low whistle. "Now we're talking underground."

We met an hour later in the back booth of a diner where the waitress knew Donell by name but didn't bother asking about me. I slid the pad across the table.

He studied the columns without speaking, his thumb tapping against the Possible list. "This one's solid," he said, pointing at a community organizer who'd lost funding last year for refusing to water down her demands at city hall. "And this one… might be good, but you gotta keep him away from anything direct. He talks too much."

We went by name until the list was smaller but stronger.

"This is your first circle," Donell said finally. "Small enough to keep it airtight, big enough to make noise when it's time."

"It's not just noise," I said. "It's a signal. A counter to the Sleeping Pill. We can't wake everybody at once, but we can wake the ones who've been pretending to sleep.

Donell nodded. "And when they wake up?"

"Then we show them the crows aren't invincible."

I noticed one perched on the signpost outside the diner, black eyes fixed on us. It didn't flinch when we stepped into the street.

Chapter 28
Bloodlines

Kristen was home three days after the hospital released her, arm still in a sling, face mottled with yellowing bruises. She'd insisted I come by, said there was someone I needed to meet.

Her place was a narrow brick house on the East Side, a porch light glowing against the early evening dark. When I knocked, the door opened to a woman in her late sixties, tall, wiry, eyes sharp enough to cut through you.

"You're Bushvill," she said, not a question.

"Yes, ma'am."

She stepped back to let me in. "I'm Lorraine. Kristen's mother. Sit down. She's upstairs getting herself together."

The living room smelled faintly of pine and old books. On the wall above the sofa hung a framed black-and-white photo of a young man in a leather jacket and beret, his eyes steady, his jaw set. I didn't have to ask.

"That's her father," Lorraine said, following my gaze. "James Brooks. He was a Panther before you were even a thought in your mama's mind."

I nodded. "She never mentioned it."

"She doesn't mention it because most people wouldn't understand. They think the Panthers were about violence. James was a proponent of free breakfast, community patrols, and education. They put a target on his back for that, not for the guns."

Kristen came down the stairs then, moving slow, her hair pulled back, a loose sweatshirt hanging off her good shoulder.

"You met my mother," she said, easing into the chair across from me.

"She was just telling me about your father."

Kristen smiled faintly. "He taught me the fight doesn't stop just because you're tired. Or scared. Or outnumbered. He said the cause outlives you, so you'd better do your part while you can."

Lorraine sank into the couch, folding her hands in her lap. "I've seen this before, Mr. Bushvill. I've seen men and women take the fight right to the line and then step back when they realize the system doesn't just come for you, it comes for your family, your job, your name. I know they came for my daughter because of you. I'm not here to scold you. I'm here to tell you what it means if you keep going."

I swallowed. "I know the cost."

"No," she said, her voice low but sharp. "You've seen the price tag. You ain't paid in full yet. When you do, it'll be more than bruises and broken bones. It'll be people crossing the street to avoid you. Preachers are locking you out of their pulpits. Family telling you to 'let it go' for your own good. And you'll have to look in the mirror and decide if you can live with that."

Kristen leaned forward, her eyes locking on mine. "You asked me in the hospital why I'd stay in this. I didn't give you the full answer. It's because this is the same fight my father was in. Different uniforms, same war. They called him dangerous because he wanted his people fed, educated, and protected. They call us dangerous now because we want the truth out."

Her voice shook, not from fear but from anger. "And here's the thing: if they win, they don't just get to bury the truth. They get to rewrite it. My kids, if I have them, will grow up thinking the ones who took from us were the ones who saved us. That's what happens when you lose the story, you lose the right to define yourself."

Lorraine's gaze softened for the first time. "James used to say, 'The system doesn't need your cooperation, it just needs your silence.' They didn't break him, and I don't want them breaking you, either."

She paused, then nodded toward the window. "You see those wires out front?"

I looked. A pair of crows perched there, silhouetted against the streetlight.

"They've been here all week," she said. "You know, back in the Panther days, we noticed something about crows. They'd follow us to rallies, to meetings, to court hearings. My husband used to say they were keeping watch, carrying words between the living and the dead. The elders told us crows remember faces. That if you were in the fight for real, they knew. And if you betrayed the fight, they knew that too."

Her eyes held mine. "Sometimes they were just birds. But sometimes… I think they were a reminder that nothing you do, good or bad, stays buried."

I thought about the fire, about praying to both God and the devil to save my brother. Donell said those without bruises carried the real cost. Here they were two women, one who'd lived it before and one who was living it now, both telling me the same thing: you either stay the course, or you live with the shame of stepping off it.

Kristen's good hand gripped the arm of her chair. "Harris, you're close. Close enough that they're showing their teeth, if you walk now, they'll take that as proof they can scare the next one, and the next. That's how movements die, not from bullets, but from the ones who could've stood and didn't."

Lorraine's eyes narrowed. "So the question is, do you want to be remembered as the man who kept his head down, or the one who made them show theirs?"

I let the silence stretch. Outside, the wind rattled the porch steps. The crows shifted on the wire; their heads tilted toward the house.

"I'm not going anywhere," I said finally.

Kristen's smile was small but fierce. "Good. Then let's make them regret picking this fight."

Lorraine stood, heading toward the kitchen. "I'll make coffee. You're gonna need it."

When I stepped out onto the porch later, the night air was cool against my face. The crows were still there, watching. I remembered what Donell said about crows being able to remember faces. Now I knew they'd been watching longer than I'd been alive.

Maybe they were remembering mine. Or maybe they were just waiting for me to prove I'd learned what Kristen and her mother had been trying to tell me.

Either way, I couldn't let them down.

Chapter 29
Global 2000

The rain had been steady for three days straight. Buffalo's skyline was nothing but gray smudges behind sheets of water, and my mind felt just as murky. Every lead I pulled on led me somewhere darker. Every truth I found carried teeth.

The name Armand Tremaine had opened a door I didn't want to walk through, but there was no closing it now.

It was Donell who first told me about Tremaine's past. We were sitting in his car outside an all-night laundromat, watching a man in a red hoodie make the same loop around the block for the third time.

"You ever notice," Donell said, "how some kids just disappear from the block? Not the ones who get locked up or killed, those we hear about. I mean the ones who vanish without a whisper, like they never lived here at all."

I glanced at him. "Yeah. Always figured it was a family thing. Moved away, better job, better school."

He shook his head. "Sometimes. But sometimes it's because somebody picked them."

That's when he told me about Tremaine. Back then, he wasn't Armand Tremaine, the name whispered in dark corners of boardrooms and backrooms. He was just Dre from Kensington, a quiet kid with a head for numbers and an ear for music. His father was a mechanic; his mother ran a little daycare out of their apartment.

Donell remembered him from summer ball at Masten Park. Said Dre could keep score in his head, track every basket, every foul, without writing a thing down. He'd sit on the bench with a paperback novel in one hand and call out plays before they happened. The coaches laughed at first, then realized he was right.

"He was different," Donell said. "You could feel it. And so could other people."

One summer, a man in a tailored suit started showing up to the games. Didn't belong to shoes that were too clean, and the watch was too heavy. He'd sit on the bleachers with a clipboard, watching Dre more than the ball. A month later, Dre was gone.

The story was that his family moved to Atlanta because his mother's sister got sick. But the truth, Donell said, was quieter and stranger: Dre had been offered a "special program" for gifted students, something run out of a private foundation with no name on the door.

Nobody saw the moving truck. Nobody saw them pack. One day, Dre was at the corner store buying Grape Now & Laters, and the next, the apartment was empty.

"Next time I saw him," Donell said, "was ten years later. He wasn't Dre anymore. He was wearing an Armand Tremaine custom suit, accompanied by bodyguards, and drove a car with tinted glass so dark that you couldn't see the shadow of the driver. He remembered me, though. Shook my hand like we were still kids in the park. But his eyes…"

"What about them?" I asked.

"They looked like he'd been somewhere the rest of us couldn't survive."

I kept thinking about that. About how certain kids get tapped on the shoulder and told they're special, and how that word special can mean salvation or damnation, depending on who's saying it.

The more I dug, the more I saw the pattern. It wasn't just Tremaine. Other Black boys and girls from rough neighborhoods'd shown a rare spark in areas such as math, music, languages, and leadership. They'd vanish into "opportunities" nobody could question. Scholarships to schools nobody could find on a map. Internships with "think tanks" that had no website. Then, years later, they'd resurface in positions of influence, such as government contractors, lobbyists, and tech innovators, each one orbiting the same hidden network.

Donell said it was like the Panthers in reverse. Back in the day, the system marked you for destruction if you showed leadership. Now, they groom you and feed you just enough to keep you loyal, and point you where they want the influence to land.

That made sense for Tremaine. The man had a gift for strategy, for seeing five moves ahead. I could picture him as a boy, watching a game from the bench, already knowing who'd score next. Only now was the court global, and the stakes weren't baskets; they were policies, contracts, whole communities.

Later that week, I met a man named Lionel, an old friend of Tremaine's from the neighborhood. He'd tracked me down after hearing I was asking questions. We met in the back of a barbershop after hours, clippers silent, the smell of talc still hanging in the air.

"Dre was my boy," Lionel said. "We used to walk to school together. He'd help me with my homework; I'd keep him out of fights. Then one summer, poof, gone. No goodbye. His moms called once, from a number we couldn't call back, just to say they were 'somewhere safe.'"

"Safe from what?" I asked.

Lionel shrugged. "That's the thing. Nobody knew we were in danger. But Dre's mom acted like we were. Like she'd just gotten news the block was about to burn, and she had the only ticket out.

Lionel told me something else as well. He said the week before Dre disappeared, there were crows everywhere. On the school roof, on the basketball hoops, on the power lines outside his building. Dre joked that they were following him, but Lionel swore they were. "You ever see a bird tilt its head like it knows you? That's what it was like," he said.

When I asked if Dre was scared, Lionel shook his head. "Nah. If anything, he looked… ready. Like he'd been waiting for that knock on the door his whole life."

That image stuck with me, Tremaine as a boy, knowing the game was about to change, and stepping into it without hesitation. It made the present-day version of him more understandable: the calculated calm, the way he could draw people in and keep them orbiting without ever revealing the chain.

And it made me wonder: if they could take a kid from the hood and turn him into a weapon for their side, what could they do to the rest of us without us even noticing?

When I told Donell what Lionel said about the crows, he didn't blink. "Makes sense," he said. "You remember what Kristen's mother told you? That crows remember faces? Maybe they've been keeping track of him from the start. Maybe they know what he's doing now, and they're just waiting for the right time to circle back."

The thought chilled me more than I wanted to admit. Because if the crows were watching Tremaine, and they were watching me, then maybe the fight we were in didn't start with Ezra's death at all. Perhaps it began years ago, when someone decided which children would live under the weight of the truth and which ones would be its enforcers.

Tremaine wasn't just an operator with offshore accounts and quiet money. He was a phantom in a suit, moving between union halls, city boardrooms, and prison corridors with the same measured ease. He'd been back in Buffalo long enough to root himself in its soil, but not long enough to leave fingerprints.

He had his hands in everything: churches, campaign funds, charter schools, and real estate, all stitched together with one thread: silence. You didn't say Tremaine's name unless you were ready to vanish.

The deeper I dug, the more it became clear this wasn't just about keeping Ezra's voice quiet. It was about dismantling anything that could awaken people. And when I traced Tremaine's pattern, I saw something else. It wasn't new.

It was Global 2000 all over again, the quiet, calculated culling of a people through policy, economics, and engineered dependency. The plan from the 1980s was rumored to "stabilize" the Black population by controlling its growth, its resources, and its future. Back then, it was wrapped in think tank language and international development jargon. Now it was dressed up in grants, community "partnerships," and tax codes.

Ezra had been one of the few to spot the connection that Tremaine was using the 501(c)(3) leash on Black churches not just to keep them politically quiet, but to make them instruments in their own erasure.

I had more than rumors. I had names, faces, and the bricks in Tremaine's wall.

That meant going underground.

Not metaphorically. Literally.

A call to an old client, now serving a ten-year sentence in Attica, led me to The Cellar, a jazz den located under an old dry cleaner on Jefferson. It was the kind of place where the truth rolled out slow over bourbon and saxophone lines.

The room was bathed in blue light when I arrived. A sax player was bleeding Coltrane into the walls, and the crowd leaned back into the sound like it was medicine. Rudy "Keys" Jackson was nursing a drink in the far corner. Rudy had once played piano for half the city's church choirs before sliding into side work that kept his pockets lined up and his name out of the paper.

"You brought the rain in with you," Rudy said without looking up.

"I'm looking for the man who holds the umbrella," I said.

That got a low chuckle. "Ain't nobody holdin' umbrellas in Tremaine's world. Just folks hopin' the thunder don't get too close."

We talked in pieces, like old jazz riffs. Names slid across the table between sips.

• DeShawn Pettis a real estate lawyer with two cell phones and a burner bank account.

• Reverend Lionel Gates a pastor of Everlasting Truth Ministries, whose sanctuary doubled as a laundering house for "donations."

• Sable Knox a club owner turned fixer with zoning board influence.

"You wanna know how Tremaine stays clean?" Rudy asked. "He doesn't hide. He blends. Wears a preacher's smile, a grant writer's suit, and a building inspector's clipboard. He doesn't kill folks; he funds their own burial. Gives 'em a grant, then watches them dig the hole with compliance."

I left The Cellar and drove home with the names burning in my head.

They lay out across my coffee table like tarot cards. The pattern was there if you looked hard enough: property deeds tucked into shell companies, grants funneled through "faith-based initiatives," pastors sitting on boards they had no business sitting on. Every path bent back toward Everlasting Truth Ministries, Ezra's old rival in the pulpit.

That was Tremaine's camouflage: a network of 501(c)(3) pulpits feeding into a single machine. Ezra's reparations plan, the Black Treasury, with its pooled church funds and political independence, would have starved that machine in public. That's why he was dangerous.

Ezra wasn't just trying to wake the church. He was trying to starve the empire, which had been feeding on our silence since Johnson's pen hit the 501(c)(3) paperwork.

And he wasn't planning to fight it with a sermon. He was building something underground, media, street bulletins, community radio, and door-to-door reporting. Called it The Watchtower Network. Said the pulpit wasn't enough anymore. If the shepherds wouldn't speak, the watchmen had to."

The Watchtower Network.

A whisper. A threat.

Two weeks later, Ezra was gone.

I stared out the window at the wet streets, a lone crow picking at trash by the curb. Now, Global 2000's shadow, Tremaine's network, the 501(c)(3) muzzle, and Ezra's plan were aligning.

And somewhere in the middle of it was the reason a man like Ezra didn't live to see his vision through.

I wasn't silent.

And I sure as hell wasn't done.

Chapter 30
The Storm Before the Broadcast

Harris stood at the edge of the rooftop, looking down at the city's twinkling lights, his coat flapping in the late October wind. The bitter breeze carried the scent of fire and winter, a sharp, biting warning that the season was changing, and so were the stakes. Below him, the city moved unaware, oblivious to the storm brewing behind closed doors.

The plan Ezra's plan was finally ready to be revealed. After weeks of sifting through financial records, tracking offshore accounts, dodging shadowy threats, and piecing together a puzzle that had nearly broken him, Harris was prepared to go public. Ezra hadn't died in vain. His vision of an independent, underground Black media network was bold, revolutionary, and dangerous. It wasn't just about controlling the narrative; it was about reclaiming it. From the sanitized pulpits of the 501(c)(3) church to the watered-down talking heads on television, Black truth had been co-opted, whitewashed, or silenced altogether.

Ezra wanted to change that. He had called The Watchtower a decentralized broadcast platform run through peer-to-peer encrypted networks, hosted in anonymous digital safehouses, and amplified through grassroots content creators. No corporate sponsors. No government grants. No pulpit-approved scripts. Just the unfiltered, radical truth about Black suffering, resilience, and revolution.

But Harris never got the chance to announce it.

The first sign that something was wrong came two days before the private unveiling. They were supposed to meet at an old union hall on Fillmore, a place once alive with political organizing, now barely standing, its windows boarded and its history forgotten. It had been Ezra's favorite meeting spot. He said the ghosts of real fighters still lingered in the rafters. The core group, consisting of six members, was meant to gather there to rehearse the rollout, verify encryption protocols, and finalize distribution channels.

Only four showed up.

Malik, the digital strategist from Atlanta, didn't respond to calls or texts. That was strange. Malik never ghosted. He was known for being annoyingly early, laptop in hand and coffee in the other. But he didn't show.

And then there was Nia, Nia Sharpe, who as to be the face of the movement.

She had been a journalist, once a mainstream one. CNN. Then MSNBC. Then BET. Her on-screen poise and piercing questions had once won her awards. Then one day, she disappeared from the airwaves. Rumor was that she had refused to read a script about a police shooting in Chicago, one that painted the dead Black teenager as a gang-affiliated thug rather than the church drummer and aspiring violinist he really was. After that, the network quietly buried her. But Ezra had found her, pulled her out of exile, and given her a new mission. She was to be the voice, the anchor, the face of The Watchtower Signal.

And now she was dead.

They found her in a downtown hotel, an upscale, immaculate, and soulless establishment. The cause of death: fentanyl overdose. Wrapped in sheets, eyes glassy, mouth slightly parted. No note. Just her phone, wiped clean. No pills. No residue. No visitors logged at the front desk.

The media called it tragic. Said she was likely depressed, hinted at a fall from grace, cited anonymous sources talking about "pressure" and "personal demons." Harris knew better.

She didn't use. Ever. Not even weed. She was vigilant about her image, her health, and her clarity. She fasted every Friday. Prayed every morning. Carried a leather-bound copy of The Fire Next Time everywhere she went.

Harris knew it was a message. Not just to him but to everyone involved. Back off. Disappear. Or end up like her.

The meeting that followed was tense, thick with fear. The four remaining members argued behind locked doors and closed blinds.

Malik was still missing. Nia was gone. And Harris was now the only one who had all the pieces: the bank codes, the location of the server nodes, the passwords, the launch protocol. Everyone else had been compartmentalized by design. It had been Ezra's failsafe; too many revolutions died because the whole plan lived in too few people.

But now Harris was the plan.

"We have to go public," he said, his voice low but firm. "Right now. If we delay, we lose control. They want us to scatter. We do that, Ezra's vision dies with us."

"You don't get it," said Alicia, the encryption coder, her hands trembling. "If they got to Nia, and Malik's MIA, who's next? You? Me?"

"They already know who we are," Harris snapped. "They're counting on fear to do their work. We have the proof. The shell companies, the dirty grant money, the tithes rerouted into PACs — everything. We can show the people how the 501(c)(3) muzzle is being used to kill the Black prophetic voice. We expose it. All of it."

The room fell quiet.

Then an old voice broke through.

"Ezra knew they'd come for him," said Bernard, the retired radio operator from Buffalo's old AM stations. He'd once helped broadcast coded messages during the sanitation strikes in the '60s. "He told me that we don't cry if anything ever happens. We don't retreat. We broadcast anyway. We speak. We rise."

Alicia wiped her eyes.

Tremaine's name was still unspoken in the room, but everyone felt him like a ghost sitting at the head of the table, listening, watching. Harris had seen his reach, the web of influence that tied megachurches, private security firms, media conglomerates, and shady nonprofits into a single knot of silent suppression. Ezra had called Tremaine "The Gatekeeper" not because he kept people out but because he decided which truth got to walk in.

The stakes had never been higher.

Back at his apartment, Harris stared at Nia's last message to him. It wasn't a call or a text. It was a voice memo she had recorded on a burner app, set to auto-send if she didn't disable it within 48 hours.

It was short.

"If they get me… don't let this die with me. Ezra's right. The people need their own signal. Don't blink, Harris. Don't you dare blink."

He played it twice more.

Then, with trembling hands, he opened the encrypted folder marked WATCHTOWER_FINAL. The servers in Ghana, Oakland, Toronto, and others stood by. The protocol was clean. The countdown was set.

And for the first time in weeks, he allowed himself to hope.

But hope was serrated sharply at the edges. He would need protection, backup, and a contingency plan. The next move had to be perfect.

Because the next move would either wake the sleeping masses… or get him killed.

Chapter 31
First Watch

The first move couldn't look like a move.

If Tremaine's people even suspected what I was building, they'd smother it before it breathed. The Watchtower Network had to come alive like a rumor, something no one could prove but everyone could feel.

I started with the streets.

Donell and I sat in my kitchen with a stack of mock church bulletins that Yolanda had designed on an old laptop. On the front: a generic image of clasped hands and a verse from the Book of Proverbs. On the inside: scripture, yes, but woven between the lines were Ezra's words, stripped of his name but heavy with his intent. The pulpit must be free. The treasury must be ours. The sleeping pill is sweet but fatal.

The back page was the only real giveaway, featuring a single crow silhouette in the corner and a QR code that didn't lead to a church website, but to an encrypted server.

"Are you sure you want to release that in the wild?" Donell asked, holding one up to the light.

"It's the point," I said. "Make it look like a sermon. Make it sound like a sermon. But let it read like a warning."

The physical drops were simple. Donell knew the janitors at half the churches on the East Side, the ones who didn't ask too many questions when a new stack of literature showed up in the vestibule. We planted bulletins in choir rooms, food pantry bags, and even under windshield wipers outside Sunday services.

By the time the first bulletins were in the offering trays, I'd sent the same message out digitally, not to everyone, but to a dozen trusted contacts, all on different secure channels.

The digital version hit harder. It opened with a grainy image of Ezra's handwritten note: God doesn't ask Caesar. Then it laid out a stripped-down map of how the 501(c)(3) lease worked and how it tied directly to the Harmony Fund's grants. No names. No addresses. Just enough for anyone awake to start connecting dots.

The final line was the same in both versions: The watchman sees the sword coming. Who will blow the trumpet?

We didn't wait long for the reaction.

Two days after the drop, Donell spotted a pair of unfamiliar sedans parked across from his place. The same models, different plates, were swapped out every few hours.

Yolanda's phone lit up with messages from pastors she hadn't spoken to in years, most of them pretending they just wanted to "catch up," but circling questions about whether she'd "heard anything strange going around."

And me? I came home to find a single crow feather taped to my door, pinned under a copy of one of our bulletins.

I returned home to five crows perched on the line across the street from my apartment.

The crows had seen the smoke. Now they'd started looking for the fire.

Chapter 32
The Signal Breaks Through

The room was quiet except for the hum of the equipment. Cables coiled across the floor like black snakes, cameras set and waiting. The countdown clock on the monitor reads twenty-four minutes until broadcast.

Yolanda stood by the window, looking out over the city. The glass reflected her face and, faintly, the glow of the screens behind her. In her hand was a worn Bible, the leather soft and frayed from years of Ezra's fingerprints. She turned the pages like she was afraid they might tear.

"Micah three, eleven," she murmured, almost to herself. "Her leaders judge for a bribe, her priests teach for a price, and her prophets tell fortunes for money. Yet they lean on the Lord and say, 'Is not the Lord among us? No disaster will come upon us.'"

Her voice caught on the last line. She closed her eyes, seeing Ezra's face the last time he'd preached that verse. He'd said it slow, letting each word land like a hammer. Not to condemn the people, but to strip the mask from the ones standing over them, feeding them poison while quoting scripture.

"That was his favorite," she said, turning toward me. "He said it was the blueprint for the times we're living in. Leaders who sell justice, preachers who sell the Word, prophets who sell comfort. And all the while, they act like God's still on payroll."

She looked back out the window, her reflection half-shadowed. "He used to say if you ever wanted to know the health of a nation, look at its pulpits. If they're clean, the streets will follow. The whole place rots from the top down if they're dirty."

She flipped a few more pages, stopping at Matthew seven fifteen. Her lips tightened. "'Beware of false prophets, who come to you in sheep's clothing but inwardly are ravenous wolves.'"

Her voice was low now, almost a whisper. "Ezra would read that one after Micah, like it was the answer to the riddle. This is who Micah's talking about, the wolves dressed in the choir robe, the ones who smile while they count your offering. He said the sheep's clothing wasn't just about deception, it was about comfort. Wolves make sure you feel safe before they sink their teeth in."

She turned to me, the weight in her eyes cutting through the low light. "That's why this broadcast matters. It's not just exposing the corruption, it's naming the wolves, so the sheep can stop pretending they don't see the blood on the wool."

I glanced at the clock. Twenty minutes. "You ready?"

She gave a small laugh that wasn't joy. "I'm past ready. But I keep thinking about something Ezra said after we returned from that conference in D.C. You remember that hotel lobby preacher who told him he needed to 'tone it down' if he wanted funding?"

I nodded. "Yeah. He didn't take it well."

"He told me in the elevator, 'If I tone it down, I might as well be one of them. And God didn't call me to be one of them. He called me to call them out.'"

She rested her palm on the Bible. "That's what we're doing tonight and calling them out. The bribe-takers, the price-tag prophets, the wolves who've been fed at the table while the flock starved. And if they come after us, that's fine. At least the people will know who they're dealing with."

I thought about Ezra, about the times I'd seen him walk into a room full of powerful men and leave it quiet, not because he shouted them down, but because the truth had a way of making noise without raising its voice.

"Ezra used to tell me," she went on, "that scripture is like a mirror; most folks tilt it until they like what they see. He refused to tilt it. And that's why they hated him."

The clock ticked down. Nineteen minutes.

Outside, the city lights blurred in the glass. The Bible's reflection in her hands seemed to merge with her own shadow.

"You know what else he said about wolves?" she asked, her tone shifting.

"What?"

"That they're patient. They'll run alongside the flock for miles, not attacking, just waiting for the right sheep to slow down. And they'll wait years if they have to. He said that's why we can't wait anymore because the flock's already slowing down, and the wolves are close enough to smell the fear."

She closed the Bible and held it to her chest. "Micah three, eleven for the rot. Matthew seven, fifteen for the face it wears. And tonight, we rip that face off in front of everybody watching."

Donell called out from across the room. "Fifteen minutes."

Yolanda nodded without looking back. Her eyes stayed fixed on the city, like she could see the whole network we were about to expose: the pastors, the politicians, the donors, the handlers, and the wolves.

She turned to me one last time before walking toward the set. "When we start, remember this isn't about us. It's about ensuring the flock knows the shepherd's been bought, and the pasture's been poisoned. If they still want to graze there after that, at least it's their choice."

I watched her, the Bible still in her hand. For a moment, in the glow of the cameras, she looked like she was about to walk into a pulpit. And I realized maybe she was just not the kind you find in a church.

We didn't launch with fanfare, a ribbon-cutting ceremony, or press releases. It was just a grainy video, black and white like the old days, except the clarity was in the message. Ezra's voice cut through the static like prophecy handed down through broken speakers, a sermon without a sanctuary.

We uploaded it to platforms they couldn't trace, couldn't choke. Harriet's Signal. Nubian Pulse. Old FTP servers that hadn't been touched since George Bush was in office. And we didn't label it as Watchtower Signal because Ezra's vision was never about branding. It was about building.

Initially, the analytics appeared disappointing. A few hundred clicks. Some bounced. Others ghosted. But we knew the kind of people who lingered weren't here for spectacle, they were here for substance. Ezra's voice wasn't built to go viral. It was built to go deep.

And it did.

By day three, a church in Atlanta had printed out the transcript and read it from the pulpit. By day five, a group in Baltimore had posted a QR code in subway stations, directing people to a mirrored link. There were no names, no leaders, just the Watchtower Network watermark and the word "Awake."

Donell leaned over the map we had pinned to the wall, with a red thread running from Buffalo to Birmingham, from Ferguson to Flint. "We started a fire," he said. "Not a big one yet. But dry ground only needs a spark."

We watched as the MANNA Covenant's roots took hold. One church in Oakland severed its 501(c)(3) status live during service, ripped the paperwork in half, and burned it in a communion dish. Another in Memphis rewrote their bylaws to form a neighborhood reparations trust, funded entirely from pooled tithes and a few small Black-owned businesses.

Some called it radical.

Others called it prophecy.

Ezra had called it obedience.

But with each ripple, the crows came closer.

That week, a city councilman in Pittsburgh lost his seat after leaked emails showed he'd funneled funds to a nonprofit linked to Tremaine's network. A Black pastor in Newark, one of Tremaine's quiet men, was found on video contradicting his own sermon, caught in a backroom negotiation with a developer. The tape was grainy, but the voice was his clear as day.

People were beginning to ask the right questions. And that's when the noise started.

Not literal. Not yet.

The noise came in the form of phone calls from numbers with no caller ID, empty cars parked outside my apartment, a city code violation slapped on my door, emails warning of pending audits every tactic subtle enough to deny but loud enough to distract.

I ignored them. We all did.

Then the firewall breach happened.

Donell burst into my office, laptop in hand. "They hit one of the nodes in Dallas," he said. "Encrypted server went dark. Someone ran a tracer through one of the church admin logins."

I nodded, already pulling up the emergency distribution protocol. "They're hunting the source."

Donell's voice dropped. "They think it's you."

I didn't answer. The truth didn't need confirmation. The system was waking up to our noise. And I knew they'd come for the megaphone first.

"Then we go smaller," I said. "Decentralized. Each congregation runs its link. No central hub. Only guidance, not governance."

"You sure?"

I looked at the blinking cursor on the screen and remembered Ezra's voice. "Build it so it doesn't need you."

"I'm sure," I said.

That night, we met in the basement of a borrowed building with half-finished drywall, exposed pipes, and the hum of purpose in the air. There were about twenty of us. Some were pastors. Other teachers. A nurse. A young barber with three kids and a distrust of banks. Donell stood beside me, silent but steady.

I passed around flash drives like communion wafers. Each one held the core files: Ezra's original video, the blueprint for the MANNA Covenant, and instructions on duplicating the network.

"This isn't about rebelling," I told them. "It's about remembering that our churches were never meant to be tamed. That our voices weren't born with gag orders."

One of them, a woman named Tasha who ran a community garden in Cleveland, raised her hand. "What happens when they come for us?"

I paused. Then, I answered with what I knew was true. "They will. But not before we wake up a few more. And if we do this right, they won't know who to shut down. Because it won't be one voice, it'll be a thousand."

Another hand went up. A younger man, face still carrying the softness of teenage years. "What if it's not enough?"

Donell answered before I could. "Then we die with our eyes open. That's more than they gave Ezra."

By the time the meeting ended, we'd planted the Covenant in three new states and agreed on the next ten. I walked out into the street and saw a crow sitting on the lamppost. Not watching this time, waiting.

The wind shifted.

I knew what came next.

Tomorrow would not be quiet.

But for the first time since Ezra's death, I didn't need quiet.

I needed thunder.

And it was coming.

Chapter 33
Salt in the Wound

The streets were slick with late October rain, and Buffalo felt like it was trying to shed something. Maybe guilt. Maybe history. Maybe both. I kept my collar up as I walked the perimeter of what used to be St. Luke's. The stained glass was gone, the steeple gutted, and scaffolding now held the building's spine upright like a patient waiting for its final surgery.

Inside, they were prepping it to become a wellness hub, the kind with yoga mats and grant-funded posters on the wall, the kind that preaches balance instead of justice. Progress, they'd say. Ezra would've called it embalming the church with language that smelled clean but meant nothing.

Donell was already there, pacing in the back near what had been the pulpit. He didn't look at me when I walked in. Just said, "You ready?"

"Doesn't matter if I am. The clock's already ticking."

He nodded and handed me a flash drive. "Clean copy of the MANNA Covenant files. We've split them across three networks: encrypted backups and decentralized broadcast platforms. We start the drop tonight."

I looked around at what used to be holy ground. "You think anyone's ready to see the church this naked?"

"They better be," Donell said. "Because Tremaine isn't waiting."

We sat down on the steps of what had once been the altar. Donell pulled out a folder. Inside were names, photos, bank statements, and digital breadcrumbs.

"They turned our prophets into property managers," he muttered. "Sermons into compliance scripts. And this city... this city fed itself on the silence."

I thought about Ezra. About the crow on my windowsill. About the silence that had become policy. I thought about the informants in pulpits and the federal language in grant proposals that turned fire into fog.

"We start tonight with Watchtower Signal," I said. "And the Watchtower Network pushes the rest in waves. Harriet's Signal picks it up by morning. Nubian Pulse, then The Brown Channel. We bury the algorithm in truth until it chokes."

Donell looked over. "You ever think we're too late? Have the people already chosen the sleeping pill?"

I shook my head slowly. "I think some of them want to wake up. They just forgot what truth tastes like. We remind them. Bitter, maybe. But real."

There was a noise outside, just wind through broken glass, but it made both of us tense. We were past the point of paranoia now. This was war, fought in information and silence, in sermons and source code.

"We launch with Ezra's final sermon," I said. "The unedited one. The one they buried."

Donell smiled faintly. "You got the courage to voice it?"

I looked at the dusty altar in front of us. "I've got the grief. That's enough."

Ezra's Last Sermon – "The Watchman's Cry"

"Ezekiel said, 'Son of man, I have made you a watchman for the house of Israel; therefore hear the word at my mouth, and give them warning from me.'"

Beloved, the watchman is not here to sing you to sleep. The watchman is not here to count the offering and pat you on the head on the way out. The watchman stands on the wall, eyes open, while you rest, to see the enemy coming from a long way off.

And I see them.

I see them in our pulpits, wearing fine suits paid for with grant money meant for the poor. I see them in back rooms with politicians, trading your future for a handshake and a photo op. I see them in the bank accounts of men who preach Jesus on Sunday and obey Caesar all week long.

They tell us, "Stay out of politics, preacher. Just preach the Gospel." But the same book they quote from says the Spirit of the Lord is upon me to preach good news to the poor, to set the captives free, to proclaim liberty. How do you set captives free if you won't name the chains?

They say, "Don't talk about race, don't talk about injustice, you'll lose your 501(c)(3)." Well, I say if your tax exemption costs you your tongue, you've sold your birthright for a bowl of soup. The church has become the quietest place in town while the streets burn and the prisons overflow.

Some of you don't want me to talk like this. You want me to make you feel good. You want a lullaby, not an alarm. But I'm here to wake you up.

You've been drugged by a doctrine I call The Sleeping Pill. It tells you to endure, but never resist. To pray, but never protest. To forgive, but never fight for your children's future. And while you've been sleeping, they've been taking.

But I tell you today, no more.

No more bowing to Pharaoh's system. No more renting pews in a government-owned church. No more prosperity gospel that fattens the pastor and starves the people. The kingdom of God is not a business; it's a revolution.

And I'll tell you something that might cost me my life: we are going to build our own table. We are going to pool our resources, buy our own land, create our own schools, feed our own children, and elect our own leaders. We will not beg for crumbs from the master's table; we will bake our own bread.

They may come for me after this. They may smear my name, pull our funding, or try to silence this voice. But you can kill the watchman, and still the wall will stand if the people rise.

So rise.

Rise like your ancestors rose when they had nothing but faith and a will to be free. Rise like the morning after a long night. Rise, because if you stay asleep, you will wake up in a world where your grandchildren have no name, no home, and no God they recognize.

This is the watchman's cry. The enemy is not coming. The enemy is here.

Choose this day whom you will serve.

We stood. Rain dripped through the ceiling in steady, indifferent beats. I thought about Ezra's line: 'They don't destroy prophets.' They repurpose them.

Not this time.

"By the time they hear it," I said, "the crow will already be in the house."

Donell nodded. "Then let's make sure it sings."

We left the ruins of St. Luke's, each of us carrying a piece of what Ezra died to build. It wasn't a resurrection.

But it was a revolution.

Chapter 34
The Sound Underground

The truth carried a weight. Not the kind you could measure in pounds or store in files. It was the kind that sat on your chest when you woke up and didn't leave until you did something about it.

We were past the phase of discovery now. Past secrets and whispers. What we held in our hands could shift the balance. The MANNA Covenant wasn't just a theory anymore; it was a detonator. And Buffalo was the test site.

The night after cracking Ezra's files, Donell and I sat in the dim backroom of The Nubian Pulse studio. The old FM radio boards had been gutted, replaced with podcast mics, encrypted streaming equipment, and two screens running fiber-level VPNs. No commercial sponsors. No digital fingerprints. Just pure, unfiltered signal.

I stared at the mic for a long time before speaking.

"You ready for this?" I asked Donell.

He nodded once. That was Donell. Not loud. Not reckless. But if you had him on your side, you were never alone.

"This platform," I said, adjusting the gain on the mic, "isn't about making noise. It's about making frequency. Something that vibrates in the bones. Wakes the ones who forgot they were born to stand."

"Let's give 'em the alarm clock," Donell said.

We hit record.

Transmission of the Watchtower Network went live at 8:16 p.m. on a Wednesday.

It wasn't polished. We weren't broadcasters or influencers. But it was true. And truth, like crow wings, flaps whether you're ready or not.

I introduced the message by reading Ezra's words, his voice layered underneath mine, pulled from an old voicemail Donell had saved. It was raw, broken in places, but powerful.

"Micah three, eleven," he began, his voice low, deliberate. "Her leaders judge for a bribe, her priests teach for a price, and her prophets tell fortunes for money. Yet they lean on the Lord and say, 'Is not the Lord among us? No disaster will come upon us.'" He let the verse hang. You could almost hear the quiet in the room where it was recorded.

"That's not ancient Israel," he said. "That's us. That's the American Black church in 2025."

"Before 501(c)(3), our churches were the headquarters of the fight. They weren't just Sunday sanctuaries. They were schools. They were banks. They were safe houses. They were where we strategized against oppression and planned to win ground for our people.

Now? Now they're franchises. Stage lights, LED screens, smoke machines, dopamine factories. You leave feeling good but powerless. You get the high, but none of the healing. The Word has been traded for the show.

And they tell you it's a blessing."

"Do you know how much we give? Fourteen billion dollars a year in tithes and offerings from Black churches in America. Fourteen billion. And yet our neighborhoods look the same. Our schools are underfunded. Our hospitals are under-equipped. Our people are over policed.

That money should be used to build our future. It should be creating an economic base for the Foundational Black American community. But it isn't because it's been hijacked."

He leaned forward now, voice tightening.

"That's what the MANNA Covenant is about. A unionized church network. One tithe system. One collective fund. No strings from the state, no gag order from the tax code. Our dollars would build our banks, our schools, our health clinics. We'd create our own jobs, our own media, our own safety nets.

But the system doesn't want that. So, they give us pastors who are bought, boards that are compromised, and doctrines that sedate. They feminize our men, harden our women, and tell us that role reversal is progress. They destroy the design and then dare us to question it."

"You want to know how Jesus responded when the temple became a marketplace? He flipped the tables. He drove them out. He made a whip and used it. That was the fight. That was the example.

And if you claim His name but won't call out the wolves in the pulpit, then you're not following Him, you're following the ones counting coins at the table He overturned."

"They'll say I'm divisive for this. They'll say I'm attacking the Body. But the Body's been poisoned, and the shepherds are the ones holding the cup. You don't heal that by staying quiet.

This may be the last time you hear me speak. If it is, remember this: the church was never meant to be a safe space for cowards. It was meant to be a staging ground for soldiers."

His tone softened, but only slightly.

"Micah three, eleven for the warning. Matthew seven fifteen for the face it wears Beware of false prophets, who come to you in sheep's clothing but inwardly are ravenous wolves.

The sheep's clothing now is a three-piece suit and a wireless mic. The wolves are patient. They'll run alongside the flock for years, waiting for you to slow down. Some of them will even sing with you.

And when they bite, you won't see it coming because you were too busy enjoying the show."

"If I'm gone when you hear this, don't waste time on my name. Take the Covenant and run with it. Unionize the pulpits. Redirect the tithes. Build the future God gave us the vision to build. And if they come for you, make them show their teeth.

I'll see you on the other side." "They'll call it rebellion. I call it repair. We can't beg for justice from the same hand that profits from our silence."

We rolled through the files in small pieces enough to spark. We hadn't named all the pastors yet, and we didn't mention Tremaine by name. Not yet. We let the people hear the system first: the shell companies, the property transfers, and the gag clauses baked into faith-based grants.

We ended the broadcast with a prayer, but not the kind that puts you to sleep. The kind that wakes bones.

"May the sleepers stir. May the watchmen rise. May the church remember it has a sword, not just a choir."

And then we cut the feed. By morning, the messages started pouring in. Not on public channels, those were too easy to monitor. But through the shadow line Donell had built: encrypted dropboxes, burner email chains, and dead Wi-Fi zones in laundromats and libraries.

Some were just gratitude.

Others? Leaks. More names. More proof. More pastors like Carr, who had swallowed their conscience for a grant.

One anonymous voice stood out.

A young woman. Said she worked in the Harmony Fund's policy division. Said she knew what happened to Ezra's grant application.

"It wasn't denied," her message read. "It was flagged as destabilizing language. Sent straight to Homeland."

We knew they were watching. But Homeland?

That meant Ezra's ideas weren't just inconvenient. They were classified as threats.

I sat on the fire escape that night, staring out over the city. Buffalo didn't look dangerous from up here. Just tired. Like an old boxer sitting between rounds, bleeding from the ears but still breathing.

Three crows landed on the edge of the roof beside me.

"Y'all following us now?" I muttered.

One crow tilted its head. Maybe it was my imagination, but it looked... approving.

Donell came out behind me with two cups of coffee.

"They hit one of the pages," he said.

"Which one?"

"Watchtower Signal's backup blog. Crashed the server around 2 a.m."

I sipped. "Means we're getting through."

"Means they're listening."

We both sat in silence. No fear. Just focus.

"What now?" Donell asked.

I looked down at the list Ezra's list. The one with twenty churches that hadn't sold out. Not yet.

"We bring the trumpet to them," I said. "City by city. Pastor by pastor. If they won't come to the mountain, we become the storm."

Donell smiled.

"You're preaching now."

I nodded. "Just doing what Ezra would've done."

The crow cawed once. Loud. Sharp. A warning or a blessing. Hard to tell.

Didn't matter.

The Watchtower Network was no longer a theory.

It was alive.

And the truth had found its own underground railroad.

Chapter 35
Judas is Inside the Room

We were building momentum, but momentum attracts weight. And weight, if you're not careful, crushes more than it carries.

The Watchtower Network was live, breathing, and spreading. Small churches from Atlanta to Oakland sent word through encrypted channels. A pastor in Detroit uploaded his own breakdown of the 501(c)(3) lease. A deaconess from Newark sent her church's deed, which proved that it had been quietly sold two years ago to a shell company tied to Sable Equity Holdings.

We weren't alone.

But someone among us was a mouth without a conscience.

Donell was the one who noticed first.

"This message got scrubbed," he said one night, holding up his phone. "Completely. It was in the inbox this morning. Now it's gone from both ends. No trace. And our internal mirror didn't catch the usual download echo."

That didn't just happen by accident.

"You thinking we've got a leak?" I asked.

Donell nodded, slow and heavy. "Not a leak. A Judas."

We'd spent months building the inner circle of the Watchtower Network. Donell handled infrastructure and ops. Yolanda vetted all media and theology before it went live. We had six others, each with different skills, backgrounds, and scars. One of them had compromised us.

The Leak

Kristen called me just after midnight. Her voice had that clipped, flat tone she used when forcing herself to stay calm.

"Harris," she said, "I think I found him."

I was sitting at my desk, staring at a spreadsheet I'd been too tired to make sense of. "Found who?"

"The leak. The one scrubbing our files."

I could hear her typing on the other end, the rapid staccato of keys. "I've been working my network the last few days. Off-the-record calls. People I trust. One of them in D.C. owed me a favor. I gave him three server signatures tied to our missing data. He traced them."

"To where?"

"To a secure login. Encrypted. On paper, it's listed under the account of someone doing 'consulting oversight.'"

She let the pause stretch.

"Christopher."

It took a second to land.

"Christopher?" I said. "Our Christopher? The one sitting in on our planning?"

"The same."

I leaned back in my chair. "You sure about this?"

"That's the thing," she said. "It's not even subtle. He's logging in during and right after our meetings. And the pattern repeats every time we lose data: names disappear from our lists, files become blank, and drafts vanish. It's surgical. Someone with access and clearance."

She told me she'd run the server logs against timestamps from our cloud backups. The erasures always happened within thirty minutes of him logging in. And he wasn't just deleting things, he was sending data out.

"My source says the packets were bouncing through two dummy servers before landing on a private IP in Delaware," she said. "Guess who owns it?"

I didn't answer.

"A holding company with a board seat tied to one of Tremaine's fronts."

I stared at the wall, picturing Christopher in those meetings, polite, unassuming, always with a legal pad and pen, the guy who nodded along when we talked about security protocols, the guy who asked thoughtful questions about Ezra's old contacts, about where the Covenant plans were stored.

"Why him?" I asked.

Kristen exhaled hard into the phone. "Because he's invisible. He doesn't set off alarms. He's the guy you'd hand the keys to because you think he's too careful to wreck the car."

Her voice dropped lower. "Harris, we've been talking like we had time. We don't. Every time he logs in, we're bleeding. If I'm right and I'm right, Tremaine's already got half of what we've been building."

I rubbed my temples. "You tell anyone else?"

"No. Just you. If I tell Donell, he'll go at him head-on, and we can't afford to spook him yet. If we're going to stop this, we need to catch him in the act. With proof."

Kristen's reporter instincts were all over this. She didn't just want the leak stopped; she wanted it documented and exposed.

"I've got an idea," she said. "We plant a file. Something tempting. Harmless to lose, but loaded with a tracking beacon. We give him a reason to take it, and when it lands in Delaware, we'll have him dead to rights."

"You sure you can do that without tipping him off?"

Her tone sharpened. "Harris, this is what I do. You forget, my father taught me to spot a fed before I could spell the word."

That's when she brought him up, her father. The Panther.

"He used to tell me, 'The most dangerous one isn't the man in the uniform. It's the one in the suit, sitting two chairs down, smiling while he takes notes.' Christopher's exactly that. The kind who'll sell you while he's offering to help you pack." Her voice cracked just slightly.

"I don't want to see another movement bleed out because we didn't take the mole seriously."

I promised her we'd set the trap. She promised me she'd have the beacon file ready by morning.

Before she hung up, she added, "One more thing. My mom always said the crows followed the Panthers not just to watch, but to remember. If they're watching now, they'll know we saw him. And they'll be watching to see what we do next." When the line went dead, I just sat there in the dim light, the spreadsheet still open in front of me. Christopher's name on our roster now looked different. Not a colleague. Not even an enemy. Something worse, someone who'd been here the whole time, feeding the wolves while we talked about building fences.

I looked at the list.

And then I looked at Christoper.

Christoper had been with us from the jump. Charismatic. Reliable. A former IT engineer who'd left the corporate world to become a storefront preacher. He knew how to move in and out of rooms and disappear without being forgotten. He also had a brother facing a federal charge, something about wire fraud and kickbacks tied to a city-funded mentorship program.

They'd offered Christoper a deal. I knew it before he said it. When we finally confronted him in the backroom of our eastside safe house, his silence told me everything.

"Just say it," Yolanda said, arms folded.

Christoper looked like he wanted to speak. But something in his eyes, maybe regret or fear, hardened his jaw shut.

"You gave them names," Donell said flatly.

Christoper nodded once.

The silence that followed was heavier than anything I'd felt since Ezra's death. Not just betrayal. Not just breach. But grief. Christoper wasn't just a comrade, he'd been family. We'd eaten together, prayed together. He'd stood at Ezra's funeral with tears in his eyes and fire in his heart.

Now he was the fracture.

"I had no choice," he finally said, voice barely above a whisper. "They said they'd make it go away. My brother's case. They knew everything about who we met with, what we planned to release next."

I wanted to scream, but I didn't. That's not how war works. In war, you hold the scream until you're alone. You hold the rage until it can be weaponized.

"You didn't just risk us," I said, "you handed them a map."

Cristopher looked down.

"I didn't give them everything," he said.

"That's not a confession," Donell said. "It's a prayer."

We voted that night. Not for vengeance. For preservation.

Christoper would no longer have access to the network. His accounts were scrubbed. His name was removed from our encryption cycles. We didn't expose him. That would've been easy. Instead, we did what Ezra would've done; we told him to repent, to protect who he still could, and to never cross our line again.

As he left, I saw the weight on his back. A man carrying both betrayal and the realization that he'd just lost the only real movement left.

That night, I lit a candle.

Not for him.

For the people we were still fighting for.

For Ezra.

For every child sitting in a pew while their pastor preached obedience, dressed in the gospel.

I went back through Ezra's files, this time slower. I was looking for the roots beneath the roots, and that's when I found it.

An old voice message. Never opened. Never played.

From Reuben Ellis.

The lawyer.

Ezra's legal architect.

Howard Law, class of '98, he'd been the one they said might "finally change the system from the inside." He'd clerked for a federal judge who used to call him "the conscience in the room," then went straight into civil rights litigation. In those years, Reuben didn't just talk about justice, he made it happen. He went after redlining cases in Baltimore, fought wrongful evictions in Philly, and even got a class-action suit against a national bank past motions to dismiss. That was the case that caught Ezra's attention.

They met in D.C. during a quiet reception after a congressional hearing on community reinvestment. Ezra was already building the bones of the MANNA Covenant in his mind, though back then it didn't have a name. He discussed pooled church resources, self-determined economic policy, and utilizing tax-exempt leverage to establish genuine political autonomy.

Reuben liked the fire in his voice. He offered to run the legal side to structure the Covenant in a way that would survive both IRS scrutiny and political sabotage. For a while, it worked. They drafted bylaws, vetted accountants, and even mapped out the transition from a faith-based economic bloc to a political third rail. This movement could push Foundational Black American issues to the forefront without needing permission from the Democrats or Republicans.

That was when the betrayal came.

A woman Reuben had gone to law school with, Marcia Dennings, was now a rising star in the Congressional Black Caucus. She'd been his debate partner once, someone he trusted enough to share early drafts of the Covenant's plans. She'd promised to "quietly shop it" to friendly ears. Weeks later, he got wind of a closed-door meeting where the Covenant had been painted as "a dangerous nationalist movement" that could "fracture essential Democratic voting blocs."

It wasn't just rhetoric. The smear was entered into the Congressional record to ensure it would surface in any future federal review. That language alone could lead to churches being audited or stripped of their status if they even considered joining.

Then came the warning shot. Reuben's motorcycle accident, the one that shattered his collarbone and nearly killed him, wasn't an accident. The driver was never found, though a witness claimed the car had government plates. Soon after, he got an anonymous letter: "You have been seen. Stop before you're stopped."

He went underground after that. Moved apartments twice in the same month. Gave up his license "temporarily" for health reasons and started showing up only in places where cell signals didn't reach.

When Donell finally tracked him down for me, he looked thinner than his Facebook profile, his eyes sharper but more guarded. He kept his back to the wall, like every seat was still a negotiation. And when I asked about Marcia, he didn't say her name, just called her the Judas from D.C.

"She didn't just betray us, Harris," he said, voice low. "She gave them the playbook. And now every step you take is a move they've already war-gamed."

I helped Ezra build the MANNA Covenant's financial framework before going underground after a motorcycle "accident" nearly killed they thought he was gone. But the message was clear.

Then I realized Rod had been small. The real Judas? It was much higher up.

Someone in Congress.

And someone who used to call Reuben Ellis "brother."

We called a meeting the next day. No live streams. No paper trail. Our small group, plus Reuben, patched in via a secure line. He sounded tired but alive.

"I told Ezra they'd come," he said. "I just didn't know how soon."

"Why now?" Yolanda asked. "Why this moment?"

"Because we got too close," Reuben replied. "Too coordinated. The MANNA Covenant wasn't just a theory; it was an engine. A living structure. Once we hit critical mass, we could've forced local banks to change their lending practices. We could've pulled Black voter blocs into collective bargaining coalitions."

"And someone inside knew," I said. "Someone who wanted that door shut."

Reuben went quiet.

Then: "Congresswoman Janelle Price. CBC. We were in law school together. I thought she was with us. But she's been playing on both sides. She warned Tremaine. That's why Ezra died."

It wasn't just betrayal anymore.

It was an assassination.

Political.

Spiritual.

Systemic.

And we were just getting started.

The Watchtower Network was wounded, but alive.

And we still had names.

We had the crows.

We had the files.

And we had the flame.

Chapter 36
Salt in the Sanctuary

The next day, I walked into New Life Restoration Cathedral under a fake name and a borrowed suit.

It was one of Tremaine's crown jewels, polished, rehearsed, and funded. The choir sang in perfect harmony. The ushers wore earpieces. The pulpit had a countdown clock to keep the sermon from running past forty minutes. They called it an efficient ministry. I called it a corporate rollout.

Crows didn't fly over this building. I'd started to notice that. Something about it kept them away. Maybe it was the frequency of silence. Perhaps it was the decay beneath the marble.

Pastor Langston Reese was the main attraction. Clean cut. Six-figure smile. And a sermon that sounded like a PR team had written it.

"We are a community," he said, pacing with a lapel mic. "We are change agents, not agitators. We're here to show the world that faith is peace."

I heard the subtext clearly.

Faith is obedience. Faith is silence.

And silence is survival.

The sanctuary lights were so bright that the gold trim on Pastor Langston Reese's robe threw sparks. He stood at the pulpit with the confidence of a man who'd already been paid, hands spread wide like he was blessing the entire zip code.

"God does not wish you to be without!" Reese's voice boomed, shaking the cheap wood of the pew in front of me. "There are riches in heaven waiting for you! There's a storehouse up there with your name on it! But you gotta stand by the gate and wait to be let in."

The crowd swayed and murmured. Some shouted back, "Amen!" Others lifted hands, eyes shut tight, as if they could see the gate from where they sat.

Reese paced the stage like a general inspecting troops. "Don't you rush God's timing! There's grace in long suffering! There's blessing in the wait!"

He hit each line like a punchline, and the congregation laughed in relief, the way people laugh when they've been permitted to stay in the same place and call it holy.

I'd heard this kind of sermon before the prosperity loop. Keep your eyes on the afterlife, keep your pockets open now, keep telling yourself that what you don't have here will be made up for in some celestial layaway plan.

Ezra's voice cut through my memory like a blade: "The kingdom of God isn't a waiting room. It's a workshop. You don't stand by the gate; you build the gate. You don't suffer for grace, you suffer for change."

I remembered one of his sermons; he leaned on the pulpit until the wood creaked, staring down the congregation like he was tired of hearing his voice bounce off the walls. "Heaven isn't a bribe for patience," he'd said. "It's a blueprint for action. And if you think God's plan is for you to wait empty-handed while the wicked build walls around what He gave you, you're not reading the same Bible I am."

Reese's choir hit a chord, and the organ swelled under him as he painted a picture of jeweled gates and endless mansions. People were on their feet now, shouting, crying, fanning themselves with church programs.

Ezra's words felt like they belonged to another planet where God didn't need a middleman to release what was already yours. Reese promised them wealth if they endured; Ezra had told them endurance without resistance was just captivity with better lighting.

I leaned back in the pew, letting the sound wash over me. Reese's voice was a smooth tide, lulling them into a holy nap.

Ezra had been a fire alarm. Reese was a lullaby.

And in this city, the lullabies were winning.

Reese's name hadn't come up in Ezra's files, but his financial backers had. Three separate LLCs are connected to Sable Equity. One of them had just acquired two blocks of East Side housing for a "redevelopment initiative." The residents? Mostly displaced elderly and single mothers.

That wasn't redevelopment.

That was gentrification with a gospel gloss.

I sat in the back, pretending to nod and be fed. But all I felt was the burn behind my eyes. The same kind I used to feel when I saw kids come into our group homes with bags full of trauma and court papers.

Reese closed with a prayer about alignment with city leadership.

I walked out before the amen.

Donell was waiting in the car across the street. Engine running. Phone in his hand.

"They launched a smear campaign," he said. "Local radio just ran a segment questioning Ezra's mental health. Said he was 'under pressure' and 'may have been manipulating church funds.'"

I didn't blink. "Who paid for it?"

"Sponsored by a group called Horizon Faith Partners. They're tied to Global 2000. And get this, they've partnered with three city churches in the past year to offer 'public safety' grants."

"Surveillance," I said.

"Exactly. Cameras, facial recognition, community 'reporting portals.' All tied to city contracts."

"They're building a digital plantation," I muttered. "And calling it ministry."

That night, I recorded another episode of The Watchtower Signal.

No studio. No fancy mic. Just me in my office, one lamp, and Ezra's file spread out behind me like scripture.

I spoke from the gut.

Not as a journalist.

Not even as a detective.

But as a man who'd had enough.

"They killed him," I said into the mic. "Not with a bullet. With silence. With isolation. With the system they've built around our pulpits, our pastors, and our people. Ezra tried to give the church back to the people, so they labeled him a crazy person. For that, they watched him drown."

I paused.

Then I told again.

About the 501(c)(3). The preachers, about the shell companies. About Global 2000's ghost protocol and the Restoration Covenant.

And I ended it with one sentence:

"The sleeping pill is a lie. And it's time we spit it out."

We didn't wait for permission to upload it. Yolanda blasted it across every Watchtower Network node text thread, encrypted inboxes, and old-school USB drops at barbershops and bus stops.

Within 12 hours, it was downloaded 340,000 times.

Within 24 hours, it had been flagged for removal from every mainstream platform.

But the people already had it.

And that's when the calls started coming in.

Churches in Jackson, Philly, and Oakland. Preachers who'd been quiet suddenly asked for copies of the MANNA Covenant. A group of young organizers from Memphis asked for a meeting. They said they were building a sister network. They called it The Trumpet Ring.

A pastor from Alabama left a voicemail that ended with, "Y'all got a place at the table down here. We ain't all asleep."

We were waking them up.

One file. One sermon. One scar at a time.

But not all the messages were friendly.

That night, someone threw a rock through the front window of Donell's apartment. Wrapped in a piece of scripture.

Romans 13.

Submit to the governing authorities.

"They're quoting Paul now?" he said, sweeping up glass.

"They're scared," I said.

"Good," Donell replied.

Two days later, Yolanda got a call from a source inside City Hall.

"There's a list," she told me. "Of churches to monitor. Pastors and to discredit. Your name's at the top."

I didn't flinch.

"Let them watch," I said. "We're not done."

Yolanda nodded, eyes blazing.

"No," she said. "We're just getting loud."

In the dead of night, I walked back to the church Ezra once pastored, Jordan House Ministries.

It was boarded up now.

But the front steps still remembered his weight.

I sat on them for a while, listening.

And finally, the crows came back.

Three of them.

They didn't caw.

They didn't circle.

They just perched watching me like they'd been waiting.

Waiting for me to speak.

Waiting for the trumpet.

And I knew then, deep in my ribs, that it wasn't Ezra's church anymore.

It was ours.

It was theirs.

It was waiting to be filled with truth again.

And we were ready to bring the fire.

Chapter 37
The Shepherd's Shadow

There's a certain silence that only follows betrayal.

Not the loud kind, not the kind you scream into a pillow or chase down an alley. I'm talking about the silence that folds itself into your skin, the kind that makes even the birds quiet.

That was the silence I sat in when I found out about Pastor Herb.

I'd known Ezra had enemies. Some wore badges. Some wrote grants. But Herb? Herb was family at least once. Ezra had mentored him. Fed him when he was broke. Laid hands on him when he doubted his own calling.

And Herb repaid him by selling his name to Tremaine's network.

Yolanda told me first. She didn't want to.

She brought over a thin manila folder, heavy in the way that only truth can be. Inside were emails, payments, and a transcript from a closed-door clergy meeting in which Herb called Ezra "divisive and unstable."

He'd been rewarded with a new building, a seat on the City Faith Council, and a bump in his grant allocations for youth programs that didn't exist.

I didn't speak for a long time after reading it.

Just stared at a photo I had of Ezra and Herb, taken five years ago at a community prayer breakfast. Ezra had his arm around him. Herb was smiling like a man who believed in resurrection.

Donell sat across from me, arms folded.

"He was the Judas," I said.

Donell nodded. "And he kissed him in full view."

We knew we had to move.

Herb's church, Living Harvest Cathedral, had become a nerve center for Tremaine's newer operations. It was flashier than the others. Housed in a converted high school gym, it had a security team, LED screens, and a branded coffee shop in the lobby.

But we weren't there to sip lattes.

Donell had intercepted internal files showing that Living Harvest was being used as a staging point for new faith-based contracts tied to surveillance tech, one of which was titled "public safety discipleship."

They were using God's name to install state-funded eyes inside sanctuaries.

We posed as consultants: Donell, me, and a contact from Nubian Pulse who could pass as a grant auditor. Inside, the walls were white and glowing, but the air smelled like desperation.

Herb came out wearing a lavender robe and matching crocodile shoes.

He didn't recognize me at first.

But when he did, he smiled that same pastoral smile that used to mean something.

"Harris," he said. "Well, look at this. What brings you to my house?"

"This ain't your house," I said. "And we're not here for fellowship."

His smile didn't break.

Donell stepped forward. "You remember Psalm 82?"

Herb blinked.

"Defend the poor and fatherless," Donell said. "Do justice to the afflicted and needy."

Still nothing.

"Ezra preached that," I added. "Right here, years ago. Before you turned his name into currency."

The smile faltered.

"You think you're doing something righteous," Herb said, voice low. "But you're risking the very thing Ezra wanted to protect. Stability. Order. Access."

I shook my head.

"You sold your voice for access. You mistook a leash for a collar of honor."

"You don't understand the system," he snapped.

"I do," I said. "That's why we're burning it down."

We didn't stay long. Just long enough to plant a copy of the MANNA Covenant flash drive in every bathroom and slide it onto the media team's server under a disguised file name: "Sunday Graphics 08.19."

Let the truth go viral where his sermon couldn't reach.

That night, Yolanda got a call from a source in DC.

A senator's aide. Young. Nervous.

He'd seen Ezra's name in a Department of Homeland Security memo flagged under "subversive religious rhetoric."

The watchtower had caught the wrong eyes.

"They're calling it digital sedition," the aide said. "Your names are in it. They've tied the Watchtower Network to potential civil unrest."

We'd expected this.

I called a meeting at Donell's place: me, Yolanda, Donell, Rudy "Keys" Jackson, and our new Memphis contact, Simone. She was sharp, perhaps twenty-five, and already building decentralized communication networks in three cities.

"This is where it changes," I told them. "We're past sermons. Past signals. They know we're real. They know we're not going away."

Donell leaned in. "So, what's the move?"

"We split the network. Multiple leaders. No central mouthpiece. We doubled our data encryption. Triple our community organizing."

Yolanda added, "We turn every pulpit that's willing into a mouthpiece for truth. We make it impossible to kill this from the top."

Simone nodded. "The shepherd is dead. But the watchmen are alive."

Before we broke, I pulled out something I hadn't shown anyone yet.

Ezra's last journal entry.

I had scanned it from a tattered notebook Yolanda found at the bottom of his desk drawer.

It read:

"If I am taken, let them know I didn't fall in silence. I blew the trumpet. I named the chains. Let them call it sedition. Let them call it madness. But never let them say I was mute. The shepherd may sleep, but the watchmen must stand."

The room went still.

I looked around at each of them.

"We don't mourn like the world mourns," I said. "We build. We remember. And we rise."

Outside, the sky was black again.

But this time, the crows flew in circles watching.

As if to say: the shepherd has fallen.

But the flock is moving.

And the wolves are running out of time.

Chapter 38
Blue Notes and Bullet Points

By the time morning came, I hadn't slept. I sat on the edge of my bed, shoes still on, and my jacket across my lap like a bulletproof vest I had forgotten to take off. The room smelled like old, musty books, black coffee, and the cologne my uncle used to wear when trying to smell sober.

Donell sent me a text at 6:04 a.m.

They hit Bramble's archive. Fire. Nothing left.

I didn't respond right away. I just stared out the window, watching the blue light of dawn press against the street. Buffalo looks beautiful when something terrible is about to happen, like it's trying to apologize ahead of time.

Bramble had been our elder, the one who still wore Malcolm on his tongue and Baldwin in his eyes. He kept records. Real ones. Names. Documents. He wasn't tech-savvy, but he had a room full of paper that could indict half the council and every faith-based initiative Tremaine had ever funneled funds through.

Now it was ash.

I called Donell. "Any word on Bramble?"

"He's alive. Shaken, but alive. He wasn't home."

"And the records?"

Donell exhaled. "Gone."

I closed my eyes and leaned back. "Then they're desperate."

"Or just getting started."

We called an emergency session of what we were now calling The Watchtower Circle, an inner ring of Watchtower leaders nationwide.

No Zoom. No phones. Face-to-face only, in a library basement off Bailey Avenue that still smelled like the '70s.

Yolanda walked in first, all business. Simone came next with two reps from Atlanta and Detroit. Donell locked the door behind them.

I wrote the word Resurrection on the whiteboard.

"We have to assume we've been infiltrated," I began. "Files, feeds, phone logs, burn it all. Start clean."

Donell nodded. "We go analog. Everything physical. Couriers. Drop locations. Weekly verbal check-ins. If you can't say it to someone's face, don't say it."

Yolanda added, "And we go spiritual. Not just information warfare. This is soul warfare. Tremaine's strength is in the spirit of silence. We weaponize truth and testimony."

Simone stepped forward. "I've got three podcast platforms, five indie radio hosts, and twelve church newsletters ready to push signal. But we need a unified language. A campaign."

She passed around a sheet of paper titled:

Sermons from the Watchtower: 12 Points for a Free Church

I read the first few lines aloud:

- The church without truth is a theater.
- The 501(c)(3) muzzle is not the voice of God.
- Economic justice is spiritual justice.
- A government grant cannot sanctify the silence it requires.

"This is a doctrine," I said.

"It's a fire," Simone replied.

We left the meeting with assignments. I was tasked with initiating The First Broadcast, a public leak of a sermon from Ezra that had never aired. It had been recorded on a tape cassette, found in a box labeled "Only if I'm gone."

It wasn't polished.

It wasn't safe.

It was perfect.

Back at the office, I slid the cassette into an old boombox I kept for nostalgia and hit play.

Ezra's voice came through grainy but alive.

"If you're hearing this, it means I didn't make it. But don't mourn me. Finish me. We were never supposed to be safe in this world. Not when the truth costs this much. You want revival? Then burn the leash. Preach without a muzzle. Love without permission. Organize without waiting. The church must come out of Babylon. We must come out… or rot inside it."

It wasn't just a request. It was a charge. A line drawn in the sand by a man who knew the system would sooner bury him than let him breathe. And now it was my line.

I'd spent years dancing around the edges of purpose, half in, half out, trying to make peace with a God I wasn't sure still wanted me. But hearing Ezra, it was like God cut through the static. Like he'd been watching me dodge my own calling and finally stepped into the room.

This wasn't about playing detective anymore. It wasn't about clearing Ezra's name or even exposing Tremaine. This was redemption work. My redemption.

If it meant I wouldn't make it either, so be it.

I thought about all the nights I'd stared at the bottom of a bottle, thinking I'd run out of chances. I thought about the people I'd let down, the truth I'd kept quiet when I should've spoken. Maybe this was the one thing I could do that would balance the ledger.

Ezra had carried it as far as he could. Now it was my turn.

I whispered to the empty room, "Alright, Ezra. I'll finish you."

It hit me in my chest.

Not grief.

Not guilt.

Something holier.

That night, I stood at the same window I'd watched the crows from a hundred times before.

They weren't there.

Just silence.

And I realized maybe they were waiting on us now.

Chapter 39
"Old School revival."

We launched just after sunrise.

No press release. No tweetstorm. No slick video with piano music and soft lighting.

Just paper.

Stacks of it.

Folded by hand, printed at Truth Press, delivered door to door by the same kids who once ran flyers for church picnics and fish fries. Now they carried revolution in their backpacks. Rolled copies slipped under doors, pinned to barber shop corkboards, tucked behind windshield wipers outside payday loan offices and liquor stores.

The Watchtower Signal.

Black ink on white pages. The mouth where the church had once gone mute.

The first issue began with Ezra's final sermon, which was never aired or edited. It wasn't soundbite theology; it was thunder. His voice and cadence were captured raw from an audio file hidden in a folder marked "Do Not Save."

It started like this:

"The 501(c)(3) tax code is a leash. And some of y'all done got so used to it, you think it's a necklace. That ain't no jewel, saints. That's a shackle dressed in Scripture."

Ezra didn't hold back.

He called out the preachers who'd traded their pulpits for grant money. He named the foundations laundering silence through community partnerships. He spoke of the MANNA Covenant, not as a fantasy, but as a commandment.

"God doesn't need Caesar's permission to bless His people. And we don't need a city permit to tell the truth."

It hit like lightning. Not because it was new. But because it had been buried.

By noon, The Watchtower had gone digital, mirrored across grassroots platforms like Nubian Pulse and Harriet's Signal. No Facebook ads. There was no algorithm, just code, signal boosts, and a sacred kind of word-of-mouth.

And the calls started.

Not the ones from the press.

The ones from the elders.

Those who remembered when sermons could still harm the state.

Some were angry.

Some were crying.

But all of them were awake.

Back at Truth Press, Donell stood at the old printer feeding fresh stacks through.

He looked different in that room, like a soldier who had finally found his battlefield. He wore an oil-streaked shirt, had ink on his hands, and had eyes lit with something righteous.

"They're trying to trace the digital footprint," he said without looking up. "They'll come knocking."

I nodded. "Then we'll just get louder."

He grinned. "Operation Pentecost?"

"Exactly."

That's what we called it, a nod to the Book of Acts, the day the church stopped waiting in upper rooms and started walking through fire with tongues of truth.

We'd broken the first seal.

The next step was scale.

The idea was simple: decentralize everything.

Each city would have its own version of The Signal. Local names. Local faces. One shared blueprint. We sent encrypted packages to Detroit, Atlanta, St. Louis, and Tulsa. Not to influencers. To janitors, crossing guards, barbers, and retired teachers, the ones who knew where the pain lived.

Inside each packet was Ezra's sermon. The MANNA Covenant outline. Instructions for printing. Suggested scripture. A phone number that rang once, then played a recording:

"If you're listening, you've been trusted. Don't let silence steal your voice. This is The Watchtower. You are not alone."

Later that night, I stood on my porch and watched the crows gather again.

Three on the line.

One on the roof.

They didn't cry. They watched.

Like they knew the air had shifted.

Like they were keeping score.

The Watchtower was now out in the world. The MANNA Covenant was breathing. The silence had cracked.

But the storm hadn't passed.

It was coming.

And this time, it would knock on every pulpit that took federal money with one hand and silenced dissent with the other.

I stepped inside and locked the door.

Tomorrow, we'll start naming names.

Tonight, I'd pray.

Not for safety.

But for clarity.

Because when the sky falls silent, and the crows stop watching...

That's when you know the enemy has moved.

And I had work to do before the morning.

Chapter 40
The Audit's

The knock came before sunrise.

Three short raps. Pause. Then two more.

I didn't move. Just watched the shadows stretch long across the floor.

Donell stirred on the couch, one hand already on the piece he kept tucked in his waistband. We didn't talk. We didn't have to.

I peeked through the blinds. Black sedan. Tinted windows. Government plates.

IRS.

Or someone wearing its skin.

The man they sent was too polite. He wore a windbreaker with no logo and a smile that said, "This is just routine."

"Mr. Bushvill," he said, "we're following up on some activity related to business registration violations. Mind if we step inside?"

I didn't let him finish the rest of the sentence. "You can leave the paperwork on the stoop."

He didn't blink. Just tucked a folded form under the welcome mat like we were exchanging takeout.

As he turned to leave, he said, "This isn't about you. Not yet."

Donell exhaled sharply when the car disappeared around the corner. "They're coming faster than I thought."

I nodded. "They're trying to cut the oxygen before we spark anything bigger."

The audit was just the beginning. In the next forty-eight hours:

- The printer at Truth Press jammed permanently. Sabotage.

• Yolanda's phone was cloned. She found out when she called me, and I answered twice.

• One of our community drop spots in Detroit was raided for "code violations."

• And Rudy "Keys" Jackson went missing.

Just like that. Gone.

We called a midnight meeting at the safehouse on Woodlawn.

No lights. No phones inside. Just a circle of chairs, a shared notebook, and the hum of fear we didn't say out loud.

Yolanda was the first to speak. "This is the retaliation phase."

Donell nodded. "They're gonna hit soft targets first. Confuse the channels. Make us doubt the network."

I flipped open the notebook. Inside was a copy of the MANNA Covenant, annotated in Ezra's hand. One note stood out, written in red:

'The machine doesn't bleed when you wound it. It bleeds when you expose it.'

That was the moment I knew what our next move had to be.

Not defense.

Exposure.

Donell had been digging into Sable Equity's deeper holdings. One name kept floating to the top: Marrow Capital Partners.

A private equity group out of D.C., Quiet. Hidden behind a hedge fund that claimed to do "urban revitalization."

In the last ten years, they've bought:

• Twelve Black churches across five states.

• Six community centers.

• Four faith-based rehab programs.

•   And the building that used to house the Monroe Street Community Center, the one Robison Erns once swept clean every morning.

That's when it hit me.

They weren't just buying property.

They were buying memory.

Erasing the places where resistance had once lived.

We crafted our second wave.

If the watchtower Signal had been the trumpet, this would be the scalpel.

We leaked excerpts of the MANNA Covenant to small community radio stations. We had teenage poets reading Ezra's notes between jazz sets. We snuck QR codes into church bulletins that led to hidden pages with maps of church property takeovers and quotes from Frederick Douglass.

And we hacked the Everlasting Truth Ministries livestream.

Right in the middle of Pastor Lionel Gates's Sunday sermon.

The screen went black.

Then Ezra's voice rang out:

"If your church has never made the city nervous, it might not be a church. It might just be a stage."

The live chat froze.

Then it exploded.

Back at the safehouse, we sat in silence. The air was thick with heat and anticipation.

"We just crossed the line," Yolanda whispered.

"No," I said. "They crossed it years ago. We just started drawing one back."

Donell tapped the folder in his lap. "This next part... It's gonna get people hurt."

I met his eyes. "They're already hurting. But now, they'll know why."

Outside, the wind had changed.

The crows hadn't come back yet.

Which meant the system was shifting.

Tremaine had stayed silent since the first Watchtower Signal drop. No message. No move.

But silence was his move.

He was waiting.

Planning.

And we weren't naïve enough to think we'd struck a killing blow.

No.

We'd just let him know we were willing to strike at all.

Chapter 41
The Ones Who Stayed Awake

We called it The Maroon Council.

Not officially. There were no filings, no paperwork, no branded sweatshirts. But word spread, like all sacred things do, without needing permission.

It started with seven young people, mostly students, a few organizers, and one poet who hadn't spoken in front of a crowd until Ezra died. They came not because we promised them safety but because we told them the truth.

The system was built to outlast outrage.

That the church had been compromised.

That survival required memory, not mercy.

Donell called them "the ones who never really fell asleep." I just called them the future.

We met in the basement of a closed charter school on Fillmore. The heating was unreliable, the walls were tagged with ghosts, and every chair wobbled like it had seen better years.

But the spirit?

It was loud.

They brought laptops, maps, burner phones, and routers. One of them, a girl with locs and a t-shirt that read "Read Assata," was building a mesh internet node so that when the city shut off the Wi-Fi, the people could still communicate.

Another had already started designing pamphlets using AI voice mimicry, Ezra's voice reading scripture paired with policy breakdowns and 501(c)(3) warnings.

It wasn't a protest.

It was a counter-sermon.

Yolanda watched from the back, arms crossed, eyes soft.

"They're doing what we never thought we could," she said. "They're not trying to fix the church. They're building one."

I nodded, too full to speak.

Ezra would've wept if he'd seen it. Or maybe he had. In a dream. In a warning. In those long pauses before he answered a question, it was as if he already knew how deep the cut would go.

Donell leaned in. "They wanna push a multi-city signal drop next month. Coordinated. Underground church houses. Spoken word at subway stations. Community breakfasts with lectures on church laundering. They're calling it" he chuckled, "Operation C.R.O.W."

I raised an eyebrow.

"Churches Reclaiming Our Wealth," he said, grinning like a proud uncle.

Back in my office that night, I sat alone with Ezra's drive plugged into the monitor. The crows were outside again, three of them, perched like sentries on the power line.

I whispered something under my breath, not a prayer, but close: We're still coming.

The MANNA Covenant was no longer a document. It had breath, bone, and blood. It lived in the kids cracking code in abandoned classrooms, in the pastors finding their courage again, and in the single mothers printing flyers on their lunch breaks.

And maybe most of all, it lived in the sound of the crows.

Not crying.

Not warning.

Just waiting.

Like Ezra once said, "The crow isn't a prophet of death. It's a witness."

The next day, we tested our first flash signal.

Donell had a burner laptop tethered to four routers in a storage unit in Niagara Falls. The signal bounced through two VPNs, hit a dummy site posing as a Black hair care store, then launched The Watchtower Signal into inboxes tied to every media contact, faith network, and grassroots org on our encrypted list.

The video opened with Ezra's voice:

"They gave us churches to calm us, but the gospel was always a sword."

Ezra's Sermon "Behind the Walls"

"Let me tell you something about complicity," Ezra's voice rang out, low and steady at first, the kind of tone that made you lean in because you knew the next part wasn't going to be easy to hear.

"When a crime happens in the daylight and the guilty wear suits, it doesn't get called a crime, it gets called policy."

"1994. Crime Bill. You know the one. The one Joe Biden put his name on, smiling, shaking hands. The one that came for our men like a harvest. And here's the part that should keep you up at night: they didn't do it alone. Black pastors stood behind it. Black officials signed the dotted line. Some of them prayed over it. And they told you it was for your safety."

He paused, letting the words settle like dust on polished shoes.

"It was estimated that the bill would touch one in three of our men. One in three! Think about your block, your family, your pew. Take three men, remove one. What's left? A home missing a father. A child missing a protector. A woman carrying weight God never intended her to carry alone."

"But what if… what if the Black church had stood together then? What if we had locked arms and said, 'Not this time. Not our men. Not our sons.' What if we had been one voice, one body, one wall the enemy couldn't scale? You think they could have pushed that bill through with a hundred thousand pulpits shouting it down? You think they could have built those private cages as fast as we could have filled the streets with protest and prayer?"

"But we didn't. We stayed behind our walls. We held revivals while the buses came to take our brothers away. We counted tithes while they counted sentencing points. And now, thirty years later, we are watching our children die in these streets, gunned down in our own zip codes, while the church still sits behind those same walls, singing the same songs, waiting for a heaven we could be building right here."

Ezra's voice broke sharp on the last words, but he didn't back away.

"Church, you cannot heal a city you refuse to touch. You cannot claim to shepherd a people you've left in the pasture while the wolves circle. The crime didn't stop with the bill. It lives on every time we stay silent. Every time we trade the cries of our children for the comfort of our walls."

"You want to know why I speak the way I do? Because the crime's still happening. And every pulpit that stays quiet is another accomplice."

Then it cut to archival footage of marches, funerals, and sermons, a map of seized church properties, and audio from Tremaine's men discussing grant compliance tactics.

At the end, one phrase lingered on the screen:

"The sleeping pill wears off when the soul remembers."

We watched it on a projector in the basement.

No one spoke.

One of the council members, a kid named Isaiah with a stutter, stood up and whispered, "Let's do it again."

Donell clapped once. "That's how it starts."

Yolanda added, "And this time, we don't stop."

I walked to my office that night through the fog. Buffalo was thick with it, wet and heavy, swallowing the sound.

I passed three churches. Not one had its lights on.

And yet, I heard music.

Drums. Low. Rhythmic. Familiar.

Someone, somewhere, was preparing for resurrection.

When I got back to the office, I found a letter slid under the door.

Unmarked envelope. No name.

Inside, one sentence written in black ink:

"You've made the top of the list. But so did he."

Taped below it: a photo of Ezra in front of City Hall.

Behind him, in the shadows, was a man I hadn't seen in years.

Armand Tremaine.

Watching.

Smiling.

Waiting.

Chapter 42
The Devil in the Balcony

I held the photo for a long time.

Ezra. City Hall. Tremaine in the background like a shadow that forgot to leave.

It wasn't just surveillance. It was a stage direction. A reminder. Tremaine wasn't hiding. He was watching. He'd been watching.

The crows were back, too, pecking at something in the alley when I left the office that morning. One of them flew up and hovered just long enough to stare me dead in the eyes. Donell called it a warning. I called it a rehearsal. For what, I didn't know yet.

We met Reuben Ellis at a warehouse turned co-op near the Fruit Belt Line. The lawyer who helped Ezra draft the MANNA Covenant looked more tired than before, like sleeping had become a habit he couldn't afford.

"You're on the radar now," he said as I shook his hand. "Congratulations. It's the same list Ezra made. The same one I made."

Yolanda folded her arms. "Then why are you still breathing?"

Reuben offered a half-smile. "I got lucky. A motorcycle accident broke my spine but saved my life. Tremaine's people thought I was dead. I let them keep thinking that."

He handed me a hard copy of the MANNA Covenant annotations, including financial flowcharts and court-ready language, in the margins. "This version goes deeper.

The envelope was heavier than it looked. Yolanda had slid it across my desk without a word, her eyes saying whatever she wasn't ready to say out loud.

Inside was a single stapled document, crisp but worn at the edges. Across the top, bold letters: THE MANNA COVENANT Mutual Aid Network for the New Awakening.

I leaned back, scanning the preamble first. Ezra's voice was in every word: "We will not wait for Pharaoh's rations. We will not bow to Babylon's laws of silence. We will live free, and we will live together."

I'd read manifestos before. This wasn't that. This was a battle plan dressed like scripture.

Then I hit the first line of the first section:

"Each participating congregation will commit 50% of its tithes and offerings to a shared Black Treasury Fund."

I sat up. Fifty percent. Half the money from every plate, envelope, and text-to-give transfer had gone from the bank accounts the pastors were used to controlling to a pooled fund that no government or corporate hand could touch.

I kept reading. The fund would bankroll housing, healthcare, education, legal defense, and small businesses. It would also fund scholarships not just for preachers or seminarians, but for law students. A stable of lawyers, ready to defend the Covenant in court and write laws of its own.

Ezra wasn't just building a network of churches. He was building a parallel government.

I read about the Covenant Learning Centers, about youth being taught Black history, African heritage, finance, and law. About the Watchmen assigned to monitor systemic threats. About a political clause that cut both parties off at the knees, no endorsements for any candidate who had a record of harming Black communities.

Then I hit the part that explained why Tremaine would see this as a personal threat:

"Churches in the Covenant will refuse grants or funding that restrict our ability to preach the whole truth or organize our communities. We will not be silent in exchange for Babylon's bread."

That was the knife to the gut for men like Tremaine. Cut off the grant money, cut off the leverage. Without that leash, pastors could speak freely or, worse, organize freely.

By the time I reached the closing declaration, I knew exactly why this document hadn't seen daylight.

"…We will be the wilderness table where our people eat, drink, learn, defend, and rise in strength until no one can take from us again."

I set it down slowly.

This wasn't a covenant. It was a loaded weapon.

And in a city like ours, you didn't leave a weapon like this lying around unless you were ready to use it.

The MANNA Covenant

(Mutual Aid Network for the New Awakening)

Preamble:

"Just as the Lord fed Israel in the wilderness with manna, so too will we feed, protect, and sustain one another in this wilderness of injustice. We will not wait for Pharaoh's rations. We will not bow to Babylon's laws of silence. We will live free, and we will live together."
Ezra Abrams

1. Mutual Provision

• Each participating congregation will commit 50% of its tithes and offerings to a shared Black Treasury Fund.

• This fund will provide emergency support for housing, healthcare, education, legal defense, and business start-ups for members of the Covenant.

• The Treasury will operate with full transparency to its members, but no government oversight and no corporate sponsorship — funded by us, for us.

2. Economic Sanctuaries

• We will build community-owned businesses, grocery stores, clinics, credit unions that keep our dollars in our neighborhoods.

- Members of the Covenant commit to buy Black, bank Black, and hire Black whenever possible.

3. Education for Liberation

- Establish Covenant Learning Centers within our churches to provide after-school tutoring, adult literacy programs, and vocational training.

- Teach Black history, African heritage, and civic rights alongside practical skills, finance, entrepreneurship, and trades.

- Train our youth in media literacy to counter propaganda, and prepare them to lead in technology, law, policy, and the arts.

- Educate our members on legal rights, court processes, and self-advocacy, so no one stands before a judge alone or uninformed.

- No child in the Covenant will be left behind to the mercy of underfunded public systems we will teach our own until our children outgrow the limits placed on them.

4. Legal Guard

- Cultivate a stable of lawyers within the Covenant funded scholarships for law students, mentorship programs, and guaranteed legal work upon graduation.

- Maintain a rotating roster of defense attorneys, civil rights lawyers, and policy advocates ready to defend our members in court, challenge unjust laws, and draft our own.

- Deploy these lawyers not only in crisis, but in legislative rooms, city councils, and negotiations shifting us from reactive defense to proactive power.

5. Political Independence

- No pulpit within the Covenant will endorse a candidate tied to policies that harm Black communities, regardless of party.

- All churches will vet local and national legislation as a united body before it passes, and speak publicly against laws that threaten our people.

6. No Sleeping Pill Doctrine

- Churches in the Covenant will refuse grants or funding that restrict our ability to preach the whole truth or organize our communities.

- We will not be silent in exchange for Babylon's bread.

7. Watchmen at the Gate

- Every church will appoint Watchmen to monitor systemic threats police violence, predatory lending, school closings and alert the network immediately.

- All information will be shared through a secure communication system across the Covenant.

8. Unity of Purpose

- Disagreements between churches will be resolved internally, with reconciliation as the goal.

- Division is a weapon of our enemies; unity is our shield.

Closing Declaration:

"We enter this Covenant knowing that manna was given daily enough for the day, enough for the journey. We will not hoard; we will not withhold. We will be the wilderness table where our people eat, drink, learn, defend, and rise in strength until no one can take from us again, and the church pews will fill up again."

Signed this day,

I flipped to a page marked with a red paperclip. The heading read: Faith-Based Fiscal Compliance: The New Plantation.

Later that night, Donell and I met at The Maroon Council's usual spot. The youth had transformed the basement into a war room with whiteboards, projectors, and encrypted devices. They had diagrams of Tremaine's influence mapped like a disease: churches, banks, schools, even hospitals.

A girl named Amari presented the newest connection.

"This man," she said, pointing to an older councilman in a suit, "was on the advisory board of a nonprofit that funneled money into Sable Equity. Guess who wrote the bylaws?"

She clicked the mouse.

"Armand Tremaine."

The whole room exhaled.

We planned our next move: simultaneous micro-sermons broadcast from underground cell towers. Preachers outside the 501(c)(3) system. Three-minute messages. Truth with no tax leash.

I was slated to deliver the first.

I hadn't preached in years.

The church I chose was the last one Ezra ever spoke.

They'd since replaced the sign out front. Removed his name from the plaque. Painted over the mural he'd helped design.

But they hadn't cleared the balcony.

I climbed up there thirty minutes before the signal drop. Sat in the same spot where Ezra used to pray before he preached. The wood still had a dent where his cane leaned.

I pulled the mic from my coat and synced it to the transmitter.

Donell's voice crackled through my earpiece. "You're live in three... two..."

I stood.

"My name is Harris Bushvill," I began. "And this is not a sermon. It's a severance."

I paused.

"For too long, we've confused obedience with salvation. We've confused comfort with covenant. But real faith is not silent. It cannot be leased. It cannot be filed under section 501(c)(3)."

The youth in the war room cheered quietly behind their laptops.

"I come not to preach revival but rebellion. Not against God. But against the men who wear His name like a mask and His people like a chain."

I ended with Ezra's words:

"The gospel was always a sword. Some of y'all just got used to being stabbed by it."

Then the line went dead.

I left through the back alley.

The same crow from earlier sat on the dumpster, watching.

"Not tonight," I told it.

It cawed once, then flew off toward the lake.

Back at my office, the power flickered. I reached for the flashlight, but the door creaked before I could touch it.

Donell stood there.

"They took down three of the broadcast spots," he said. "Two others stayed up. One preacher in Detroit called out the IRS by name. Went viral in two hours."

"Damage?"

He shrugged. "Too early to say."

We sat in silence.

Finally, he pulled a flask from his coat and handed it to me.

"Tonic water," he said. "But if we make it through this, I'll buy you the good stuff."

I took a sip. Bitter. Clean.

Like truth.

On my desk was another envelope.

No return address.

Inside: a screenshot.

Ezra's face blurred in surveillance walking into a building we hadn't identified yet.

But at the corner of the photo, partially visible, was a sign:

"RESTORATION BANK COMING SOON."

Donell leaned over my shoulder. "You are thinking what I'm thinking?"

I nodded. "Ezra was about to launch a financial weapon.

The crow outside shrieked once, then fell silent.

Chapter 43
The Bank That Wasn't Supposed to Exist

The sign in the photo had been half-obscured, like God Himself had redacted it.

RESTORATION BANK COMING SOON

Ezra had been standing just outside the entrance, not smiling, not posing, just waiting, like he knew something was about to begin. Or end.

We traced the image metadata back to an industrial district off Bailey Avenue near the old freight yard. It was the kind of place you'd never look twice at, and that was the point.

Donell drove. Neither of us spoke.

When we arrived, there was no sign, just a crumbling red brick warehouse with faded graffiti and boarded-up windows. But something buzzed under the surface. The locks were new, the cameras were wireless, and there were fresh tire tracks in the snowless gravel.

We circled back to the rear alley and slipped through a broken door someone had tried too neatly to disguise.

Inside, the past whispered.

The smell hit first cedar and ink. Then the silence.

It wasn't abandoned. It was paused.

Chairs still arranged. Paper still stacked. A black filing cabinet hummed like it had never stopped guarding secrets.

"This is it," Donell whispered.

The space had been divided into three rooms: the lobby, the office, and the vault. The vault door was open.

Inside, we found rows of safety deposit boxes, most of which were empty. But one sat labeled with Ezra's handwriting:

REDEEM THE TITHE.

Donell cracked it open with bolt cutters we'd packed in the trunk. Inside was a black satchel and a handwritten letter.

If you're reading this, I'm gone.

And if I'm gone, it means I didn't back down.

Inside this satchel is the paperwork, routing codes, and contacts for The MANNA Bank. This isn't charity. It's justice. We've tithed to silence long enough.

Now let us tithe to liberation.

—Ezra

We brought the satchel back to the office and locked the door behind us. Yolanda, Reuben, and Amari were waiting.

When Donell dumped the contents onto the table, it wasn't just routing numbers and contact sheets; it was infrastructure a fully mapped plan for a digital banking cooperative built outside the federal system, utilizing blockchain validation and Black-owned credit unions as satellite nodes.

Ezra had named it The Covenant Ledger.

The title page read:

MANNA Digital Banking Cooperative – Independent Economic Network

"Wealth without permission. Power without leash." Ezra Abrams

I scrolled through.

Step One: Every participating church redirects 50% of its tithes and offerings to the Black Treasury Fund.

Step Two: Funds are distributed into satellite accounts at Black-owned credit unions, each acting as a node in the network.

Step Three: Transactions are recorded on a private blockchain ledger, validated by multiple nodes to prevent fraud or external tampering.

There were diagrams illustrating how it worked: one showing the local church deposit being fed into its "home" credit union, and another showing the blockchain ledger verifying transactions across the network in real-time.

The kicker?

Phase Two – Public Wallet Integration: A mobile app already in prototype, allowing members to send or receive funds directly, bypassing traditional banks altogether.

And then there was the most dangerous section, Legal Containment Strategies.

A memo from Reuben Ellis outlined how the network would be incorporated under a cooperative non-profit shield, using multiple jurisdictions to make it nearly impossible for the IRS to freeze funds without triggering a lawsuit in every state where a node existed.

It wasn't just banking. It was an economic recession.

The file even had marketing materials, a draft flyer with Ezra's picture:

"MANNA: Our Money, Our Future. Join the network. Build the gate. Fund the freedom."

I leaned back in my chair, and the weight of it settled over me. This wasn't a vision board. This wasn't a plan waiting for someone to give it the green light.

This was infrastructure.

It was ready.

And it explained everything why Tremaine's feeders were tracking me, why Yolanda carried the ledger like it was a live grenade, why Ezra had been killed before he could take the next step.

Because if this were launched, it wouldn't just threaten Tremaine's cut.

It would make his whole operation obsolete.

Donell leaned in, scanning the diagrams. "These nodes are real?"

"Two churches. One credit union. Already running."

He let out a low whistle and pulled up a chair. "Alright, let me tell you why this scares people like Tremaine and not just Tremaine. This is the kind of thing that gets your name on watchlists."

I didn't say anything, just let him work.

"First," Donell tapped the screen, "Fifty percent tithes. That means every pastor who signs on is cutting their personal budget in half. No more shiny SUVs, no more padded 'building funds.' That alone makes enemies inside the church."

He scrolled down to the blockchain flowchart. "Second, this ledger? The second the money hits the Treasury, it's clean. Untraceable by the feds because there's no federal bank in the loop. Tremaine can't skim it. Politicians can't freeze it without triggering fifty lawsuits at once."

He opened the "Legal Containment" memo. "Third, this right here? Ellis is playing chess. He's using multi-state incorporation like body armor. To shut this down, you'd have to fight in every jurisdiction at once, and each fight drains their budget while the network keeps running."

Donell leaned back, eyes narrowing. "And then you got the app. That's the nail in the coffin. If the second generation can send money directly to each other's phones without Bank of America or Chase in the middle, the entire control grid cracks. No overdraft fees. No approvals. No waiting period for bail money or legal retainers. A cop snatches somebody up on Friday night, they're out before sunrise, no fundraising, no begging a judge."

I was already thinking it, but hearing him say it made it heavier. "It's freedom money."

He nodded. "And that's the one thing they can't afford to let circulate. You move money like this, you move power. And once power shifts, the people holding it now? They can't get it back without blood."

We sat in the office's hum for a moment. Outside, the street was quiet except for the rumble of a bus and the faint flap of wings overhead.

"Question is," Donell said finally, "now that you've seen it, what will you do with it? Cause I can tell you one thing, Tremaine already knows you have it."

I glanced at the screen one more time. Ezra's words glared back at me from the flyer: Our Money, Our Future.

"I think," I said, "we're past the point of doing nothing."

"This isn't just a bank," Yolanda said, eyes scanning the packet. "It's a sovereign economy."

Reuben nodded. "It's the kind of thing that got Marcus Garvey deported. The kind of thing that made King start talking about redistribution before he was murdered."

Amari pulled up a laptop and typed in one of the server codes. A secure site is loaded.

It launched.

"You understand what this means?" I said to the room.

"We've got to protect it," Donell answered. "But we also need to use it."

I nodded. "Not just to hold money but to fund the Watchtower Network. Community media, street clinics, food security teams, housing cooperatives."

Reuben spoke slowly. "It'll make us targets."

"We already are," I said. "We're just deciding whether we'll be targets with leverage or with nothing but prayers."

Amari looked up. "If we go live with this… Tremaine will show his face."

Donell nodded. "Good. I'm tired of shadows."

We spent the next seventy-two hours replicating the ledger data and encrypting copies across trusted nodes in three cities, seven platforms, and two off-grid servers. If they hit us, we'd rise again. That was the promise.

I broadcast a midnight message on the fourth night through The Brown Channel.

I didn't use my name.

"The Restoration Bank is real.

The Covenant is real.

Your tithe is no longer chained to silence.

It is now your weapon.

Use it.

Or lose it."

We watched the views climb: 10,000. Then 100,000. Then 1000,000.

By sunrise, our inbox was full.

Questions. Volunteers. Congregations asking how to join.

At 8:13 AM, my burner phone buzzed.

Unknown number.

I answered.

The voice was low. Unhurried.

"You've opened a door you can't close, Mr. Bushvill."

I didn't speak.

"You were warned. Ezra was warned. And yet… here we are."

I leaned back in my chair. "If you're going to make a threat, make it interesting."

"No threat," the voice said. "Just letting you know the sermon's over. The judgment begins now."

I stared out the window. A single crow flew past. Not circling. Just moving.

No audience. No applause.

Just a black silhouette against a gray sky.

Watching.

Waiting.

Chapter 44
The Sermon

We didn't light the match.

We just stopped hiding the gasoline.

That was the message Donell left with every pastor who called and every Black-owned bank that emailed asking if this was real. Reuben stayed up three nights straight writing the legal framework for local church buy-in. Yolanda recorded an orientation video in her living room: plain backdrop, no filter, just truth.

"This ain't a hustle," she said. "This is an exodus."

Within a week, we had over sixty churches expressing interest. Most were small storefronts, house gatherings, or pop-up ministries. But that's who Ezra built this for. Not the stadium preachers with ten-man entourages. The foot-washers. The food-bank faithful. Those who never appeared in the city budget report but knew the names of every elder on their block.

The sleeping church was stirring.

And Tremaine felt it.

The blowback didn't start with a bullet or a break-in.

It started with a nationwide press release.

"Local Extremists Linked to Unauthorized Financial Platform."

They named no one. They didn't have to.

We were called radicals. Disruptors. A "potential threat to municipal cohesion."

The Restoration Bank was labeled "unregulated" and "potentially fraudulent."

They even used our own language against us.

A tithe of resistance.

Reparations without permission.

They quoted Ezra without saying his name.

It was the kind of calculated smear that didn't need to prove anything; it just needed to plant doubt.

Then the banks started freezing accounts.

Amari called from the office. "Regions pulled their support. Chase flagged Donell's name. And the App Store just delisted Nubian Pulse."

I didn't curse. I didn't scream.

I opened the window and listened.

Nothing but wind.

And crows.

"We expected this," I said during the team call that night. "They can't kill the story, so they'll kill the platform."

Reuben leaned in. "Then we move back to analog. If they want a digital war, we give 'em something older. Flyers. Street teams. Spoken word. Cassette tape energy."

Yolanda smiled. "The gospel got here on foot. It'll survive this."

Donell looked at me. "We're still good on backups?"

I nodded. "Three mirrored servers. Two cold storage drives. One off-grid rig at the Harriet House."

"Then we've got what we need," he said.

At 2:47 a.m., I got the next call.

This time, it was personal.

"This is Tremaine," the voice said.

He didn't sound how I imagined. No snake oil. No growl. Just… smooth.

Like silk over a knife.

"You made your point," he said. "Now it's time to bow out."

I waited.

"I can make you disappear quietly. Or I can make your movement implode spectacularly. Choose your cross, Mr. Bushvill."

I kept my voice steady.

"I didn't come for a cross. I came for the keys."

Click.

By sunrise, five more churches joined.

By noon, the Brown Channel was broadcasting again through an independent server in Ghana.

That afternoon, Reuben leaked internal grant emails showing city officials redirecting funds from Black-owned youth orgs into white-led nonprofits with "cultural competency language."

One quote stood out:

"Let them preach. They're easier to manage when they're shouting into a microphone than sitting on a zoning board."

Ezra's voice echoed like a ghost through time.

They don't fear our praise. They fear our plans.

That night, Yolanda and I sat in the parking lot outside New Morning Church, one of the first to join the Covenant. The moon was full. The crows were quiet.

She turned to me.

"You ever wonder if we'll make it to the other side of this?"

"Every day," I said. "But then I remember what Ezra said."

"What's that?"

I looked up at the glowing steeple, the paint peeling, but the light holding.

"He said sometimes God doesn't part the sea. Sometimes he sets the water on fire and says, 'Walk anyway.'"

She smiled, then leaned her head on my shoulder.

We didn't speak after that.

We just listened.

To the silence.

To the waiting.

To the world about to catch flame.

Chapter 45
Liberation Sunday

It wasn't an uprising. Not yet. But it was a hum under the floorboards, a long-awaited murmur turned movement.

We called it Liberation Sunday.

No press releases. No social media countdowns. No slick branding. Just word of mouth, encrypted messages, and handwritten bulletins were passed from pastor to pastor, much like communion. The goal was straightforward: every church in the Restoration Covenant would deliver the same sermon at the same time on the same day.

The subject?

The Sleeping Pill.

Ezra's phrase. His fire.

The message: the gospel we were taught had been drugged. The church had been domesticated and rendered harmless by tax exemptions, prosperity grifts, and patriotism wrapped in scripture. And the same institutions that once feared our organizing had now learned how to subsidize our silence.

That Sunday, we were going to say it out loud.

Donell met me at the warehouse on Fillmore, where we kept our print operations. He looked like he hadn't slept, but his eyes still burned with that old street energy, the kind that made threats feel like invitations.

"We've got confirmations from eighty-nine churches," he said. "Twelve cities. Twenty-two states."

"Canada?"

"Three congregations in Toronto. One's got a Black queer activist choir. Ezra would've loved that."

I smiled. "He would've cried."

Donell smirked. "And then called it biblical."

We both laughed, for the first time in days.

Then I got serious. "Tremaine?"

"Scrambling. They're trying to get ahead of the story. Leak counter-sermons. Remind folks about tax compliance. One bishop in Atlanta just told his flock that 'true obedience is patriotic.'"

I winced. "That's the drug talking."

Donell opened a crate and handed me a folder. "These are the pulpits. Every sermon has the same spine, but each preacher has their own verses to weave in. Personal touch."

"What about Everlasting Truth?" I asked.

He shook his head. "Still quiet. Too quiet."

We coordinated the rollout like a choir setlist. Harlem at 9:00 a.m., Chicago at 10:00, Oakland at noon. Buffalo was last. Prime time.

Reuben called it a symphony of truth.

Yolanda called it war in a whisper.

At 10:03 a.m., my phone lit up. A small church in Tallahassee had just gone live. The pastor, Sister Lenora Wright, was preaching about the tithe as a protest.

"…we give, not because we're obedient, but because we're building something they can't tax, touch, or take."

Amen.

At 11:15, word came from Detroit. Pastor Malcolm Liles read from Ezra's notes directly:

"The 501(c) (3) was never about partnership. It was a leash with gold threading. And when a man loves his leash, he forgets how to run."

By noon, we had more than sixty pulpits on livestream.

Some were interrupted. One in Baltimore lost audio. A storefront in Cincinnati had its power cut mid-sermon. But most kept going.

The gospel was moving without permission.

I stood in the balcony of New Morning Church, watching Yolanda deliver our city's sermon. She wasn't flashy. She didn't shout.

But she was surgical.

"There is a doctrine," she said, "that tells us to endure, not resist. To obey, not organize. It calls itself holy. But it smells like Rome."

A murmur rippled through the room.

"The Sleeping Pill," she continued, "was administered to our grandparents through 'integration.' It was given to our fathers through grants and city partnerships. And now, they offer it to our children through Instagram theology and pacified faith."

She stepped back from the podium, eyes glassy.

"But I believe the body is waking up."

Silence.

Then a single voice from the back: "So do I."

Then another: "Amen."

Then a roar.

Not of chaos. Not of protest.

Of clarity.

Outside, the air felt different.

Tremaine's network had money, media, and silence.

But we had something else.

Momentum.

At midnight, we gathered back at the office. The board was covered in pins, each with a pulpit that flipped the script.

Amari pulled out a bottle of ginger ale. "This counts as communion?"

"Tonight it does," I said.

Donell raised his glass. "To Ezra. And to the churches that finally said something real."

"To waking up," Yolanda added.

And we drank.

That night, I didn't sleep.

Not because of fear.

Because I knew what was next.

Tremaine wouldn't sit this out.

He would respond. With something bold. Something brutal.

But I was ready.

Liberation Sunday was not a finale.

It was a declaration.

And the Watchtower was still lit.

Chapter 46
The Fire Sermon

Tremaine didn't strike with a bullet. That would've been too loud, too final. He struck with the discrediting of his favorite weapon. And this time, he aimed it straight at Donell.

It started with a blog post.

Anonymous. Sloppy grammar. Just enough truth to feel dangerous. "Former convict turned activist caught laundering funds through Watchtower shell accounts." It was posted at 6:17 a.m., and by 8:00, it had been picked up by a half-dozen "urban watchdog" platforms.

Yolanda called me in a panic. "They're framing him, Harris. They're trying to break the movement by making our cleanest brother look dirty."

"He's not clean," I said, already reaching for my laptop. "He's honest. That's what makes him dangerous."

The documents attached to the article were doctored sloppily. Donell's signature was cut and pasted from old court transcripts and applied to fake ledgers and cash deposit slips. But to the untrained eye, it looked convincing.

Tremaine was testing the network, testing us.

He didn't just want to stop the message.

He wanted to divide the messengers.

Donell walked into the warehouse just as I scanned the metadata of the files. "They're amateur," I told him. "Whoever made these didn't even scrub the time stamps. The documents were created two days ago on a Mac registered to an LLC in Arlington. It traces back to a consulting firm tied to the city."

Donell didn't flinch. "So, this is what retaliation looks like."

I nodded. "Not with violence. With shame. With suggestion."

He sat down, tired but not broken. "Ezra used to say, you don't have to kill a prophet to silence him. Just question his character enough, and the crowd will do the rest."

"They're scared," I said. "Liberation Sunday worked."

Donell looked me in the eye. "Then we double down."

That afternoon, we dropped the Fire Sermon.

Ezra's voice was pulled from old audio files and blended with new footage. A voiceover, layered with images from the movement, the Restoration Covenant blueprint, and the footage from Liberation Sunday. It ran for fifteen minutes.

Donell edited it himself.

We pushed it through our underground media network, The Brown Channel, Harriet's Signal, Nubian Pulse, and The Watchtower's secure stream.

No sponsors. No monetization. Just truth.

Ezra's voice rang out like thunder in a quiet room.

"If they kill your name, stand anyway.

If they lie on your record, walk anyway.

If they shame your past, preach anyway.

Because the fire isn't in the sermon, it's in the living."

The sermon ended with a simple slide:

We Will Not Be Silent.

By nightfall, hashtags had already started trending:

#DonellStands

#RestorationFire

#EzrasCovenant

And then came the counterstrikes.

One city threatened to freeze funding to churches "in violation of federal tax compliance."

A known pastor in D.C. publicly condemned the Watchtower Network, calling it "radical and dangerous."

Two smaller churches were evicted from their properties, leases quietly revoked by landlords tied to Sable Equity Holdings.

But something Tremaine hadn't counted on happened.

People didn't run.

They stood.

And Donell?

He became the face of the resistance.

Late that night, Yolanda came by the office. She had a look in her eye somewhere between grief and pride. "This is becoming what Ezra hoped," she said.

"He always hoped was," I replied. "The world just caught up."

She walked to the board and pinned a photograph of Ezra in mid-sermon, hand raised, sweat on his brow.

"We can't let this die."

"We won't," I said. "But we've got to be smarter."

Donell stepped in from the other room, holding a new draft of Ezra's third-stage plan. "You two ready to move past sermons?"

I raised an eyebrow. "What's next?"

He dropped the folder on the table.

Phase Three: Economic Exodus.

Ezra's plan wasn't just theological. It was tactical.

A collective divestment. A credit union charter. A mutual aid web across every participating church. Exit strategies from federal partnerships. Legal shields. Land trusts.

The Restoration Covenant was only the beginning.

The Fire Sermon had bought us time. Now it was time to buy our freedom.

Together.

Chapter 47
Exodus Math

You don't announce an exodus with a press release.

You whisper it through barbershops. You fold it into prayers for fellowship hall. You bake it into the sweet potato pies at repast dinners and hum it through the final verse of a benediction. That's how we began.

Phase Three was never about protest signs or fiery tweets. It was about disappearing from the system that fed off us, one account, one dollar, one voice at a time. Ezra had drawn it out in plain language. Don't ask to leave the plantation; walk off quietly with the other field hands and take the tools with you.

We called it The Exodus Math.

The numbers had always been there.

Sixty million Black people in America. Roughly half are affiliated with a church. Multiply that by ten million households, and you have a sleeping economic giant, twenty billion dollars moving through pulpits annually. And most of it was tied up in sermons and stage lights, in mortgages and megachurch mortgages. Not movement. Not freedom.

Ezra had written in his notes:

Restoration Covenant National Plan

Annual Budget: $20,000,000,000

Time Horizon: 10 years (with measurable outcomes every 2–3 years)

Guiding Principles:

• Economic Independence – Circulating dollars inside the community before they leave.

- Institutional Power – Creating structures that endure beyond individuals.

- Cultural Integrity – Rooting progress in FBA history, values, and identity.

- Generational Transfer – Ensuring children inherit assets, not just memories.

Phase 1 — Foundation & Stabilization (Years 1–3)

Goal: Stop the economic bleeding, stabilize vulnerable households, and create the base for sustainable growth.

Budget Allocation: $5.2B/year (~32.5% of budget)

1. Debt Relief & Credit Repair ($1.2B)

o Establish community credit unions to consolidate high-interest debt into low-interest, no-fee loans.

o Free credit repair and financial literacy counseling.

2. Black-Owned Bank Expansion ($800M)

o Expand existing Black-owned banks and establish 10 new regional banks in underserved cities.

o Guarantee deposits with Covenant-backed insurance.

3. Housing Security Fund ($1.5B)

o Buy and rehab foreclosed properties for affordable ownership by FBA families.

o Partner with Black contractors for renovation work.

4. Community Food & Health Hubs ($800M)

o Build or retrofit centers combining grocery co-ops, urgent care, and mental health clinics.

5. Emergency Assistance Reserve ($900M)

o Rapid deployment grants for disaster relief, prevention, and medical emergencies.

Phase 2 — Infrastructure & Workforce Development (Years 3–6)

Goal: Build the backbone of self-sufficiency — jobs, skills, and essential services owned by the community.

Budget Allocation: $5.6B/year (~35% of budget)

1. Vocational Training & Apprenticeships ($1.2B)

o Partner with unions and Black tradespeople to train in construction, electrical, plumbing, welding, coding, and renewable energy.

2. FBA Business Accelerator ($1.5B)

o Provide grants and low-interest loans for Black-owned businesses in strategic sectors (construction, agriculture, tech, manufacturing, logistics).

3. Transportation & Logistics Cooperatives ($900M)

o Establish trucking, delivery, and rideshare co-ops owned and operated by FBA workers.

4. School-to-Enterprise Pipeline ($1B)

o Charter schools with a STEM/entrepreneurship focus and guaranteed post-graduation internships.

5. Healthcare Workforce Initiative ($1B)

o Fund nursing, physician assistant, and medical technician training to place FBA professionals in underserved areas.

Phase 3 — Political Leverage & Cultural Restoration (Years 6–10)

Goal: Convert economic power into political influence and cultural protection.

Budget Allocation: $3.2B/year (~20% of budget)

1. FBA Policy Institute ($500M)

o National think tank to produce policy proposals and lobby for reparations, economic protections, and civil rights enforcement.

2. Media & Narrative Ownership ($900M)

o Fund FBA-owned news outlets, film production companies, streaming platforms, and social media spaces.

3. Land & Agriculture Fund ($800M)

o   Purchase farmland for FBA food sovereignty projects.

o   Teach sustainable farming to youth in urban and rural areas.

4. Legal Defense Network ($500M)

o   National legal team for civil rights, voting rights, and wrongful convictions.

5. FBA Cultural Archives & Museums ($500M)

o   Preserve, teach, and celebrate FBA history through physical and digital spaces.

Ongoing Reserves & Contingency Funds

Budget Allocation: $2B/year (~12.5% of budget)

•   Covers inflation, market fluctuations, and emergency scaling for successful programs.

Projected Impact (10 Years)

•   Homeownership: +25% in FBA households.

•   Black-Owned Business Growth: 200% increase in sustainable enterprises.

•   Employment: Reduction in FBA unemployment to under 4%.

•   Economic Circulation: Average FBA dollar circulates 8–10 times before leaving the community.

•   Political Representation: Doubling of elected officials openly advocating FBA-specific policy.

"Our wealth isn't missing. It's just misassigned."

"Fourteen to sixteen billion," he began. "That's how much we give every year in tithes and offerings through the Black church in America. That's not an estimate, that's the truth.

And here's the other truth: right now, most of it is going to maintain buildings, pay salaries, and keep the lights on in sanctuaries that can't light up our communities.

But if we united that money, if we pooled it into one covenant fund, we could rebuild the FBA nation inside a nation. And I'm going to tell you exactly how."

In his notes, he wrote down Micah 3:11, and it read:

"Her leaders judge for a bribe, her priests teach for a price, and her prophets tell fortunes for money. Yet they lean on the Lord and say, 'Is not the Lord among us? No disaster will come upon us.'"

"That's us now. Bought pulpits, rented prophets. A gospel of comfort when God gave us a gospel of conquest. And I mean conquest over poverty, over ignorance, over systems designed to break us.

So here's my blueprint, and if I'm gone when you hear this, take it and run with it."

Phase One: Foundation and Stabilization (Years 1–3)

Ezra leaned forward, resting his elbows on the desk.

"First, we stop the bleeding. Five-point-two billion a year goes into stabilizing our people.

We eliminate predatory debt by creating FBA-owned credit unions that consolidate high-interest loans into low or no-interest loans. We also fix credit scores for free.

We expanded into ten new black-owned banks in the first three years, specifically in cities where the nearest bank is now a liquor store.

We spend one and a half billion dollars a year to buy back foreclosed homes, rehab them with our own contractors, and sell them back to FBA families at cost.

We bring together fresh food, urgent care, and mental health services in the same building as community hubs that nourish both your body and your spirit.

And we keep nine hundred million in a rapid-response fund so no family in our network ever faces eviction or a medical crisis alone."

Phase Two: Infrastructure and Workforce (Years 3–6)

He sat back, his tone sharpening.

"The next three years, we will build the spine. Five-point-six billion a year goes into jobs, training, and industry.

We offer apprenticeships in a range of trades, including construction, electrical, plumbing, welding, coding, and green energy. Our young people will know how to build, fix, and own.

We launch a business accelerator, offering grants and loans to Black-owned companies in construction, technology, agriculture, and manufacturing.

We start FBA-owned trucking and delivery co-ops, so the supply chain is in our hands.

We open charter schools that don't just teach to tests; they teach ownership, they teach enterprise, and they guarantee internships upon graduation.

And we train our own medical workforce nurses, techs, assistants, placing them in underserved neighborhoods so we're not begging for help from outside."

Phase Three: Political Leverage and Cultural Restoration (Years 6–10)

Ezra's voice dropped low now, the way a man speaks when the next words might get him killed.

"The last phase, three-point-two billion a year, is where the fight shifts from survival to sovereignty.

We build a policy institute, our think tank to write the laws we need, and a lobbying arm to get them passed. Reparations. Land protection. Economic safeguards for FBA communities.

We invest nearly a billion dollars in FBA-owned media newsrooms, film companies, and streaming platforms, ensuring that outsiders can't rewrite our stories.

We buy farmland, so our food supply isn't in somebody else's hands. We teach our children about farming so they know where their meals come from.

We build a national legal defense network to support civil rights cases, address wrongful convictions, and combat voter suppression. If they touch one of us, they answer to all of us.

And we create archives and museums so our history is preserved, taught, and never erased."

Ezra paused, looking into the lens like he could see who'd be watching years later.

"Some of you will say, 'Ezra, that's too much money.' No, it's the money we already give. The problem is we're giving it to a system that eats it and gives nothing back.

We have to unionize our churches. We have to centralize the tithes. We have to stop thinking like customers in God's house and start thinking like shareholders in His kingdom."

He leaned closer now, his voice tightening into something like a dare.

"They've feminized our men and hardened our women because they know divided households are weak households. They've traded our fight for LED lighting and a dopamine rush.

You want Jesus? Jesus wasn't a stage act. He flipped the tables. He made a whip. He drove the thieves out of the temple.

So either you're flipping tables with Him, or you're sitting with the ones counting coins while they rob your people."

Ezra placed both hands flat on the desk.

"This is the plan. It works if we work it. Sixteen billion a year. Ten years. Economic independence. Institutional power. Cultural integrity. Generational transfer.

If I'm not here when you hear this, don't let it die with me. The enemy will tell you to pray about it instead of doing it. Don't fall for that.

Faith without works is dead.

Now go do the work."

In the silence afterward, you could almost hear the weight of what he'd just laid down, not a sermon, but a will. A covenant.

And if you were in the room when it was read, you knew two things:

He meant every word.

And the people he was talking about would kill to keep it from happening.

Donell built the first ledger, a parallel economy framework. It wasn't flashy. It was simple. Mutual aid funds were tracked anonymously through encrypted platforms. Food co-ops were established in abandoned storefronts. Legal clinics were funded with tithes. Land was bought in trust.

Yolanda, whose gift had always been seeing the soul in the structure, organized the ten-member Exodus Circles inside each church, committing to redirecting resources every Sunday. They pooled rent, groceries, and childcare funds not for charity, but for sovereignty. You helped the person beside you because you knew they'd help you when the lights got cut or the landlord knocked twice.

It wasn't socialism.

It was FBA sovereignty and survival.

The old heads said it reminded them of what the church used to be before 501(c)(3), before pastors became CEOs, before revival looked like concert lighting and fog machines.

But not everybody was happy.

Some pastors bucked. Some threatened excommunication. One even called Ezra a "false prophet of economic rebellion" during a televised sermon.

Didn't matter.

We weren't playing their game anymore.

We had our own.

Word got out.

Not through news outlets, they wouldn't touch us.

But through whispers. Crow feathers tied to doorknobs. USB drives dropped in offering baskets. QR codes scribbled on bus stops that led to sermons you couldn't find on YouTube, and lessons about tithes becoming tools.

We built a data farm underneath a closed-down bingo hall. Called it The Nest.

The crows started coming back everywhere.

Symbol by design. Reminder by presence.

And that's when Tremaine struck again.

A dozen churches received sudden IRS audits.

Two community credit unions had their FDIC applications frozen.

A bishop in Atlanta who'd quietly pledged his entire network to the Covenant was arrested on a 20-year-old charge for "financial misconduct." Old, stale, and timed to the second.

And yet… no one flinched.

They saw the game now.

The system had gone from seducing us to surveilling us, from inviting us in to locking the gates behind us.

The Exodus was on.

Donell and I met at The Nest just after midnight, weeks into Phase Three.

He looked tired. Not defeated. Just carrying.

"You think we're ready?" he asked, running a hand over his face.

I looked at the map we'd built, churches circled in red, blue lines for supply routes, green dots for aligned pastors, and yellow stars for already launched Exodus Circles.

"No," I said. "But neither were the Israelites."

He chuckled. "You comparing us to Moses?"

"Hell no," I said. "I'm just saying sometimes all you get is a staff, and a promise."

He nodded slowly. "Then we'd better start walking."

Ezra's final message played in my head like a hymn.

"They gave us a theology of chains. We're writing one of the keys."

We weren't asking for reparations anymore.

We were rebuilding them.

One transaction at a time.

One circle at a time.

One pulpit taken off the leash at a time.

Because freedom isn't a moment.

It's a muscle.

And we were learning how to flex.

Chapter 48
The Leak

It started with a single manila envelope slipped under the door of our office at The Nest.

No stamp. No return address. Just the words "For the Watchmen" scribbled in blue ink across the front.

Donell found it just after dawn, still rubbing the sleep from his eyes and carrying a box of coffee for the early crew. He didn't even make it to his desk before ripping it open.

Inside were two items: a typed letter on congressional stationery and a photocopy of a classified report marked "CONFIDENTIAL: INTERNAL REVIEW – Faith-Based Partnerships and National Stability."

And just like that, the whispers became undeniable.

The document read like a strategy manual, but for control, not uplift.

It traced back decades of post-9/11 expansions of domestic surveillance, redacted memos from Homeland Security, and a targeted partnership program nicknamed Pulpit Watch. The mission? Monitor and manage Black churches under the guise of "community stabilization" and "radicalization prevention."

But the true purpose was simpler: compliance maintenance.

In the margins, someone had scrawled in pen.

The meeting wasn't on any official schedule. There were no cameras or transcripts. The conference room was in the back of a downtown D.C. hotel, with curtains drawn and the catering table pushed against the wall.

Standing Committee Room. A row of lawmakers is seated at a long table facing the gallery. Behind them, a CCTV feed displays a projected map of the MANNA network, including nodes, blockchain flows, smartphone apps, and credit union locations.

Committee Chair (Rep. Williams, CBC member):

The committee will come to order. We are here today to discuss the so-called MANNA Digital Banking Cooperative. This proposal outlines a digital, blockchain-based banking network that would divert fluxes of church tithes directly into independent nodes, effectively creating a parallel, unauthorized financial system.

Ranking Member (Rep. Larson):

Thank you, Chair Williams. At first glance, this may appear to be innovative fintech or faith-based mutual aid. But any system operating entirely outside traditional federal regulation, especially one with digital wallets capable of bypassing voter engagement systems problematic. How do we ensure there is no disruption to federal financial stability or election integrity?

Rep. Jackson (CBC Banking Liaison):

I rise not to defend state overreach, but to protect democracy. The threat here isn't hypothetical; diverting funds off the ledger, especially from historically oral tradition networks like churches, risks disenfranchising voters. If cash becomes intangible, and if the Treasury doesn't show up at the local precinct to power polling stations, then what happens to the ballot box? This isn't just about money, it's about civic participation.

Rep. Greene (R-state):

So you're suggesting that decentralized finance could tamper with voting? That's hyperbole. People still cast ballots. Digital wallets don't disable polling places.

Rep. Jackson:

It's not hyperbole. When those wallets become the currency for coordinating race-targeted get-out-the-vote efforts, they can divert funds, block independent civic groups, and suppress turnout. Especially in Black communities historically targeted by redlining and voter suppression.

Rep. Meyers (CBC member):

Let's be clear: Federal policy has already failed Black and Brown financial inclusion. Look at the legacy of Freedman's Bank; expropriation of wealth from our communities has been systemically extracted from financial systems before GovInfo. Ezra's plan is a reaction to decades of being locked out. This cannot be criminalized simply because it resists existing power structures.

Rep. Larson:

We can't ignore the legal precedent. Any financial application that enables transfers across state lines without federal oversight may conflict with treasury regulations, money laundering laws, and FDIC insurance protocols.

Rep. Jackson:

Alternatively, we can view it as civil disobedience, a system deliberately built to serve Black communities when the federal system has failed them. Is preventing a vote more important than empowering a community?

Rep. Williams (Chair):

We must balance innovation with oversight. The committee will request testimony from banking regulators, voting experts, and civil rights advocates before taking further action.

A senior Congresswoman who had spent years branding herself as "the voice of the people."

"Let's not pretend it's going to die," she said, her voice carrying the confidence of someone used to steering the room. "If anything, Ezra's death has made it more dangerous. People romanticize martyrs. We must take the air out of this before it builds more momentum."

A younger Congressman, eyes still sharp from his first term, leaned forward. "With all due respect, are we sure we want to oppose this on record? Publicly, I mean? The optics could"

"That's exactly why we won't oppose it publicly," she cut in. "We'll say we 'share the goals' while making sure the execution is impossible. We frame it as unworkable, 'not inclusive enough,' and we slow-walk it into irrelevance." An older Senator cleared his throat. "The unionized church model is the real threat. Fourteen to sixteen billion a year pooled in one place? That's a war chest. That's more money than most PACs can dream of. They could buy media, fund candidates, and operate outside the donor class's leash. We can't have that."

He looked around the table. "Our job is to make sure the money keeps flowing the way it's flowing now, diffuse, scattered, and easy to influence."

A staffer clicked on a projector. The screen lit with bullet points under the header: DISRUPTION STRATEGY – RESTORATION COVENANT.

1. Reframe as an Extremist

o   Use friendly media outlets to paint the Covenant as a separatist, exclusionary movement.

o   Highlight any language about "Foundational Black Americans" as divisive, anti-immigrant, or anti-coalition.

2. Co-opt the Messaging

o   Launch a "Unity Faith Initiative" with similar rhetoric but tied to federal grants and 501(c)(3)-compliant churches.

o   Position it as "Ezra's dream, responsibly managed."

3. Divide the Leadership

o   Identify ambitious pastors within the Covenant's orbit and offer them platform opportunities, funding, or committee appointments in exchange for "shaping the mission."

o   Pit them against each other over funding priorities.

4. Bury in Committees

o   Push for a national "Faith Accountability Bill" that increases financial reporting requirements for any religious coalition over a certain size.

o   Frame it as "transparency" but make compliance so costly that the Covenant stalls.

5. Leverage Social Pressure

o Quietly pressure Black-owned banks and contractors to avoid direct partnership with the Covenant to avoid "political controversy."

The Congresswoman tapped the table. "The beauty of this is we don't have to kill it outright. We just have to weaken it until it collapses under its own weight. You make it toxic to partner with, you slow down the money, you keep it under constant audit, eventually, the dreamers get tired."

The younger Congressman shifted in his seat. "You realize if this gets out, we'll look like we're working against our own people."

The Senator gave a dry smile. "We're working for the people. Just not the way Ezra wanted. He was an idealist. Idealists don't last long in this town."

A staffer in the corner, who'd been silent until now, spoke up. "There's another angle. Tremaine already has his hooks in certain mega-church pastors. If we lean on those relationships, we can get them to steer their congregations away from the Covenant quietly. Sermons about 'avoiding division in the body,' that kind of thing."

The Congresswoman nodded. "Good. Spiritual language is the best cover. No one wants to argue with God from the pew."

They moved on to messaging. Talking points. Sound bites that could make it onto Sunday morning shows without raising suspicion.

• "We honor Ezra's vision, but we have to make sure it serves all communities, not just some."

• "Unity means inclusion, and inclusion means we can't leave anyone out, not immigrants, not other faith traditions."

• "Pooling resources is fine, but without oversight, you risk exploitation."

The phrases were smooth, focus-grouped, and designed to sound like concern while cutting the movement's legs.

As the meeting wrapped, the Congresswoman gathered her notes. "Remember, no one in this room is to be quoted on this. If anyone asks, we support community empowerment. And we support Ezra's legacy." She gave a thin smile. "We just get to decide what that legacy looks like."

When they left the room, the table was littered with empty coffee cups and half-eaten pastries. The projector screen still glowed faintly with the last slide:

"Containment, Not Confrontation."

Somewhere out there, people were still watching Ezra's recording, feeling inspired, ready to act.

And in here, behind locked doors, plans were already in motion to make sure that inspiration never had the chance to become power.

"They were never afraid of riots. They were afraid of resurrection."

Donell and I sat in silence after reading it through, the weight of confirmation settling like ash on our skin.

"They've been planning this for years," he said.

"No," I replied. "They've been betting on us staying asleep."

The letter accompanying the report was brief and signed with only a single initial, "A."

It read:

"I sat in those rooms. I heard the language. 'Faith-based coordination units.' 'Demographic fatigue management.' They speak in code, but the code means us. Ezra was right. I couldn't save him. But maybe this helps save the rest of you.

Release it. Burn their lies to the ground."

Donell looked up. "You think it's our ally in Congress?"

I nodded. "Has to be. She was always the wildcard."

had brief contact with her early on, back when he was still speaking softly about the need for a new order. She'd been a rising star in the Congressional Black Caucus, beloved for her eloquence but always skating the line between reform and revolt.

After Ezra's death, she went silent.

Now we knew why.

We brought the document to the full Watchtower council that night. Yolanda read it aloud, tremblingly, the words echoing off the warehouse walls like scripture from a stolen Bible.

Every name on the advisory board. Every note about surveillance partnerships. Every clause about controlling the narrative inside Black churches.

"They didn't just want to neutralize us," she said, closing the folder. "They wanted to harness us. Turn pulpits into perches."

The crows outside seemed to scream in agreement.

And then, Donell stood.

"I say we drop it," he said. "No edits. No spin. Just the raw, bloody truth."

Heads nodded around the table.

"But not on platforms they control," I added. "No Facebook. No Twitter. Not even the so-called Black media. We leak this through The Watchtower Signal. Through Harriet's Signal. Through Nubian Pulse, Brown Channel, Radio Diaspora, and airdrop zines at churches already inside the Covenant."

Yolanda leaned in. "If we do this, there's no coming back."

"I'm not trying to go back," I said. "I'm trying to go through."

Within forty-eight hours, the leak had reached every city with a Watchtower presence.

Printed flyers landed in barbershops from Detroit to Atlanta.

Encrypted files were shared via church Wi-Fi routers, disguised as sermons.

Community radio stations in North Philly, Compton, Houston, and Jacksonville ran the report like it was morning scripture.

And the people?

They didn't riot.

They remembered.

Remembered every quiet dismissal, every denied grant, every sermon that felt like sedation instead of salvation. The report confirmed what many had already suspected: we'd been managed like livestock with hymnals.

Now, we were wide awake.

Backlash came quick.

Cable news called it a "radical disinformation campaign."

Faith-based coalitions denounced us publicly.

One pastor we knew had been on our side suddenly turned before sunrise, his building surrounded by federal vehicles. That night, his sermon was broadcast nationwide, calling us "agents of confusion."

But we didn't blink.

The Watchtower Network had never been built on the approval of the powerful. It was born from whispers, carved out of exile, shaped by those who'd learned to make miracles with scraps.

And now, with the leak confirmed, we have something new to report.

Momentum.

Ezra had always said:

"They won't give you freedom. They'll give you distractions, platforms, and sound bites. You'll have to take the freedom. Quietly. Completely."

And as I looked across the room at Donell, Yolanda, and the others, I knew we weren't just exposing the system.

We were escaping it.

One truth at a time.

They finally said it out loud.

"Domestic Faith Insurgency."

It appeared first in a leaked intelligence assessment from the Department of Homeland Security. A 38-page internal document, stamped CLASSIFIED, was released, which named the Watchtower Network as the leading influence in a new category of civil disruption:

"Decentralized religious radicalism rooted in ethnonational identity and theological dissent from federal grant-based doctrines."

Translation?

Too Black.

Too independent.

Too ungoverned.

The report framed Watchtower sermons as "coded speech." Labeled FBA reparations proposals as "non-governmental financial organizing." And reclassified Watchtower churches as "faith-adjacent civic structures hostile to federal influence."

The phrase that stuck out the most?

"Theology as sedition."

Cable news lit up like a war room.

One anchor said:

"This isn't about race, it's about order."

Another asked:

"Should faith-based institutions lose legal protections if they challenge the nation's foundational narrative?"

And a third, in a clip that would go viral for all the wrong reasons, said:

"At some point, even prophets need permits."

Back in the shadows, Harris watched the coverage from a motel room with peeling wallpaper. He was off-grid now, but never offline. He saw the headlines. The panic. The coordination. The script.

And he smiled.

Because the truth was finally loud enough to scare them without needing to scream.

But it wasn't about him anymore.

In the Bronx, a 17-year-old named Makai Evans livestreamed a sermon from the steps of a shuttered school, holding a bootleg Watchtower reader like it was scripture.

"They don't fear violence," he said to 6,000 live viewers.

"They fear Black faith with no leash."

"They fear an offering plate that doesn't pass through D.C."

His voice cracked from nerves, but not from doubt.

"We don't need no bishop's permission.

We already got the bones."

In Houston, Marisol Parker, age 19, led a classroom of third graders in a weekly "Remembering Service."

They didn't say the Pledge.

They read quotes from Ezra.

They called it:

"The Unbroken Church."

A parent complained.

Marisol was fired.

Three days later, two more teachers in Baton Rouge picked up the ritual and invited her to train them.

The Watchtower wasn't collapsing under pressure.

It was replicating.

Not like a church.

Like a code.

A virus of truth passed silently, untraceably, from generation to generation. Offline. Off-script.

It no longer needed livestreams or fancy websites.

It had become oral again.

Secret again.

Holy again.

The way truth had always traveled when it was hunted.

Back in Washington, the CBC issued a statement.

Hooks, looking gaunt and tired, stood at a podium flanked by American flags and federal seals.

"We urge all citizens, especially our youth, not to be misled by seductive rhetoric that weaponizes Black pain for political theater."

And then came the warning:

"There will be consequences for those who align themselves with unregistered theological insurgencies."

She never said the word "Watchtower."

She didn't have to.

It was now a ghost in the system, untraceable, unkillable.

And the youth?

They weren't waiting for it to be proven legitimate.

They had already decided it was theirs.

In a basement in Newark, four teenagers held a communion service with dollar store grape juice and cornbread.

They read from a worn copy of Ezra's notes.

They baptized each other in a sink.

They closed by reciting a new creed.

One that had no author.

One that belonged to all of them.

"We are the children of the buried.

We do not ask to be seen.

We remember in code.

We pray in truth.

We serve no empire.

We worship with our feet.

And if the prophet falls, we finish the sermon."

Somewhere, Harris heard it whispered through a burner audio feed.

And for the first time in weeks, he let himself cry.

Not from fear.

But from relief.

He had lived long enough to see the bones not just rise…

…but march.

Naming the Fire

It started with a press conference.

White House Rose Garden. Mid-morning.

The sun was out, but everything felt colder.

Standing behind the seal of the United States, flanked by the Secretary of State and the Attorney General, President Kayden McClure adjusted the mic. It uttered five words that would echo across the globe:

"The Watchtower Network is dangerous."

She didn't say violent.

She didn't say armed.

She didn't have to.

The language was familiar and calculated. Enough to trigger new sanctions, freeze accounts, and justify surveillance expansions without ever firing a shot.

"We believe this organization, though not officially recognized as a structured entity, has inspired decentralized actions that challenge constitutional order, exploit religious protections for political radicalism, and coordinate with unregistered domestic and international actors."

Journalists scribbled. The stock market dipped. Pulpits nationwide went silent.

And behind the scenes, the paperwork began moving.

A formal petition to the United Nations Security Council:

"To designate Watchtower-affiliated entities as part of a transnational ethno-theological insurgency posing a threat to global stability and national sovereignty."

In simpler terms?

They were trying to label it.

The news broke within hours.

CNN. BBC. Al Jazeera.

Headlines screamed:

"U.S. Seeks Global Terror Label for Black Faith Movement"

"From Preaching to Extremism? Watchtower Under International Scrutiny"

"Gospel, Guilt, and Geopolitics"

And with that, the scramble began.

African governments were the first to weigh in.

Kenya condemned the Watchtower outright, eager to preserve U.S. aid and defense contracts.

Nigeria called the movement "reckless" and "divisive."

South Africa initially said nothing.

But the real surprise came from Barbados.

Prime Minister Ayanna Clarke, young, unbought, and barely out of her forties, stepped to the mic that evening, holding a single sheet of paper.

"This is not about a threat to the people."

This is about the truth that no longer asks permission.

Foundational Black Americans have a right to their own name.

They have a right to demand what is owed.

And they have a right to build faith that is not colonized by tax codes and non-profit grants."

She folded the paper.

"The Caribbean will not support any resolution that criminalizes lineage, truth, or ancestral clarity.

If memory is a threat to empire, let empire tremble."

Within 48 hours, Jamaica, Trinidad, and even Guyana echoed her stance.

And in Ghana, a group of Black historians, archivists, and reparations scholars released an open letter titled:

"We Are Not Buffers: In Defense of FBA Specificity"

It trended across African Twitter for three days.

Harris watched it all from a laptop in a borrowed van parked outside a farm in Humboldt County.

He didn't speak. He just kept refreshing the screen.

Yolanda finally broke the silence. "You see what you did?"

"No," Harris said quietly. "I see what Ezra did."

Meanwhile, in Geneva, the United Nations Human Rights Commission convened an emergency panel.

The U.S. delegation was confident.

They cited Watchtower's coded language.

The encrypted broadcasts.

The mass withdrawal of Black churches from traditional tax systems.

They even played a clip from Harris's speech at the Baltimore pulpit months earlier:

"We are not clapping for the empire anymore."

The delegate paused dramatically.

"This is not theology. It is insurgency with liturgy."

But just as the room prepared to nod along…

…a quiet voice interrupted.

The Nigerian ambassador long thought to be in Washington's pocket cleared her throat.

"And what do we call the Catholic Church when it lobbies for immigration rights?

What do we call the Zionist movement when it organizes faith-based funding structures across nations?

What do we call white Christian political blocs when they advocate for gun rights in the name of scripture?

Do we call those things terrorism?"

Silence.

Then she leaned forward.

"Or is it only when Black people remember where the bones are buried?"

The room didn't applaud.

But something cracked.

That week, the vote on the U.S. resolution stalled.

Russia abstained. China offered no comment. France called for "further review."

And Barbados?

Barbados voted no.

Flat-out.

So did Ghana.

So did Trinidad.

And in a last-minute shock, South Africa abstained, citing "complexity of historical entanglements."

The resolution failed.

The U.S. delegation left red-faced.

The Secretary of State canceled their post-vote presser.

And in Watchtower safehouses around the globe, encrypted messages flew:

"The world just blinked."

Chapter 49
Sons and Daughters of Thunder

We were holed up in the back of the old print shop we'd been using as a meeting space. The air smelled like dust and ink, and the hum of the old offset press in the corner felt like a pulse in the room.

Donell sat on a folding chair, scrolling something on his phone, while Yolanda leaned against the worktable, sipping cold coffee from a paper cup. I had my notebook open, half listening, half just letting the quiet wrap around me.

"You ever notice," Donell said without looking up, "how the kids ain't scared the way we were?"

Yolanda tilted her head. "Scared of what?"

"Everything," he said. "Scared of losing jobs, scared of cops, scared of saying the wrong thing in the wrong room. These young ones… they'll livestream a protest while the tear gas is still in the air. They'll put a name on a flyer before they even check if they're on somebody's list. They don't even think about lists."

I leaned back, letting the chair creak. "That's because they don't know enough to be afraid yet."

"That's exactly why they need to take over," Donell said. "We're too careful now. Too… calculated. We think about consequences before we think about possibilities. They think the other way around."

Yolanda smiled faintly. "They're smarter than we were, too. Not in that they know more history, most of them don't, but they know tech like it's a second language. They can build platforms in a week that would've taken us months. They can run circles around surveillance if we just teach them where to look."

I thought about that for a minute. The old guard had instincts, patience, and war stories. But the new guard had speed, creativity, and no inherited fear of the system's boundaries.

"When we came up," I said, "we had to learn where the walls were before we could figure out how to climb them. These kids? They're born with a ladder in their hands. They might put it on the wrong wall sometimes, but they're moving. And moving fast." Donell finally looked up from his phone. "That's what scares me, though. They can move faster than we can keep up, and if we don't hand them something solid, they'll build on sand."

Yolanda set her cup down. "Then we make sure they've got the foundation. Not by preaching at them, but by showing them where we bled so they don't have to."

I could see Ezra in my head then, talking about "passing the mic before it's too late." He'd said the movement couldn't just be a generational relay race where the baton got dropped because we were too proud to let go.

"You know the difference between us and them?" I said. "We learned to work inside the cracks of the system, like water slipping through. They're ready to break the wall entirely. And maybe that's what it's going to take."

Donell grinned. "They're already doing it. These young people don't go to City Hall for permission; they set up in the park and make it happen. They don't wait for grants; they crowdfund. They don't worry about credentials; they worry about results.

And these YN'S don't look to the old guard for approval, which is why the old guard doesn't know what to do with them."

Yolanda's voice softened. "The old guard still thinks it's about respectability. About making the right friends and saying the right words. The kids don't care about that. They're not here to be liked. They're here to be heard."

The press in the corner clicked off, leaving the room quiet. I closed my notebook and looked at both of them.

"If we don't continue bringing them in, the system will," I said. "And they'll twist that idealism into something toothless. That's how they've been doing it for fifty years. But if we give them the keys early, the knowledge, the history, the strategies, we make it harder to turn them."

Donell tapped his phone against his leg. "You think they'll even want to take it from us?"

I thought about the marches I'd seen, the livestreams from neighborhoods I hadn't set foot in for years, the faces lit by phone screens in the middle of the night.

"They already have," I said. "The question is whether we're going to guide them or just get out of their way."

Yolanda smiled, but it wasn't light. "We can do both. Guide them enough to keep them from getting swallowed whole, but step back enough to let them make their own mistakes. That's the part nobody likes, letting them mess up. But that's how you learn what not to repeat."

I nodded slowly. "Then that's the plan. We set the foundation. We pass on the history. We show them the traps before they step into them. And then we give them room to run."

For a moment, none of us spoke. The weight of what we were talking about hung in the air, not just the future of the movement, but the reality that we wouldn't always be here to see it through.

It wasn't about building something we could control. It was about building something that could outlive us.

The meeting took place in a back room of an old art gallery that now doubled as a youth tech lab. From the outside, it looked like another half-funded community space. Inside, it buzzed like a bootleg think tank. Computers hummed. Cords ran like vines across the floor. Walls were covered in whiteboards layered with code, quotes, and unfinished battle plans.

This was the New Guard. The next wave.

And I wasn't leading this meeting. I was just sitting in the corner, watching something beautiful grow.

Donell stood up front beside a tall, wiry 17-year-old named Zion, who had once been kicked out of school for printing radical poetry on the district's printers. Now he was designing encrypted social channels for The Watchtower Network.

"Y'all aren't volunteers," Donell told them. "You're witnesses. That means what you say matters. What you don't say? That might matter even more."

Around the table were ten others. Some still wore their charter school IDs around their necks. One had an ankle monitor. Two were formerly involved in church youth groups that had been quietly silenced after Ezra's death. All of them had eyes too tired for their age, and a hunger that scared even me.

Donell passed out a copy of The Restoration Covenant. Not the full blueprint, just enough to light the match.

Zion leaned in, voice steady. "This isn't just about leaking documents or crashing systems. This is about narrative. They've owned our story for 400 years. That ends now."

The room nodded.

Later that night, Yolanda and I sat in the hallway outside the lab. She had her knees tucked to her chest, hoodie over her braids. I had a styrofoam cup of coffee going cold in my hands.

"You think they're ready?" she asked.

"No," I said. "But neither were we."

She laughed quietly. "That Zion kid… He reminds me of Ezra."

I nodded. "Same fire. Same refusal to ask permission."

"They're going to need armor," she said.

"They already have it," I replied. "Truth. Each other. And the fact that they've seen the inside of the machine. They know the lie. That's more protection than we ever had."

The 9th Pew, as they called themselves, chose their own names for operations.

Thunderbird was their encrypted messenger app.

Church Underground was a podcast-style audio drop that paired historical resistance movements with local testimonies.

Ghostwire was the anonymous hotline they built to let kids across the country report pastors, principals, and nonprofit execs connected to Tremaine's network.

They weren't just replicating our work; they were refining it.

We had laid the bricks.

They were building cathedrals with no doors.

One night, Zion pulled me aside.

"Can I ask you something?"

"Shoot."

"When you were our age… were you afraid?"

I thought about that. About being 16 and watching my uncle fall asleep drunk in his chair with a Bible in his lap. About finding copies of books my dad read like "Tell me how long the trains been gone" and "Native Son" and old sermons on cassette tapes in my mother's closet. About knowing something was broken in the world but not yet having the language to name it.

"I was afraid of being alone," I said. "Afraid that if I saw too much, spoke too much, I'd be left out there to die."

"You were."

I smiled. "Yeah. But then I stopped being afraid of that, too."

Zion looked down at his shoes, then back up. "I think I'm almost there."

The next phase wasn't about me anymore.

It was about building systems they couldn't dismantle.

Community food hubs disguised as pop-up farmers' markets.

Youth-run media labs inside libraries.

Underground worship nights using code word RSVPs and encrypted GPS pings.

Kids were preaching now not from pulpits, but from headphones and livestreams, their voices cutting through the fog like trumpets.

They weren't asking for permission to lead.

They were just leading.

At the next Watchtower gathering, I sat beside Yolanda while Donell introduced the Youth Council formally. Each of them stood and stated their alias.

Zion.

Phoenix.

Langston.

Marley.

Harriet.

Stokely.

Cicada.

Anansi.

Solace.

Blaze.

The Children Who Heard the Bones

They called themselves The Ninth Pew.

No one remembered who gave them the name.

But it spread like all truth in the Watchtower Network did: unannounced, undeniable, and encoded in memory.

It was whispered first in Memphis, where five high schoolers began hosting unauthorized Bible studies using Ezra's writings as scripture.

Then in Oakland, where a group of teen barbers started baptizing customers in barber chairs spraying rosewater over fresh fades, reciting lines from Harris's speeches between clippers and sermons.

By the time it reached Atlanta, the Ninth Pew had a logo, a manifesto, and a mission:

"We are the children who sat behind the elders.

We passed the note.

We caught the whisper.

We remember the silence.

And now we speak.

There were nine core members.

All under 25.

No one knew all their names.

Some were orphans of the movement, kids whose parents had vanished in raids or been blackballed for housing.

Some were preacher's kids who rejected the post-revival theatrics.

Some were street-coded, web fluent, and spiritually bilingual.

And one Makai Evans, now 18, was the first to say it publicly:

"We are not leaders.

We are inheritors."

The Ninth Pew didn't organize like a board.

They moved like a cipher.

Every message began with a memory.

Every gathering included a reading of Ezra, Harris, or one of the unnamed preachers from underground networks.

And every new initiate recited a line carved into the wall of a burned church in Gary, Indiana:

"We were born after the microphone broke.

But we still heard the bones."

Their first official action was symbolic.

They launched a Digital Altar, a decentralized network of Watchtower teachings, coded in meme format, poem, graffiti, TikTok duets, and AI-generated sermons voiced to sound like Ezra in reverse.

But it wasn't nostalgia.

It was reclamation.

A new language for the same truth.

Then came the strategy.

- They built burner curriculum maps for public schools.

- Published lesson plans disguised as art projects.

- Distributed repair grant templates for FBA elders to rebuild homes destroyed by gentrification under the name "restorative ministry."

They taught ten-year-olds how to decode sermons for policy.

They trained fifteen-year-olds to recite reparation line items like scripture.

They ran theology through group chats, band rehearsals, and trap beats.

And it worked.

Because the government had no doctrine for the youth who remembered the bones.

One of their first public broadcasts was titled:

"The Inheritance They Tried to Deny."

A girl named Janiya, seventeen, spoke into the lens with a voice like Sunday thunder:

"We're not trying to go viral.

We're trying to go forever."

She stared down the camera like a prophet's daughter.

"We've been taught everything but memory.

We've been given every gospel but the one that names us by name.

So now we make it ourselves."

CBC members tried to dismiss it.

Hooks went on Morning Joe, called the Ninth Pew "the youth wing of a dangerous ideology that refuses to evolve."

The White House released a non-statement:

"We support young leaders rooted in civic responsibility, not theological separatism."

But the Ninth Pew never responded to the press.

They responded with presence.

A march in Newark.

A shutdown of a federal grant training in D.C.

A re-baptism ceremony in Chicago, where they used water from the Mississippi River, shipped in Mason jars by elders from Baton Rouge.

Their unofficial chant?

"We're not your future.

We're your replacement."

Back in the redwoods, Harris saw them on a burner stream.

He didn't weep.

He just exhaled.

"They're already better than we were," he whispered to the trees.

Yolanda, listening beside him, nodded.

"Because they were born in the ruins," she said. "And didn't expect shelter. Just truth."

In one Ninth Pew meeting captured in grainy footage, passed like holy contraband, a new member asked:

"What happens if they kill us too?"

A girl named Bree, who was just fifteen, stood up.

No mic.

Just fire.

"Then we finish the sermon anyway.

In dance. In language. In silence. In code.

And when they raid the ninth pew…"

She looked around the room.

"We build a tenth."

And with that…

…the children of Watchtower made one thing undeniable:

This wasn't just a movement now.

It was a succession.

The gospel had new voices.

The altar had new architects.

And the bones?

The bones had students.

 I realized something.

We weren't the resistance anymore.

We were the seed.

Chapter 50
The Audit

The call came in just after noon. Pastor Ellison's voice was tight, like he'd swallowed glass.

"They're here," he said.

I didn't have to ask who it was.

By the time Donell and I pulled up to Ellison Baptist, two black SUVs were parked at the curb. Four men in suits were carrying file boxes into the side office. The gold badge on the jackets read Department of Financial Services.

Ellison met us at the door, sweat running along his temples. "They say it's a compliance review. Treasury flow, donor transparency, anti–money laundering statutes." He laughed once, dry. "They even brought their own court order."

We followed him down the hall to the fellowship room. The men were already set up at a folding table, laptops open, manila folders spread like they were planning a wedding instead of a takedown. One of them, a tall man with close-cropped hair and a face that didn't blink enough, stood as we came in.

"This is an official audit," he said, not bothering to introduce himself. "We've received information suggesting irregularities in the church's financial operations, specifically the routing of congregational tithes through non-traditional banking systems."

I stepped closer. "You mean the credit union. Which is legal."

The man's smile was small and professional. "Legality isn't the only concern. Transparency matters, Mr…?"

"Bushvill," I said.

Something flickered in his eyes, recognition.

"We'll need to see all transaction records for the past six months," he continued, "including any off-ledger accounts or pooled funds."

Ellison's hand tightened on the back of a chair. "Our ledgers are private."

"Not anymore," the man said. "Refusal to cooperate could result in seizure of assets under the Civil Asset Forfeiture Reform Act."

There it was, the weapon dressed in a suit. This wasn't about finding wrongdoing. It was about making the church feel the heat until they pulled out of the network.

I leaned against the wall, arms crossed. "You running this for Treasury or for Tremaine?"

The man didn't answer, just went back to his laptop. The clack of keys filled the silence.

Donell moved beside Ellison. "We can stall them. Get Reuben Ellis on the phone. He'll know how to wrap this up in procedural knots."

Ellison looked at me. His eyes were steady now, but I could see the calculation. If he stayed in, the church would be a target. If he backed out, he'd be safe and so would his people.

"They're trying to make an example of you," I said quietly. "If you leave the Covenant now, you're telling every other pastor it's not worth the fight."

He exhaled slow. "Then I guess I'm in the fight."

When we left, the men in suits were still working, their boxes multiplying on the table. Out on the street, I saw a crow on the church's front sign, black feathers gleaming in the sun.

One crow.

For now.

Chapter 51
Tremaine's Table

The room was dim except for the green glow of a banker's lamp on the end of the conference table. Tremaine sat at the head, jacket off, sleeves rolled, a pen spinning slow between his fingers. Two men in suits, the same type I'd seen at Ellison Baptist, sat halfway down the table, one flipping through a thin report, the other scrolling on a tablet.

"How'd our friends at Ellison's place do?" Tremaine asked without looking up.

The taller man spoke first. "Everything went as expected. He resisted at first. Then your boy Bushvill showed up. We made it clear what would happen if the church didn't comply. They're rattled."

Tremaine stopped spinning the pen. "Rattled isn't enough. I don't want them to be nervous; I want them to be isolated. I want other pastors to see that building and think, not me."

The shorter man slid the tablet across the table. "We've got four more beta-node churches flagged. Same playbook anonymous complaints to the Department of Financial Services, asset freeze warnings, compliance reviews. All perfectly legal."

Tremaine glanced at the list and smirked. "Legal is the beauty of it. You hit them with lawsuits, and they get to play the martyr. You hit them with fines and paperwork? They drown in it. No sermons about that. No photographs in the paper. Just exhaustion."

The taller man nodded. "What about the credit unions? They're the real backbone."

Tremaine leaned back in his chair, eyes narrowing. "Those are trickier. But everybody's got a lever. Loans, regulators, licensing boards… We'll find it. And when we do, the whole thing collapses."

A third man, sitting quietly in the shadows near the back, finally spoke. His voice was low, almost casual. "What if it doesn't collapse? What if this thing is as airtight as they think?"

Tremaine smiled then, the kind of smile that wasn't for show. "Then we change the air. Make it toxic to breathe inside that Covenant. No one survives in a room they can't stand to be in."

The shorter man cleared his throat. "And Bushvill?"

Tremaine's gaze hardened. "He's already halfway to the gallows. We just have to finish the paperwork. Conspiracy to commit wire fraud easy, with that blockchain mess he's playing with. Unlawful assembly, all it takes is a few photos of him at the wrong meeting. Inciting civil unrest, we let him speak in public once, then stitch his words into the narrative we want."

The taller man added, "We can have an indictment ready before summer. Keep him locked down while we mop up the rest."

Tremaine nodded slowly, then snapped the pen in half without looking away from the man. "Do it. Get him off the street before he starts believing he can win. And when you make the arrest, make it loud. I want the rest of them to hear the cuffs from here to the lake."

Outside the conference room window, a crow landed on the sill, tapping once at the glass. Tremaine glanced at it, then back to the table.

"Gentlemen," he said, standing, "let's get to work."

Chapter 52
The Raid

The safe house wasn't much - peeling paint, a leaky roof, and a mattress that remembered better days - but it was quiet. Quiet enough for me to hear the rain, steady against the glass, and the soft clatter of keys under my fingers as I worked on the laptop. Outside, a line of crows hunched on the power line, slick black in the streetlight glow. They didn't move, didn't call, just watched.

I told myself they were only birds.

The door exploded inward before I could stand. Splinters shot across the room, and boots slammed heavy on the floor. Flashlights cut the dark, and hands yanked me forward. My wrists snapped into cuffs before I could ask for a warrant. No words, just muscle and speed.

They shoved me into the back of a van. No windows, just steel walls humming with the road.

When the door opened again, I found myself in a small room with fluorescent lighting, a metal table, and two chairs. A man in a dark suit sat across from me. Clean shave. No name.

"You've been making noise," he said, voice calm. "You've got influence. The kind that moves people. But you're running in the wrong direction."

He leaned forward, folding his hands like he was offering a prayer. "You could be at the big table. Meet the right people. Get the funding. Keep your head above water."

I didn't answer.

He gave a small smile. "Or… you can keep doing what you're doing and find yourself swept under. Think about it."

"I already have," I said. "I'm not for sale."

They processed me into the county lockup before sunrise, charged with conspiracy to commit wire fraud, unlawful assembly, and inciting civil unrest, no bond. All paper-thin. The kind of charges you use to keep someone in a cage while you dismantle their life outside it.

The holding cell smelled like bleach and tired men.

Fluorescent lights hummed overhead, making the steel bench under me feel colder than it had to.

I'd been there six hours, long enough to know they weren't in any hurry to process me, which meant someone wanted me to sit in it.

The door clanged open. A man in uniform stepped aside to let in a man in no badge, no gun, just a dark tailored suit and the kind of clean-shaven calm that makes you check your own heartbeat.

He nodded at the uniform, who stepped out and shut the door behind him.

"Mr. Bushvill," he said. "You've caused quite a ripple."

I didn't bother standing. "Guess that means it's working."

He sat down across from me, crossing one leg over the other, his cufflink catching the light. "Here's the truth: you're on the hook for conspiracy to commit wire fraud, unlawful assembly, and inciting civil unrest. That combination, in federal court? You're looking at double digits."

I let that sit. I'd already figured as much.

"But," he continued, leaning in slightly, "there's an alternative. You walk away from the MANNA Covenant, denounce it publicly, say it was a misunderstanding, a bad direction, whatever story you like. In return, the charges disappear. You get a clean record, a seat on a municipal advisory board, and a stipend. Influence. Stability. You'll be alive, at the table, doing more for people than you ever will in here."

I stared at him. "You really think I'm going to sell Ezra's work for a seat next to people who'd rather burn the table than share it?"

His jaw tightened, but his voice stayed even. "You can do more for people alive at the table than dead. And believe me, Harris, if you keep going down this road, it won't be a cell you end up in. It'll be a box."

I leaned forward until the space between us was just air and bad breath. "If all I can offer my people is a seat you let me have, then I've already failed them."

We locked eyes briefly before he stood, buttoning his jacket with deliberate slowness.

"You've got heart, Mr. Bushvill. The heart doesn't beat forever."

When the door clanged shut behind him, I leaned back against the wall.

The hum of the lights faded, replaced by the memory of my brother Rick the night I thought he'd given up, when the burns kept him in bed and the pain made him quiet.

Until I found him in the basement, sweat dripping, hands shaking, lifting weights he had no business touching.

That night, I realized some fights weren't about winning. They're about not letting the other side see you quit.

I wasn't about to quit.

Three days after I told the man in the suit "no," I was still in holding.

No bail. No arraignment date. Just waiting in the fluorescent hum.

That morning, the guard's tone was different when he came for me, clipped, all business.

"Bushvill. Let's go."

They walked me to a small interview room. Two men and a woman, all dressed in suits, were waiting. The woman did the talking.

"Mr. Bushvill, during a lawful search of your residence, investigators discovered a firearm, a .38 caliber revolver, in a locked box at the back of a closet. Our preliminary records indicate this weapon may have been involved in a homicide approximately thirty years ago."

I didn't flinch, but my stomach sank. I knew exactly which gun she was talking about. My grandfather's. Old blued steel, the kind of weight that felt like history in your hand.

It had been in the family for a long time before I was born. I'd last seen it when I was twelve, before the night police lights flashed outside our window and whispers filled the block.

The taller man spoke next. "Ballistics are being run. In the meantime, we're adding murder, possession of an unregistered firearm, to your charges and potential obstruction, given you failed to disclose it during your arrest."

I almost laughed. "You tore apart my place without a warrant for a murder weapon from when I was twelve, and I'm the one obstructing?"

The woman's eyes stayed cold. "Given the seriousness of these developments, you're being transferred to a more secure facility while we evaluate the homicide connection. You are now considered a higher flight risk."

The shorter man closed the file in front of him. "And just so you understand, you won't see bail with these additional charges. Not this month. Probably not this year."

They stood and filed out without waiting for a response.

Chapter 53
The Transfer

They moved me that night.

No warning. No personal items. Just cuffs, chains, and the short walk from the cell to the transport van. The inside smelled of diesel and metal, the bench cold enough to leech the heat out of your bones.

The new facility was built with long-stay high fences, razor wire, and guard towers. The kind of place where they don't expect to see you leave until you've forgotten what the street smells like.

In my new cell, the walls were thicker, the locks heavier, and the silence louder.

But what stuck with me wasn't the move or the charges. It was the part they didn't say out loud:

Somebody wanted me buried in here long enough for MANNA to starve on the outside.

I sat on the cot and closed my eyes, seeing my grandfather's hands scarred, steady, teaching me how to clean that revolver.

"You don't carry a thing like this unless you're ready for the weight that comes with it."

I understood now.

The weight wasn't just the metal. It was history.

And history was exactly what they were trying to use to break me.

The air inside was thick with sweat and bleach, and it was the kind of place where days blur into each other.

A few nights in, a group of Muslims approached me in the dayroom. They were respectful and direct. Their spokesman sat across from me, leaning in.

"You've got a message," he said. "We can make sure it reaches further than you ever could alone. But you've got to walk with us. One banner. One alliance."

It was the same deal as the suit had offered, dressed in different colors.

"I'm not changing my colors," I told him.

He nodded once, like he already knew my answer, then stood and walked away.

They came for me after the evening count. I didn't recognize two guards wearing the kind of blank faces you see on men who've been paid to forget your name. They didn't cuff me. I was just told I had a "call."

The walk took us down the long tier, past eyes watching through bars, the walk was without the usual shouts and banging. Tonight, it was quiet. Too quiet.

They led me into a part of the prison I'd never been, an old visitation room no one used anymore. The blinds were drawn. The only light came from a desk lamp in the corner.

At the center of the room sat a man in a white kufi and a neatly pressed khaki shirt. He was older, the kind of elderly person who carried weight not from years, but from the gravity of having been listened to. His beard was gray at the chin, his eyes sharp but calm.

"Brother Harris," he said, like we'd known each other for years. "Sit."

I didn't sit right away. "And you are?"

He smiled. "Names aren't important. Let's say I'm someone who can open doors for you. Someone who can make your time in here… not just bearable, but meaningful."

I took the chair across from him, the metal legs scraping the floor.

"You've been noticed," he said. "You've got people on the outside listening to you. You've got influence. And influence, inside these walls, is a currency more valuable than cigarettes or commissary."

I kept my face still. "So what? You want me to be your mouthpiece?"

He shook his head. "Not my mouthpiece. Our partner. You want to see change? I can give you a seat at the big table. A path to effect change controlled change. The kind that lasts. But to do that, you have to play ball. Work within the structure."

"Whose structure?" I asked.

He leaned forward, resting his elbows on the table. "The one that already runs this place. You think the warden calls the shots? No. We do. Every yard has its order. Every man has his lane. When someone steps out of it, there are consequences."

I knew what he was offering: protection, access, leverage. But there was a hook in it, and hooks have a way of sinking deeper the longer you pretend they're not there.

"And if I say no?"

He didn't answer right away. He just looked at me for a long time, then sat back. "Then you keep doing what you're doing, and we keep doing what we're doing. And one day, those roads might cross in a way you don't like."

The guards came back for me. No cuffs again. Just the walk back to my cell, their boots echoing on the concrete.

Three days later, I got another "call." This time, it wasn't the head man. It was a face I knew, Fred "Slim" Redding. We'd run together on the outside, back before the streets swallowed him whole. Slim had been a stick-up kid with a laugh that made you forget he was dangerous. Now he was in a tan DOC uniform, with a crescent moon on a chain around his neck.

He grinned when he saw me. "Man, you ain't changed a bit."

"I could say the same," I told him. "Except for the wardrobe."

We sat. For a minute, it was just catching up names from the past, quick stories about who'd gone where. But then his tone shifted.

"Listen, Har," he said, leaning in. "You know how it is in here. Ain't no free agents. Everybody belongs somewhere. You rolling solo, that's a dangerous game. The brothers want to bring you in. You get a seat at the table, a voice in what goes down. You could actually make moves instead of just… surviving."

"I'm making moves already," I said.

He shook his head. "Nah. You're making noise. There's a difference. You make too much noise without the right backing, you get tuned out or tuned up. And I don't want to see that happen to you."

It was almost enough to sound like concern. Almost.

"I appreciate it, Slim," I said. "But I don't play ball."

He looked down at the table, tapping his fingers. "I told 'em you'd say that."

Something in his voice tightened my chest.

"I tried to tell 'em you was stubborn, that maybe we could work you around. But the word came down."

"What word?"

He looked up, and there was no smile now. Just the kind of tired you see in men who've traded their freedom for a little bit of power.

"You're done, Har. I'm supposed to be the one to do it."

We sat there in that dead air for a long moment, the hum of the light overhead sounding too loud.

"You gonna do it?" I asked.

He swallowed, his eyes flicking away. "I ain't decided yet. But you made it hard, man. You always gotta make it hard."

The guards came for me again, and Slim didn't look at me when I stood up.

Back in my cell, I sat on the bunk and stared at the wall, thinking about all the ways loyalty bends before it breaks.

In here, a man's word was supposed to mean something. But power had a way of sanding the meaning off words until all that was left was the sound.

Chapter 54
The Visit

They brought me to the visitation room in chains. Not because I was dangerous, but because they wanted me to look dangerous.

The room was lined with scratched plexiglass partitions and metal stools bolted to the floor.

Donell was already on the other side, leaning forward, hands folded on the counter. He looked like he hadn't slept much, but his eyes were sharp.

The guard stepped back far enough to give the illusion of privacy, which we both knew wasn't real.

"You look like hell," Donell said.

"Comes with the address," I replied.

He cut straight to it. "They're spinning this hard outside. Tremaine's people are pushing a story about the gun, making you out to be a lifelong criminal hiding behind church politics. Some folks are eating it up."

I didn't react. "Figures."

"But that's not why I'm here," he said, lowering his voice a fraction. "I've got someone who can help. Works shifts here a few nights a week. He's… old Buffalo. Grew up in the Fruit Belt. Knew Ezra. Never took Tremaine's money."

I studied his face. "And he's clean?"

"As clean as anyone in a place like this," Donell said. "he's not gonna smuggle you a hacksaw in a cake, but he can get messages in and out. News from the outside, updates on the Covenant, whatever you need."

"What's his angle?" I asked.

"He says Ezra saved his cousin from a long bid. Thinks what you're doing is worth the risk." Donell leaned closer. "But listen, you can't make him visible. If they smell he's helping, he's done. We use him quite careful. No names in the messages, nothing they can pin."

I nodded slowly. "How do I know when it's him?"

"He'll ask you if the 'choir's still rehearsing.' That's the phrase. You answer, 'on Tuesdays.' That tells him it's safe to pass the message."

The guard tapped the glass, signaling time. Donell's face hardened. "They want you to feel cut off, Harris. He'll keeps the line open. But you've got to stay sharp; this place is built to turn you into someone who talks just to hear yourself. Don't give them anything to twist."

"Tell him I'll be ready."

Donell gave the smallest nod. As he walked away, I noticed his hand tap the side of his leg twice, a habit of his when he was telling me, Trust me, I've thought it through.

Back in my cell, I sat on the cot and replayed the conversation in my head.

A friend on the inside. A thread to the outside world.

And for the first time since they locked me in here, the walls didn't feel quite as solid.

The cell was quiet except for the drip in the corner and the shouts echoing from another tier. I lay on the bunk, tasting copper and blood, when the shadow of Officer filled the doorway.

He asked," If the 'choir's still rehearsing?" "I said on Tuesdays, "He wasn't like the others, kept his head down, treated men like they were still men. We'd spoken in passing. Enough for him to know I wasn't here for what the paperwork claimed.

He stepped inside, glancing down the hall before speaking. "You don't have much time."

From under his jacket, he pulled a small digital recorder, the kind used for witness statements. "Whatever you need to say, say it now."

I sat up, my ribs screaming. "If you get caught with this"

He cut me off. "If I get caught, they'll just say I lost it in an inventory sweep. But you? You won't get another chance."

I clicked it on. My voice was low, but steady. And I prayed. Lord,

You know me better than I've ever known myself.

You know the roads I've walked, the ones I ran from, and the ones you carried me down when my legs gave out.

I've been stubborn. I've been angry. I've doubted you more times than I've believed. But tonight, I need You. Not the version I was handed in stained glass and sermons, but the God who hears the man locked in a cell with nothing but his breath and his truth.

Give me peace, the kind that doesn't care about walls or guards or the clock running down on my life.

Give me a clear mind so my words can land where they're meant to.

Don't let fear steal the strength from my voice.

Don't let pride keep me from our mercy.

If my work ends here, let it matter.

Let it wake somebody up. Let it plant something that grows long after I'm gone.

Protect Donell. Protect the people who are carrying the light now. And protect the ones who don't even know yet that they're going to have to carry it.

I'm ready for whatever You decide, Lord.

… stay close.

Amen.

Chapter 55
The Yard

The yard was wide open under a gray sky, the kind of overcast that made everything feel heavier. The fence line shimmered in the distance, topped with rolls of razor wire that caught what little light there was.

Men moved in slow, looping circuits, some on the track, some posted up near the weight benches, others in tight clusters by the bleachers.

I'd been here long enough to know the difference between a casual look and a look that meant something. Today, the air was full of the second kind.

I walked the track at an easy pace, hands in my pockets, trying to look like I had nothing on my mind. But every turn, I let my eyes sweep the yard, slow and steady.

That's when I saw him.

Slim was across the yard near the basketball court, leaning against the chain-link fence. He wasn't playing, wasn't talking. Just watching.

Our eyes met for half a second before he looked away, not quick, not guilty, just… calculating.

Two other men I didn't know were nearby, pretending to argue over a foul. They kept glancing in my direction.

If you've been in long enough, you know when the air changes. This was the change the moment before something breaks.

I kept walking. Stopping would've been the wrong move. Running would've been worse.

As I rounded the far corner of the track, I caught a glimpse of the guards in the tower. Two were watching the court, but not me. No one was looking for what was about to happen.

I thought about Slim's voice two days ago. You're done, Har. I'm supposed to be the one to do it.

And I thought about how easy it would be for him to decide today was the day.

The rules in here were simple: when an order comes down, you don't stall unless you've got a reason that'll hold up. Friendship? That doesn't hold up. Not in here.

I slowed my pace near the bleachers, just enough to scan the angles. Two exits: the gate back to the building, and the long walk across the yard past the weight pit.

Neither was good if something went down.

When I came around again, Slim was no longer on the fence. The two men who'd been by the court had split, one heading toward the benches, the other toward the far end of the track.

They were closing the space, but not too fast. That's how you do it in here, casual, like you're just crossing the yard.

I passed under the shadow of the bleachers and caught sight of Slim again, this time sitting on the bottom row. Elbows on his knees, head down like he was just resting.

But his eyes tracked me through the gap in the planks.

I walked straight toward him. No detour, no hesitation. When I stopped in front of him, he looked up slow.

"You gonna do it here?" I asked.

He didn't answer right away. Just studied myself. Then: "You could've made this easier, Har."

I shook my head. "Easy's how you end up owned.

One of the other men had drifted close now, pretending to stretch. The second was on the far side, leaning against the fence like he was watching a game that wasn't happening.

They were boxing me in.

"You know," Slim said, "if you took the seat they offered you, you could've had real pull. You could've made moves."

"Yeah," I said. "Controlled moves. Somebody else's leash."

His mouth twitched like he wanted to argue, but the words didn't come.

We sat in that moment, the noise of the yard muffled around us.

I could see it in his eyes, the calculation, the weighing of orders against whatever history we had. And I knew if he swung first, I'd be lucky to make it back to my cell breathing.

Finally, Slim stood. "Not today," he said.

He walked away, and the two others peeled off with him, like a tide pulling back from the shore.

I stayed on the bleachers for a while, watching the fence line. My pulse was still heavy in my ears.

In here, you don't celebrate walking away from something like that. You just keep walking because the order doesn't die. It just waits.

And so does the man who's supposed to carry it out.

Three nights later, the power was cut off.

I heard the footsteps before I saw the shadows. Quick. Purposeful.

A familiar voice, a voice of a friend, spoke low in my ear. "You could've lived long, Bushvill."

The first blow took my breath. The second took my balance. After that, there was only the sound of the rain outside and the weight of the crows on the wire.

The Last Transmission

It was just after dawn when Donell got the knock. Three short, one long, not the kind you answer without checking the street first.

Outside, Kemp stood with his collar turned up against the wind, an envelope clutched in his hand. His eyes kept moving, scanning the block.

"This never happened," he said, pressing it into Donell's palm. "I was never here. And if anyone asks, you've never seen me before in your life."

Donell felt the weight inside not paper, but plastic. A recorder.

Kemp hesitated at the steps. "He didn't bend. Not to them. Not to us. Paid for it." He swallowed, looking past Donell. "They'll say it was gang politics or a fight over commissary. Don't believe it. He knew this was coming. Told me it had to reach you."

The door shut behind him, and Donell locked it twice before pulling the recorder out.

The voice that filled the room was ragged, tired, but alive in a way Donell hadn't heard since Ezra. Harris spoke like he was sitting across from him, telling him what had to be done. The Restoration Covenant. The Watchtower Network. Tremaine's web. The churches feed the machine. The demand to keep pushing even when the shepherds were gone.

By the time the tape clicked off, Donell's jaw was set. There was no funeral to plan, no time to grieve. Harris hadn't given him an eulogy order.

He reached for the burner phone and started dialing. Nubian Pulse. The Brown Channel. Harriet's Signal and the many underground lines that couldn't be bought.

The crows on the wire outside shifted black against the pale morning.

It was time to wake the city.

The room had small, bare walls, one window, and a heater that rattled as if it were trying to escape the cold. But inside, it was warm.

A young mother sat on the edge of a worn couch; her newborn wrapped in a soft blanket, tucked to her chest. Her two older children, a boy and a girl, sat cross-legged on the floor, their eyes fixed on the secondhand tablet she'd propped up on a milk crate.

On the screen, the Watchtower Signal flickered to life. No logos. No theme music. Just a black screen with Harris Bushvill's voice.

His tone was quiet, clear, and measured. The kind of voice that made you sit up straighter, not out of fear but reverence.

The Final Prayer

"This is my last transmission. If you're hearing this, it means they couldn't buy me, and they couldn't scare me into silence. Donell put this where they can't touch it. Let the crows carry it."

Outside, through the slit of the window, I could see the wire. The crows hadn't moved. Still watching.

I recorded each line in the dark, long after the last crow had gone quiet. Yet he sat at my window, which was still, in the kind of silence that comes right before something breaks open. I had no plan for what to say.

This wasn't for headlines.

This was for judgment.

For the record.

For the ones who never got to speak because their tongues had been tied with funding and fear.

To the Church,

I reach out to you not as a stranger but as a son.

One raised in your pews, baptized in your waters, fed at your tables.

But I come to you now like a prophet with no robe, just scars and truth.

You were never supposed to be the gatekeepers of silence.

You were never meant to trade your voice for tax exemptions.

But somewhere along the way, your sermons stopped sounding like liberation and started sounding like sleep.

Ezra called it what it was: a Sleeping Pill.

Wrapped in scripture.

Sugar-coated in prosperity.

Swallowed whole every Sunday by people who didn't know they were being anesthetized.

To the State,

You were always listening.

I know that now.

You sent informants into our pulpits.

You wrote gag orders into our grant agreements.

You built prisons where you should have built schools,

And you called it "urban development."

You paid our prophets to sing lullabies instead of war songs.

You made our church report on us.

And you called it a partnership.

We see you now.

And we are not asleep

To the Brothers,

I know why you're tired.

I know why you've stopped showing up,

why you sit in the back with your arms crossed or not at all.

You've been told to be silent or be sinful.

You've been erased.

You've been feminized and criminalized often in the same breath.

But your rage is righteous.

And your rest is sacred.

Don't let them steal that from you.

Ezra believed in you.

So do I.

Come home.

Not to the four walls.

To the fire.

To the Watchers,

You have been faithful.

You stayed up when others slept.

You whispered truth in the dark,

carried files across state lines,

broke codes and curfews.

The crows circled not to mourn but to guard.

You knew that.

You were never paranoid.

You were awake.

To the Next Generation,

We failed to warn you.

We dressed our pain in silk and shouted clichés from stages.

We turned trauma into testimony and called it healing

when really we were just bleeding louder.

But you

you are thunder with skin.

You are sacred algorithms.

You are Zion rebuilt.

Take the blueprint.

Burn the parts that no longer fit.

Build higher.

Dig deeper.

Make this truth bulletproof.

To the Women,

You have carried the weight of our deliverance longer than we have noticed.

You sang when we were too broken to speak.

You prayed when we were too proud to kneel.

You stitched together sons who the world had already buried in statistics.

They called you emotional, but emotion was never your weakness it was your prophecy.

You built kingdoms out of kitchens, sermons out of silence, and revolutions out of whispers.

And still, they asked you to shrink to make yourself small enough to fit behind pulpits that never made room for your fire.

But you kept the oil burning.

You kept watch when the rest of us slept.

You are the keepers of both wound and weapon.

Ezra saw you too.

He said the kingdom would not come through crowns or collars, but through the hands that have always been washing,

feeding,

holding,

healing.

So rise,

not as helpmates but as heralds.

Not as background, but as backbone.

Your power does not need permission.

Your anointing was never up for debate.

You are the sound that wakes the sleepers.

You are the reason the crows still circle.

 It felt holy.

If you're hearing this, it means I'm not where I'm supposed to be. But it also means the work is bigger than the worker. The files are safe. The plan is safe. You have what you need to finish what we started. Don't look for leaders, be one. Don't wait for freedom, build it."

The newborn stirred, a soft whimper escaping as the mother gently rocked him. The older children leaned closer to the speaker, as if they could catch the warmth in the words and hold it in their small hands.

"They will tell you to be patient. They will tell you to pray for change while they legislate your chains. But you have a covenant written in your own hands, signed in your own names. Keep it. Guard it. Pass it on. And if you're afraid… remember, so was I. But fear's only the proof that what you're doing matters."

"If you're hearing this, it means the signal made it. That means they didn't kill the whole tree, just a few branches. That means you're still here, and so is the truth."

The mother didn't speak. She just rocked and gently breastfed her newborn, her eyes fixed on the screen.

"This isn't about Ezra anymore. It's not about me. It's about the inheritance they tried to bury in paperwork and protocol. It's about what happens when we finally choose to believe each other more than we believe them."

The boy leaned forward, brow furrowed. The girl reached for her mother's hand, squeezing it gently.

"Ezra called it the MANNA Covenant, our Restoration. But really, it's just a seed. One, we plant every time we tell the truth. Every time we refuse to be bought. Every time we remind our churches that silence isn't holy, we are reminded that it is not. That obedience isn't always righteousness. That justice starts at home."

The screen showed no image. Just Harris's voice, stretched out over space and time like a hand in the dark.

"If I don't make it to the next broadcast, it's okay. Don't wait for a shepherd. You are the watchmen now. You are the ones who see. You are the trumpet. Blow it."

Static buzzed, then faded.

Silence filled the room.

The mother leaned back, pressing her lips to her baby's forehead. Her boy whispered, "Is he gone?"

She didn't answer with words. She just adjusted the blanket around the newborn and nodded toward the window.

Outside, a crow landed on the power line.

It didn't caw.

I just watched it.

Chapter 56
The Last Amen

The church was packed, but it wasn't the kind of crowd that came just to be seen.

This was the kind of full where the air feels thick with grief and gratitude settling into every pew.

Harris lay in a closed casket at the front, draped in a black-and-red cloth embroidered with a single emblem: a crow in flight, wings spread over an open book.

Behind him, the stained glass threw muted light over the faces of those who'd come old fighters from the movement, young faces from the Watchtower Network, and people who didn't even know him personally but swore his work had changed them.

The pulpit mic squealed once, then settled into a steady tone. A young man stepped forward, perhaps twenty-four, possibly younger, tall and lean, dressed in a simple black suit.

He didn't carry notes. Just stood there with his hands resting on the wood like he'd been preparing for this moment without knowing it.

"My name's Isaiah," he began. "Most of you didn't know me while Harris was alive. I came up in the back row of the movement, holding cameras, running livestreams, and staying out of the frame.

But Harris saw me.

And if you knew Harris, you know once he saw you, he didn't unsee you."

A ripple of low laughter moved through the crowd, then quieted. Isaiah pulled out a letter Harris asked him to read if something happened to him.

Harris's Letter

If you're reading this, it means I'm not here anymore.

That's alright.

I never planned on living forever, just long enough to make sure the work outlived me.

I know how the game works.

They'll try to fold my name into speeches that mean nothing. Turn me into a mural on a wall they're planning to demolish.

Don't let them.

Don't let them shrink me down to something safe.

I wasn't safe.

I wasn't polite.

I wasn't here to make the enemy comfortable.

The movement isn't about me. It never was.

It's about you, the ones still breathing, still building, still running toward the fight instead of away from it.

You've got something I didn't have when I started: you've got the blueprint.

You know where the traps are.

You know how they bought the pulpits and silenced the voices.

You know the cost of playing ball with people who see you as a token, not a threat.

So, here's my last piece of advice:

Don't get on their leash, even if the collar looks like gold.

Keep your money in our hands.

Keep your faith in our God, not theirs.

And keep your eyes on the ones smiling at you while they measure your coffin.

I called it the New Black Church with walls.

Not walls to keep people out, but walls to keep the truth in.

Walls that protect our history from being rewritten and our money from being stolen.

Walls that can't be torn down with a phone call to the IRS.

You build those walls everywhere you can in our neighborhoods, in our banks, in our schools, in our minds.

Every place we control is a place they can't.

You're the new guard now.

You're faster, smarter, better with the tools this world runs on.

Don't wait for permission.

Don't ask for a seat at their table, build your own, and don't be afraid to eat alone until the right people show up.

If fear ever creeps in, remember this:

Fear's only job is to make you still long enough for someone else to put you in a cage.

Keep moving.

"I'm standing here today not because I was his protégé, but because I'm part of the generation he fought to hand the keys to.

He used to tell us, the crew, all of us who were still green, that the movement could not be a relay race where the baton drops between generations.

He said we had to take it while he was still running."

Isaiah took a breath, scanning the faces in the pews.

"Harris didn't just fight for a new Black church. He fought for one with walls, not the kind that keep people out, but the kind that keep the truth in.

Walls that could hold the weight of history without letting it be rewritten.

Walls that could protect our money from being siphoned off by hands wearing sheep's clothing.

Walls that could block the echo of the state telling our pulpits what could and couldn't be preached.

He wanted those walls to stand long after he was gone."

Isaiah's voice tightened, but he didn't pause.

"Some of y'all remember the old days, the storefront churches where the floorboards creaked and the roof leaked, but the sermons shook the block.

Where nobody had to check with a lawyer before speaking the truth.

That's the spirit Harris fought to bring back, but with a structure they couldn't infiltrate, couldn't buy, and couldn't break with a tax code."

He looked down for a moment, gathering himself.

"I remember the night Harris told me, 'The old guard has experience, but the young guard has speed, creativity, and no fear.

And we need all three if we're gonna win.'

He said we were the generation that didn't know enough to be afraid, and that was our superpower.

Now he's gone.

And the question is, what do we do with that power?"

Somewhere in the crowd, someone said softly, "Use it."

Isaiah nodded. "That's right. We use it.

The New Black Church, the one with walls, is already here. Built from the blueprint Harris helped protect. It's unionized, our tithes fund it, and it answers us, not them.

We're buying land. We're building schools. We're putting clinics in neighborhoods they forgot about until it was time to send in the police.

And we're doing it with the same stubborn refusal that Harris carried like a badge, the refusal to play ball with anyone who wanted to put us on a leash."

The crowd hummed not applause, but that deep sound church folk make when they agree in their bones.

"Harris used to say faith without works is dead. He didn't mean faith in the system, or in the institutions that sold us out a hundred times before.

He meant faith in ourselves, in God's command to build and protect what's ours.

He didn't just flip tables; he showed us how to make sure no one could set up shop in the temple again."

Isaiah stepped back slightly, his voice softening.

"I didn't know Harris in his younger days. I never saw him when he was running the streets, working cases, or fighting his way through rooms where he wasn't welcome.

I only knew him as the man who made time for anyone willing to work, whether you were an old comrade or a kid with a cracked phone trying to stream a rally.

That's the man I'll remember.

And that's the man I'm asking all of you to honor not by mourning, but by moving."

He looked out over the room one last time.

"The New Black Church with walls is standing because Harris wouldn't let them knock it down before it was built.

Now it's ours to guard, ours to grow, and ours to pass to whoever's coming next.

So when you leave here today, don't just say rest in peace.

Say, the work continues."

Isaiah stepped away from the mic.

The choir began to hum low, the organ slipping in underneath.

And as the pallbearers moved toward the casket, the crowd stood not in chaos, not in weeping, but in a kind of collective readiness.

It wasn't the end of something.

It was the last amen before the next fight.

Two months after the funeral, the air smelled like wet cement and fresh-cut lumber.

The first Covenant Hall was going up on the corner of what used to be a vacant lot, across from a row of boarded-up houses.

Now there were steel beams in the air, the thud of hammers, the whir of saws, and the sound of voices, young and old working together without waiting for permission from anybody outside the circle.

Isaiah was there, hard hat crooked on his head, clipboard in hand. He was shouting measurements to a crew of teenagers who were laughing, teasing each other, and moving with the kind of speed only youth can carry.

Every few minutes, someone would glance up at the brick façade, where the stone for the cornerstone was already carved:

HARRIS BUSHVILL THE WORK CONTINUES

Inside, the space was already taking shape.

A sanctuary at the front, not for Sunday sermons alone but for assemblies, strategy sessions, and community meetings.

Behind it, classrooms equipped with the fastest internet in the county, spaces for coding boot camps, history workshops, and small business training.

A side wing that would house the clinic, the food co-op, and the legal aid office.

It wasn't a church in the old sense, and it wasn't just a community center.

It was both, and more.

A headquarters.

Yolanda walked the perimeter with Donell, pointing out where the security systems would go.

"No dead spots," she said. "We're not building a place they can sneak into without us knowing."

Donell nodded. "We learned that the hard way."

They stopped in front of the cornerstone.

"You think Harris would like it?" Yolanda asked quietly.

Donell smiled. "He'd tell us to make it bigger. And then he'd ask how we're paying for the next one."

The money was coming in steadily now, not from grants or federal programs, but from tithes pooled across the Covenant network.

FBA-owned banks held the accounts.

Every dollar was tracked and audited by people from inside the community.

It was exactly what Harris and Ezra had preached: the unionized church structure, immune to the chokehold of 501(c)(3) compliance.

And it was working.

On the far side of the lot, a group of middle schoolers was unpacking boxes of donated laptops.

A college student, one of the Watchtower youth Harris had mentored, was showing them how to set up secure messaging apps and encrypt their drives.

"This," she told them, "is how you protect the work.

Your grandparents had to watch their phones. You have to watch your clouds.

By noon, the sound of construction gave way to the sound of drums.

A group of kids had set up in the middle of the lot, pounding out a rhythm on overturned buckets and scrap wood.

The beat carried down the block, pulling people out of their houses, drawing them toward the site.

Some came to watch. Some came to help.

Everyone stayed.

Inside, Yolanda and Donell called a break and gathered the crews in the half-finished sanctuary.

Isaiah stood in front of them, holding a photo of Harris, the one where he's leaning against a brick wall, arms crossed, looking like he's halfway between a smile and a warning.

"I don't need to tell you who this is," Isaiah said. "You wouldn't be here if you didn't know.

This building is the first of many. Harris didn't fight and bleed so we could have just one stronghold. He fought so we'd have fifty. A hundred.

Places that can't be bought, can't be bullied, and can't be broken from the outside in."

He paused, scanning the room.

"We call it the New Black Church with walls. But these walls aren't just brick and mortar.

They're our history. They're our discipline. They're our refusal to forget who we are and for whom we're building.

This is just the first."

The room hummed with quiet agreement.

Someone clapped once, and then the clapping spread, not loud, but steady, a rhythm that matched the heartbeat of the drums outside.

Later, when the sun dipped low, Yolanda walked to the edge of the lot.

She could see kids riding bikes in the street, elders sitting on porches, and the half-finished Hall standing tall against the skyline.

There was still a lot to do, but the foundation was there; it's always been, it's just in the concrete, but in the people.

The work was already bigger than any one name.

And Harris, wherever he was now, would've liked that.

Epilogue: The Watchers

They said the land was cursed, but the crows knew better.

From the telephone wires and broken crosses, they watched as the foundation was poured hands blistered, backs bent, hearts steady. The ground where the old church had fallen now carried the hum of something alive, something ungoverned.

No stained glass. No marble floors. Just wood, brick, and the smell of rain.

This time, the blueprints didn't come from grants or government boards. They came from memory from all the tongues that were once tied, from every sermon buried under silence.

The people called it The New Church, but the crows called it Return.

They gathered on the scaffolds and the steeple beams, black feathers against a clear sky. Watching. Waiting. Guarding.

They didn't sing; they didn't need to. Their presence was the hymn the same low hum that carried through Buffalo's streets long after the headlines faded and the cameras turned away.

At dusk, when the last hammer quieted and the workers wiped the sweat from their faces, one crow lifted from the roof and circled wide above the lot.

Then another.

And another.

Until the air was thick with movement black wings cutting through the sunset like ink through water.

Some said it was a sign.

Others said it was memory.

But I knew better.

They weren't mourning anymore.

They were watching faithful as ever over what was being built in the ashes.

Over what had survived the silence.

Over what refused to die.

The murder had gathered again,

not to warn this time,

but to witness.